P9-DWH-182

WITHDRAWN

WARRIORS
THE DARKEST
HOUR

WARRIORS

*Book One: Into the Wild*

*Book Two: Fire and Ice*

*Book Three: Forest of Secrets*

*Book Four: Rising Storm*

*Book Five: A Dangerous Path*

*Book Six: The Darkest Hour*

# THE DARKEST HOUR

ERIN HUNTER

HARPERCOLLINS*PUBLISHERS*

The Darkest Hour



Series created by Working Partners Limited

 Printed in the United States of America. For information address HarperCollins Children's Books, a division of HarperCollins Publishers, 195 Broadway, New York, NY 10007.

www.harperchildrens.com

---

Library of Congress Cataloging-in-Publication Data

Hunter, Erin.

The darkest hour / Erin Hunter.—1st ed.

p. cm.—(Warriors ; bk. 6)

Summary: ThunderClan's darkest hour is upon them and Fireheart, the warrior cat, must protect his clan from a threat unlike any the forest has ever seen, as the time comes for prophecies to unfold and heroes to rise.

ISBN 0-06-000007-4 — ISBN 0-06-052584-3 (lib. bdg.)

[1. Cats—Fiction 2. Fantasy] I. Title.

PZ7.H916625 Dar 2004 2003022493

[Fic]—dc21

---

Typography by Karin Paprocki

20 PC/LSCH 25 24 23

❖

First Edition

*This book is for Vicky Holmes and Matt Haslum,*
*who helped find Fireheart's destiny.*
*Thank you.*

*Special thanks to Cherith Baldry*

# ALLEGIANCES

## THUNDERCLAN

**LEADER** — **FIRESTAR**—handsome ginger tom
**APPRENTICE, BRAMBLEPAW**

**DEPUTY** — **WHITESTORM**—big white tom

**MEDICINE CAT** — **CINDERPELT**—dark gray she-cat

**WARRIORS** — (toms, and she-cats without kits)

**DARKSTRIPE**—sleek black-and-gray tabby tom
**APPRENTICE, FERNPAW**

**LONGTAIL**—pale tabby tom, dark black stripes

**MOUSEFUR**—small dusky-brown she-cat
**APPRENTICE, THORNPAW**

**BRACKENFUR**—golden-brown tabby tom
**APPRENTICE, TAWNYPAW**

**DUSTPELT**—dark brown tabby tom
**APPRENTICE, ASHPAW**

**SANDSTORM**—pale ginger she-cat

**GRAYSTRIPE**—long-haired gray tom

**FROSTFUR**—beautiful white she-cat, blue eyes

**GOLDENFLOWER**—pale ginger she-cat

**CLOUDTAIL**—long-haired white tom

| | |
|---|---|
| APPRENTICES | (more than six moons old, in training to become warriors) |
| | **THORNPAW**—golden-brown tabby tom |
| | **FERNPAW**—pale gray with darker flecks, she-cat, pale green eyes |
| | **ASHPAW**—pale gray with darker flecks, tom, dark blue eyes |
| | **BRAMBLEPAW**—dark brown tabby tom, amber eyes |
| | **TAWNYPAW**—tortoiseshell she-cat, green eyes |
| | **LOSTFACE**—white she-cat, ginger splotches |
| QUEENS | (she-cats expecting or nursing kits) |
| | **WILLOWPELT**—very pale gray she-cat, unusual blue eyes |
| ELDERS | (former warriors and queens, now retired) |
| | **ONE-EYE**—pale gray she-cat, the oldest cat in ThunderClan, virtually blind and deaf |
| | **SMALLEAR**—gray tom with very small ears, the oldest tom in ThunderClan |
| | **DAPPLETAIL**—once-pretty tortoiseshell she-cat, lovely dappled coat |
| | **SPECKLETAIL**—pale tabby, and the oldest nursery queen |

## SHADOWCLAN

| | |
|---|---|
| LEADER | **TIGERSTAR**—big dark brown tabby tom, unusually long front claws, formerly of ThunderClan |

| | |
|---|---|
| DEPUTY | **BLACKFOOT**—large white tom, huge jet-black paws, formerly a rogue cat |
| MEDICINE CAT | **RUNNINGNOSE**—small gray-and-white tom |
| WARRIORS | **OAKFUR**—small brown tom |
| | **LITTLECLOUD**—very small tabby tom |
| | **BOULDER**—skinny gray tom, formerly a rogue cat |
| | **RUSSETFUR**—dark ginger she-cat, formerly a rogue cat<br>**APPRENTICE, CEDARPAW** |
| | **JAGGEDTOOTH**—huge tabby tom, formerly a rogue cat<br>**APPRENTICE, ROWANPAW** |
| QUEENS | **TALLPOPPY**—long-legged light brown tabby she-cat |

## WINDCLAN

| | |
|---|---|
| LEADER | **TALLSTAR**—black-and-white tom, very long tail |
| DEPUTY | **DEADFOOT**—black tom with a twisted paw |
| MEDICINE CAT | **BARKFACE**—short-tailed brown tom |
| WARRIORS | **MUDCLAW**—mottled dark brown tom |
| | **WEBFOOT**—dark gray tabby tom |
| | **TORNEAR**—tabby tom |
| | **ONEWHISKER**—brown tabby tom<br>**APPRENTICE, GORSEPAW** |
| | **RUNNINGBROOK**—light gray tabby she-cat |

**QUEENS** **ASHFOOT**—gray she-cat

**MORNINGFLOWER**—tortoiseshell she-cat

**WHITETAIL**—small white she-cat

## RIVERCLAN

**LEADER** **LEOPARDSTAR**—unusually spotted golden tabby she-cat

**DEPUTY** **STONEFUR**—gray tom, battle-scarred ears
**APPRENTICE, STORMPAW**

**MEDICINE CAT** **MUDFUR**—long-haired light brown tom

**WARRIORS** **BLACKCLAW**—smoky black tom

**HEAVYSTEP**—thickset tabby tom
**APPRENTICE, DAWNPAW**

**SHADEPELT**—very dark gray she-cat

**MISTYFOOT**—dark gray she-cat, blue eyes
**APPRENTICE, FEATHERPAW**

**LOUDBELLY**—dark brown tom

**QUEENS** **MOSSPELT**—tortoiseshell she-cat

## BLOODCLAN

**LEADER** **SCOURGE**—small black tom with one white paw

**DEPUTY** **BONE**—massive black-and-white tom

## CATS OUTSIDE CLANS

**BARLEY**—black-and-white tom that lives on a farm close to the forest

**RAVENPAW**—sleek black cat that lives on the farm with Barley

**PRINCESS**—light brown tabby, distinctive white chest and paws, a kittypet

**SMUDGE**—plump, friendly black-and-white kittypet that lives in a house at the edge of the forest

HIGHSTONES

BARLEY'S FARM

WINDCLAN CAMP

FOURTREES

FALLS

OWL-TREE

RIVER

SUNNING-ROCKS

RIVERCLAN CAMP

CARRIONPLACE
SHADOWCLAN CAMP
THUNDERPATH
THUNDERCLAN CAMP
GREAT SYCAMORE
SNAKEROCKS
SANDY HOLLOW
TALLPINES
TREECUT PLACE
TWOLEGPLACE
THUNDERCLAN
RIVERCLAN
SHADOWCLAN
WINDCLAN
STARCLAN

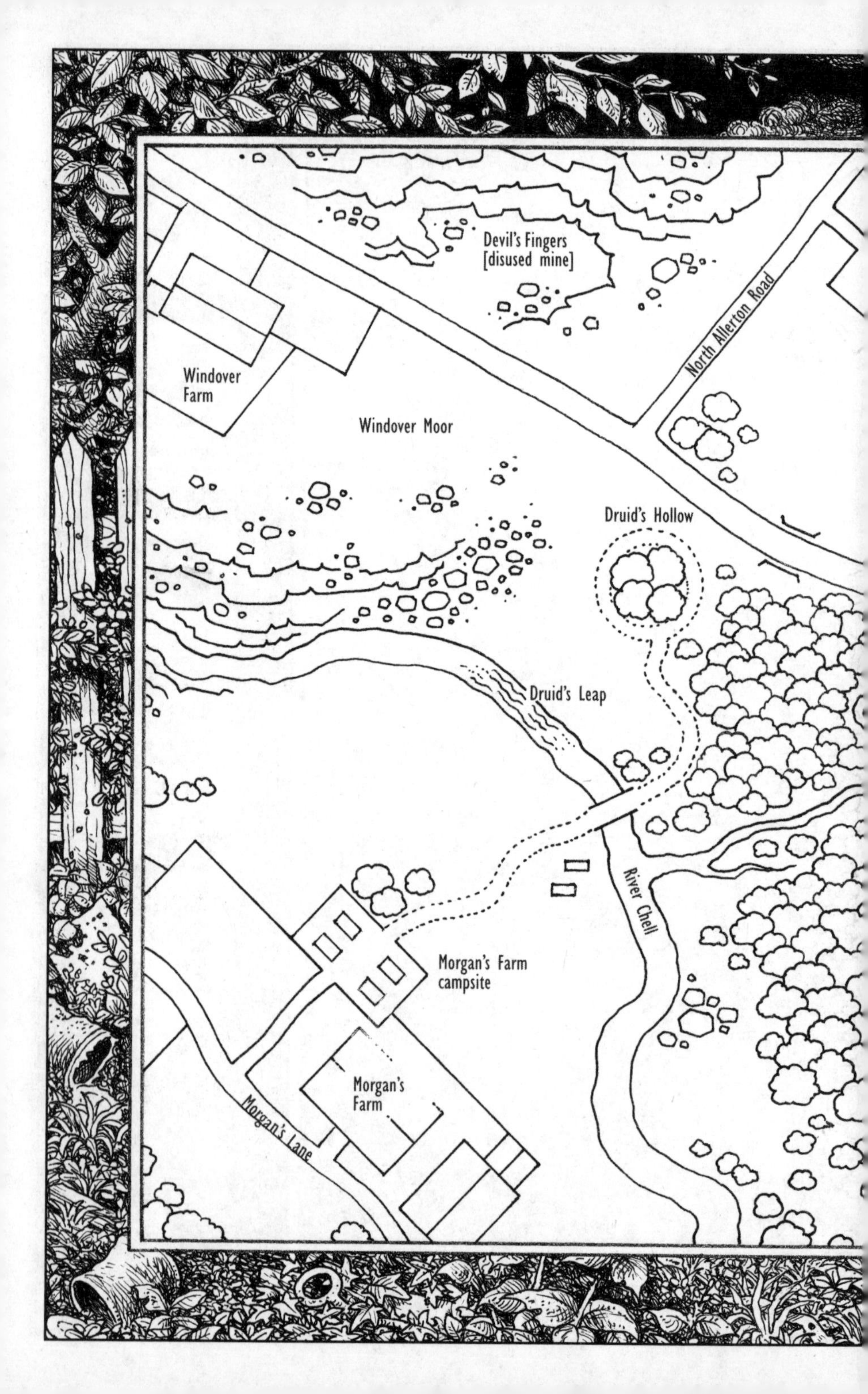
Devil's Fingers
[disused mine]
North Allerton Road
Windover
Farm
Windover Moor
Druid's Hollow
Druid's Leap
River Chell
Morgan's Farm
campsite
Morgan's
Farm
Morgan's Lane

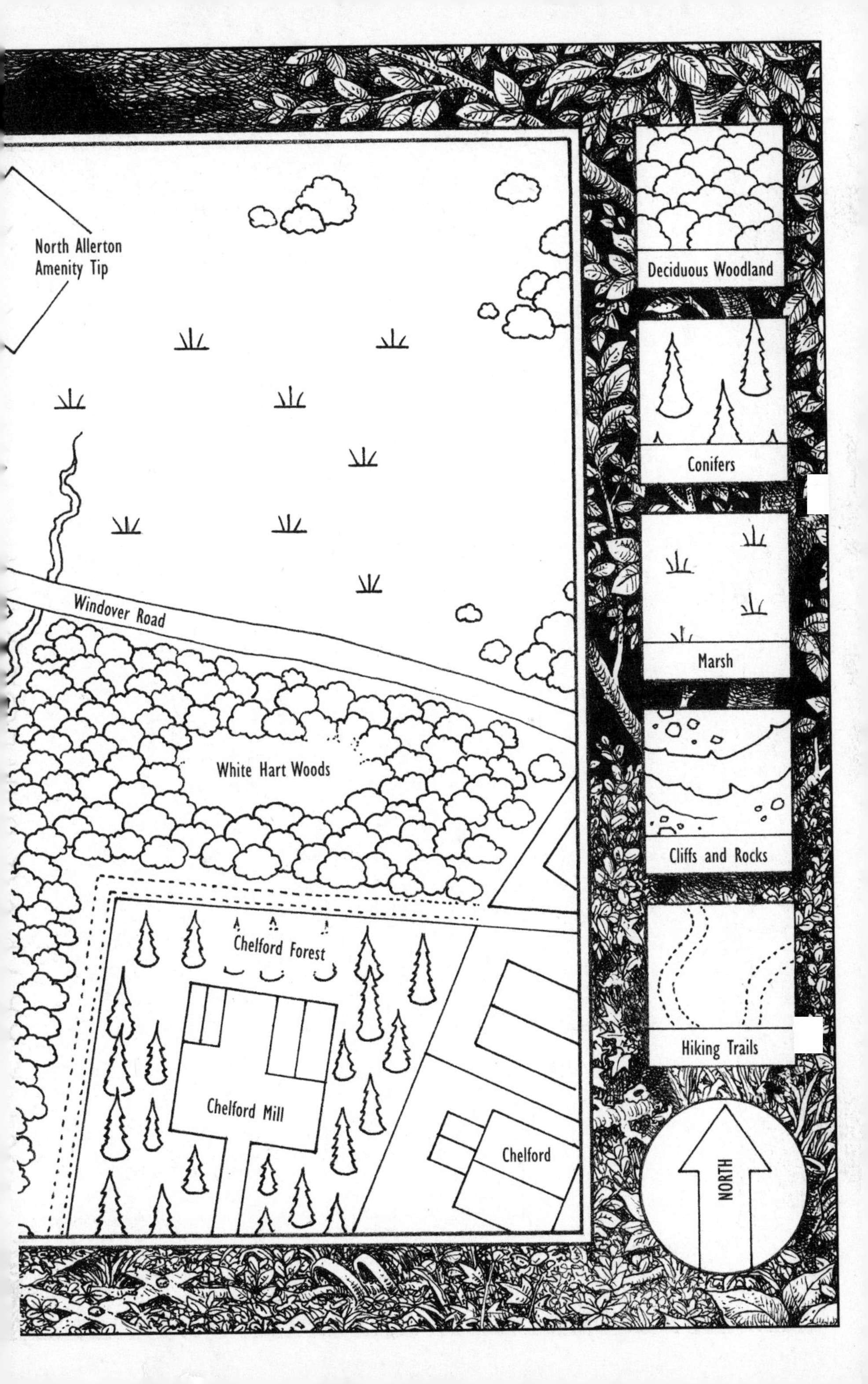

North Allerton
Amenity Tip
Windover Road
White Hart Woods
Chelford Forest
Chelford Mill
Chelford
Deciduous Woodland
Conifers
Marsh
Cliffs and Rocks
Hiking Trails
NORTH

# PROLOGUE

*Rain fell steadily, drumming on the* hard black Thunderpath that led between unending rows of stone Twoleg nests. From time to time a monster snarled past, its eyes glaring, and a single Twoleg scurried along, huddled into its shiny pelt.

Two cats slipped silently around the corner, keeping close to the walls where the shadows were deepest. A skinny gray tom with a ragged ear and bright, watchful eyes went first, every hair on his body slicked dark with the wet.

Behind him prowled a huge tabby with massive shoulders and muscles that slid smoothly under his rain-soaked pelt. His amber eyes glowed in the harsh light, and his gaze shifted back and forth as if he expected an attack.

He paused where the dark entrance to a Twoleg nest offered a little shelter and growled, "How much farther? This place stinks."

The gray tom glanced back. "Not far now."

"It had better not be." Grimacing, the dark brown tabby padded on, ears twitching irritably to flick away the raindrops. Harsh yellow light angled across him, and he flinched as a monster roared around the corner, throwing up a wave of filthy water that reeked of Twoleg rubbish. The cat let out a snarl as the water slopped around his paws and the spray drizzled down on his fur.

Everything about the Twolegplace disgusted him: the hard surface under his paws, the stench of monsters and the Twolegs they carried in their bellies, the unfamiliar noises, and most of all, the way that he could not survive here without a guide. The tabby was not used to depending on another cat for anything. In the forest he knew every tree, every stream, every rabbit hole. He was considered the strongest and most dangerous warrior in all the Clans. Now his sharpened skills and senses were useless. He felt as if he were deaf, blind, and lame, reduced to following his companion like a kit trailing helplessly after its mother.

But it would be worth it. The tabby's whiskers twitched in anticipation. He had already launched a plan that would turn his most hated enemies into helpless prey in their own territory. When the dogs attacked, no cat would suspect that they had been lured and guided every step of the way. And then, if things went according to plan, this expedition into Twolegplace would give him all he had ever wanted.

The gray cat led the way along the path and across an open space reeking of Twoleg monsters, where a swirl of color from unnatural orange lights floated on the puddles. He stopped by the entrance to a narrow alley and opened his jaws to draw in the scent of the air.

The tabby halted and did the same, disgustedly swiping his

tongue over his lips at the stink of rotting Twoleg food. "Is this the place?" he asked.

"This is it," the gray warrior replied tensely. "Now—remember what I told you. The cat we're going to meet holds command over many cats. We must treat him with respect."

"Boulder, have you forgotten who I am?" The tabby took a step forward so that he towered over his companion.

The skinny gray cat's ears flattened. "No, Tigerstar, I haven't forgotten. But you're not Clan leader here."

Tigerstar grunted. "Let's get on with it," he growled.

Boulder turned into the alley. He stopped short after just a few paces when a huge shape loomed up in front of them.

"Who goes there?" A broad-shouldered black and white cat stepped out of the shadows. Strong muscles were outlined under fur plastered to his body by the rain. "Identify yourselves. We don't like strangers here."

"Greetings, Bone," the gray warrior meowed steadily. "Remember me?"

The black-and-white cat narrowed his eyes and was silent for a few moments. "So you've come back, have you, Boulder?" he meowed at last. "You told us you were going to find a better life in the forest. What are you doing here?"

He took a step forward, but Boulder held his ground, unsheathing his claws against the uneven ground. "We want to see Scourge."

Bone let out a snort, half contempt, half laughter. "I can't imagine that Scourge will want to see you. And who's this with you? I don't recognize *him*."

"My name is Tigerstar. I've come from the forest to speak with your leader."

Bone's green eyes flicked from Tigerstar to Boulder and back again. "What do you want with him?" he demanded.

Tigerstar's amber gaze burned like the Twoleg lights reflected on the shining wet stones around them. "I'll discuss that with your leader, not his border patrol."

Bone bristled and extended his claws, but Boulder quickly slipped between him and Tigerstar. "Scourge needs to hear this," he insisted. "It could be to every cat's advantage."

For a few heartbeats Bone hesitated, and then he stepped back, allowing Boulder and Tigerstar to pass. His hostile glare scorched their fur, but he said nothing.

Now Tigerstar took the lead, treading cautiously as the light faded behind them. On either side, skinny cats were slinking behind piles of rubbish, eyes gleaming as they followed the progress of the two intruders. Tigerstar's muscles tensed. If this meeting went wrong, he might have to fight his way out.

A wall blocked the end of the alley. Tigerstar stared around, looking for the leader of these cats of Twolegplace. He was expecting an even more massive creature than the broad-shouldered Bone, and at first his gaze swept over the small black cat crouching in a shadowy doorway.

Boulder gave him a nudge and jerked his head in the black cat's direction. "There's Scourge."

"*That's* Scourge?" Tigerstar's exclamation rang with disbelief above the falling rain. "He's no bigger than an apprentice!"

"Shh!" Panic flared in Boulder's eyes. "This may not be a Clan as we know it, but these cats would kill if their leader ordered them to."

"It seems I have visitors." The black cat's voice had a brittle, high-pitched sound, like the splintering of ice. "I wasn't expecting to see you again, Boulder. I heard you'd gone to live in the forest."

"Yes, Scourge, I have," Boulder replied.

"So what are you doing here?" Scourge's voice held the faintest suggestion of a snarl. "Have you changed your mind and come crawling back? Do you expect me to welcome you?"

"No, Scourge." Boulder held the black cat's ice-blue gaze. "It's a good life in the forest. There is plenty of fresh-kill, no Twolegs—"

"You haven't come to extol the virtues of forest life," Scourge interrupted him with a flick of his tail. "Squirrels live in trees, not cats." His eyes narrowed, glinting with a pale fire. "So what do you want?"

Tigerstar stepped forward, shouldering the gray warrior aside. "I am Tigerstar, the leader of ShadowClan," he growled. "And I have a proposition for you."

# CHAPTER 1

*Watery shafts of light sliced through* the bare trees as Fireheart carried his leader to her final resting place. With his teeth clenched firmly in her scruff, he retraced the route the dog pack had taken as the brave warriors of ThunderClan lured them to the gorge and their destruction. His whole body felt numb, and his head spun with the terrible realization that Bluestar was dead.

Without his leader, the forest itself seemed different, even stranger to Fireheart than the day he had first ventured into it as a kittypet. Nothing was real; he felt as if the trees and rocks could dissolve like mist within a moment. A vast, unnatural silence covered everything. With the rational part of his mind Fireheart realized that all the prey had been scared away by the rampaging dog pack, but in the grip of his grief it seemed that even the forest was stunned into mourning for Bluestar.

The scene at the gorge replayed over and over in his head. He saw again the slavering jaws of the dog who led the pack, and felt its sharp teeth meet in his scruff. He remembered how Bluestar had appeared out of nowhere, flinging herself at the dog, driving it—and herself—over the edge of the gorge and into the river. He flinched again at the icy shock of the water as he leaped in to rescue his drowning leader, and their hopeless struggles until two RiverClan warriors, Mistyfoot and Stonefur, came to help them.

Most of all, Fireheart recalled his dismay and disbelief as he crouched beside his leader on the riverbank, and realized that she had sacrificed her last life to save him and all of ThunderClan from the dog pack.

As he bore Bluestar's body home, with the help of Mistyfoot and Stonefur, he kept pausing to scent the air for fresh traces of dog, and he had already sent his friend Graystripe to scout the territory on either side of their trail, searching for signs that the dogs had caught any of the ThunderClan cats in their desperate race for the gorge. So far, to Fireheart's relief, they had found nothing.

Now, skirting a bramble thicket, Fireheart set down his lifeless leader once more and raised his head to drink in the air, thankful to taste only the clean scents of the forest. A moment later, Graystripe appeared around a clump of dead bracken.

"Everything's fine, Fireheart," he reported. "Plenty of broken undergrowth, but that's all."

"Good," Fireheart meowed. His hope rose that the dogs that had escaped the fall into the gorge had fled in terror, and the forest once again belonged to the four Clans of wild cats. His Clan had lived through three terrible moons, when they had become prey in their own territory, but they had survived. "Let's keep going. I want to check that the camp is safe before the Clan comes back."

He and the RiverClan warriors took up Bluestar's body again and carried it through the trees. At the top of the ravine that led down to the camp entrance, Firestar paused. He briefly remembered the early morning, when he and his warriors had followed the trail of dead rabbits that Tigerstar had laid to lure the dog pack to the ThunderClan camp. At the end of the trail they had found the body of the gentle queen Brindleface, slaughtered to give the savage dogs a taste for cat blood. But now everything seemed peaceful, and when Fireheart tasted the air again he could detect only cat scent coming from the camp.

"Wait here," he meowed. "I'm going to take a look."

"I'll come with you," Graystripe offered instantly.

"No." It was Stonefur who spoke, flicking out his tail to bar the gray warrior's way. "I think Fireheart needs to do this alone."

Flashing a grateful look at the RiverClan deputy, Fireheart began picking his way down the ravine, his ears pricked for any sound of trouble ahead. But the strange silence still reigned over the forest.

As he emerged from the gorse tunnel into the clearing, Fireheart paused to glance warily around. It was possible that one or more of the dogs had never made it to the gorge, or that Tigerstar had sent ShadowClan warriors to take over the camp. But all was quiet. Fireheart's fur prickled with the strangeness of seeing the camp deserted like this, yet there was no sign of danger, and still no scent of dogs or ShadowClan.

To be sure the camp was safe, he rapidly checked the dens and the nursery. Memories came unbidden: the bewilderment of the Clan as he told them about the dog pack, the heart-pounding terror of the chase through the forest with the breath of the pack leader hot on his fur. At the foot of the Highrock, listening to the wind whispering through the trees, Fireheart thought back to the time Tigerstar had stood here, boldly facing his Clan as they discovered the true depth of his treachery. He had sworn undying vengeance as he was sent into exile, and Fireheart was sure that his bloodthirsty attempt to set the dog pack on the cats of ThunderClan would not be his last attempt to fulfill his oath.

Last of all Fireheart prowled cautiously through the fern tunnel to Cinderpelt's den. Glancing through the entrance, he saw the medicine cat's healing herbs neatly ranged beside one wall. The strongest memory yet flooded over him, of Spottedleaf and Yellowfang, who had been ThunderClan medicine cats before Cinderpelt. Fireheart had loved them both, and grief for them swept over him again to mingle with his grief for his leader.

*Bluestar is dead*, he told them silently. *Is she with you now, in StarClan?*

Retracing his steps along the fern tunnel, he returned to the top of the ravine. Graystripe was standing on watch while Mistyfoot and Stonefur gently groomed the dead leader's body.

"Everything's fine," Fireheart announced. "Graystripe, I want you to go to Sunningrocks now. Tell the Clan that Bluestar is dead, but nothing more. I'll explain everything when

I see them. Just let them know that it's safe to come home."

Graystripe's yellow eyes brightened. "On my way, Fireheart." He spun around and tore off through the forest, heading for Sunningrocks, where the Clan had gone to hide while the dogs were following Tigerstar's trail of rabbit blood to their camp.

Stonefur, crouching beside Bluestar's body, let out a purr of amusement. "It's easy to see where Graystripe's loyalties lie," he remarked.

"Yes," Mistyfoot agreed. "No cat ever really thought he would stay in RiverClan."

Graystripe's kits had been born to a RiverClan queen, and for a while he had gone to RiverClan to be with them, but in his heart he had never left ThunderClan. Forced into battle against his birth Clan, he had chosen to save Fireheart's life, and the RiverClan leader Leopardstar had banished him from her Clan. Her sentence of exile, Fireheart reflected, had freed the gray warrior to return to where he truly belonged.

With a nod of acknowledgment to the RiverClan warriors, Fireheart took up Bluestar again, and the three cats maneuvered her body down the ravine and into the camp. At last they could lay her down in her den beneath the Highrock, where she would remain until her Clan had said farewell to her and buried her with all the honor that such a wise and noble leader deserved.

"Thank you for your help," Fireheart meowed to the RiverClan warriors. Hesitating for a moment, knowing only too well the significance of his invitation, he added, "Would you like to stay for Bluestar's burial ceremony?"

"That is a generous offer," Stonefur replied, showing only a flicker of surprise that Fireheart should admit members of a rival Clan to something so private. "But we have duties in our own Clan. We must be getting back."

"Thank you, Fireheart," meowed Mistyfoot. "That means a lot to us. But your Clan will think it's strange if we stay. They don't know, do they, that Bluestar was our mother?"

"No," Fireheart told her. "Only Graystripe. But Tigerstar overheard what you and Bluestar said to each other on . . . on the riverbank. You must be prepared in case he chooses to reveal it at the next Gathering."

Stonefur and Mistyfoot exchanged a glance. Then Stonefur drew himself up, his blue eyes gleaming defiantly. "Let Tigerstar say what he likes," he meowed. "I'll tell RiverClan myself today. We're not ashamed of our mother. She was a noble leader—and our father was a great deputy."

"Yes," Mistyfoot agreed. "No cat can argue with that, even if they did come from different Clans."

Their courage and determination reminded Fireheart of their mother, Bluestar. She had given them up to their father, Oakheart, the RiverClan deputy, and the two cats had grown up believing that they had been born in RiverClan. At first they had hated Bluestar when they learned the truth, but this morning, as she lay dying on the riverbank, they had found it in their hearts to forgive her. In the midst of his pain, Fireheart was relieved beyond words that his leader had been reconciled with her kits before she went to StarClan. He alone of all the ThunderClan cats knew how much Bluestar had suffered, watching them grow up in another Clan.

"I wish we'd known her better," Stonefur meowed sadly, as if he could read Fireheart's thoughts. "You're lucky to have grown up in her Clan and been her deputy."

"I know." Fireheart looked down sorrowfully at the blue-gray she-cat lying so still on the sandy floor of the clearing. Bluestar looked small and helpless now that her noble spirit had left her body and gone to hunt with StarClan.

"May we say good-bye to her alone?" Mistyfoot asked tentatively. "Just for a few moments?"

"Of course," Fireheart replied. He padded out of the den, leaving Stonefur and Mistyfoot to crouch down beside Bluestar's body and share tongues with their mother for the first and last time.

As he skirted the Highrock he heard the sound of cats approaching through the gorse tunnel. Hurrying forward, he saw Frostfur and Speckletail creep timidly into the clearing, hesitating in the shelter of the tunnel before they dared venture back into the camp. With the same wariness, Brackenfur and Goldenflower followed.

Pain stabbed Fireheart's heart to see his cats so wary of their own home, and his eyes sought out one warrior in particular—Sandstorm, the pale ginger she-cat he loved. He needed to know that she was unhurt after the crucial part she had played in luring the dog pack away from the camp.

Fireheart spotted his nephew, Cloudtail; the white warrior was carefully escorting Lostface, a young cat who had suffered terrible injuries from the dog pack before they attacked the camp. Next Cinderpelt came limping through the entrance with a bundle of herbs in her mouth; and pushing eagerly behind her were Bramblepaw and Tawnypaw, the two newest apprentices, who were also Tigerstar's kits.

At last Fireheart saw Sandstorm padding along beside Willowpelt, while Willowpelt's three kits bounced around them, happily unaware of the crisis their Clan had endured.

A purr swelled in Fireheart's throat as he ran toward Sandstorm and pressed his muzzle into her flank. The pale orange warrior covered his ears with licks, and when he looked up at her he saw a warm glow in her green eyes.

"I was so worried for you, Fireheart," she murmured. "I couldn't believe the size of those dogs! I've never been so scared in my life."

"Nor have I," Fireheart confessed. "All the time I was waiting, I kept thinking they might have caught you."

"Caught me?" Sandstorm pushed away from him; the end of her tail was twitching, and for a heartbeat Fireheart thought he had offended her, until he saw the sparkle in her eyes. "I was running for you and the Clan, Fireheart. It felt as if I had the speed of StarClan!"

She paced into the center of the clearing and looked around, her expression clouding. "Where is Bluestar? Graystripe told us she was dead."

"Yes," Fireheart replied. "I tried to save her, but the struggle in the river was too much for her. She's in her den." He hesitated before adding, "Mistyfoot and Stonefur are with her."

Sandstorm turned to him, her fur bristling with alarm. "There are RiverClan cats in our camp? Why?"

"They helped me pull Bluestar out of the river," Fireheart explained. "And . . . and she's their mother."

Sandstorm froze and her eyes grew huge. "Bluestar? But how—"

Fireheart interrupted her by pressing his muzzle against hers. "I'll tell you all about it later," he promised. "Right now I have to make sure the Clan is okay."

While they were speaking, the rest of the Clan had appeared through the gorse tunnel and begun to gather in a ragged circle around Fireheart and Sandstorm. Fireheart spotted Fernpaw and Ashpaw, the two apprentices who had begun the race to lure the dogs away from the camp. "Well done, both of you," he meowed.

The young cats let out a purr. "We hid in the hazel thicket where you told us, and jumped out as soon as we saw the dogs," mewed Ashpaw.

"Yes, we knew we had to keep them away from the camp," Fernpaw put in.

"You were very brave," Fireheart praised them. Once again he remembered the limp body of Brindleface, the apprentices' mother, murdered by Tigerstar. "I'm proud of you—and your mother would be proud, too."

Ashpaw shrank, suddenly looking like a fragile kit. "I was *terrified,*" he admitted. "If we'd known what the dogs were like, I don't think we'd have dared to do it."

"We were all terrified," Dustpelt meowed as he came up

and gave Fernpaw a gentle lick. "I've never run so fast in my life. You two did brilliantly."

Though he praised his own apprentice equally, the warmth in Dustpelt's gaze was all for Fernpaw. Fireheart managed to hide his amusement. The brown tabby warrior's affection for her was no secret.

"You did well, too, Dustpelt," Fireheart meowed. "The Clan owes thanks to all of you."

Dustpelt held Fireheart's gaze for a moment before he gave him a little nod of acknowledgment. As he turned away, Fireheart spotted Cloudtail gently guiding Lostface past and stopped them to ask, "Are you okay, Lostface?"

"I'm fine," the young she-cat replied, though she glanced around nervously with her good eye. "Are you sure none of the dogs got this far?"

"I checked the whole camp myself," Fireheart told her. "There's no sign of any dogs."

"She was very brave at Sunningrocks," meowed Cloudtail, touching his muzzle to Lostface's shoulder. "She helped me keep watch from a tree."

Lostface brightened. "I can't see as well as I used to, but I can listen, and scent."

"Well done," Fireheart meowed. "You too, Cloudtail. I was right to rely on you."

"They've all done well." That was Cinderpelt's voice; Fireheart turned to see her limping toward him with Mousefur just behind her. "There was no panic at all, not even when we heard the pack howling."

"And every cat's okay?" Fireheart asked anxiously.

"They're all fine." The medicine cat's blue eyes glowed with relief. "Mousefur tore a claw when she was running from the dogs, but that's all. Come on, Mousefur, I'll give you something for it."

As Fireheart watched them go, he realized that Whitestorm had appeared beside him. "Can I have a word with you?"

"Of course."

"I'm sorry." Whitestorm's eyes were full of anguish. "I know you asked me to take care of Bluestar when we were fleeing from the dogs. But she slipped away from Sunningrocks before I realized she'd gone. It's my fault she's dead."

Fireheart narrowed his eyes at the older warrior. For the first time he noticed how exhausted he looked. Although Whitestorm was the senior warrior of ThunderClan, he had always seemed strong and vigorous, his white coat sleek and well-groomed. Now he looked a hundred seasons older than the cat who had left camp that morning.

"That's ridiculous!" Fireheart insisted. "Even if you had noticed that Bluestar had gone, what could you have done? She was your leader—you couldn't have made her stay."

Whitestorm blinked. "I didn't dare send another cat after her—not with the pack loose. All we could do was sit up in the trees around Sunningrocks and listen to the howling. . . ." A shudder ran through his body. "But I should have done *something*."

"You did everything," Fireheart told him. "You stayed with the Clan and kept them safe. Bluestar made her own decision in the end. It was the will of StarClan that she died to save us."

Whitestorm nodded slowly, though his eyes were still troubled as he murmured, "Even though she had lost all faith in StarClan."

Fireheart was aware of the secret they shared, that in her last moons Bluestar's mind had begun to give way. Shocked to the core by the discovery of Tigerstar's treachery, Bluestar had begun to believe that she was at war with her warrior ancestors. Fireheart and Whitestorm, with Cinderpelt's help, had managed for the most part to keep the knowledge of their leader's weakness from the rest of the Clan. But Fireheart also knew that Bluestar's feelings had changed during the last moments of her life.

"No, Whitestorm," Fireheart replied, thankful that there was some comfort he could offer the gallant old warrior. "She made her peace with StarClan before she died. She knew exactly what she was doing, and why. Her mind was clear again, and her faith was strong."

Joy tempered the pain in Whitestorm's eyes, and he bowed his head. Fireheart realized how devastating Bluestar's death must be for him; they had been friends throughout a long life.

By now the rest of the Clan had crept into the circle around Fireheart. He could see the traces of their terrible experience still in their eyes, along with fear for the future. Swallowing uncomfortably, he realized that it was his duty now to calm those fears.

"Fireheart," Brackenfur asked hesitantly, "is it true that Bluestar's dead?"

Fireheart nodded. "Yes, it's true. She . . . she died saving me, and all of us." For a moment he thought his voice would fail completely, and he swallowed hard. "You all know that I was the last cat on the trail to lead the dogs to the gorge. When I was almost at the edge, Tigerstar leaped out at me and held me down so that the pack leader caught up to me. He would have killed me, and the dogs would still be loose in the forest, if it hadn't been for Bluestar. She threw herself at the dog, right on the edge of the gorge, and . . . and they both went over."

He could see a ripple of distress sweeping across his Clan mates, like wind stirring the trees.

"What happened then?" Frostfur asked quietly.

"I went in after her, but I couldn't save her." Briefly Fireheart closed his eyes, remembering the churning water and his hopeless struggle to keep his leader afloat. "Mistyfoot and Stonefur from RiverClan came to help me when we had been swept clear of the gorge," he went on. "Bluestar was alive when we got her out but it was too late. Her ninth life was over, and she left us to join StarClan."

A yowl of grief came from somewhere among the circle of cats. Fireheart realized that many of the cats had not even been born when Bluestar became leader, and losing her now must feel as if the four great oaks of Fourtrees had been torn up overnight.

He raised his voice, forcing it not to shake. "Bluestar isn't gone, you know. She's already watching over us from StarClan . . . her spirit is here with us now." *Or in her den,* he thought privately, *sharing tongues with Stonefur and Mistyfoot.*

"I would like to see Bluestar now," meowed Speckletail. "Where is she—in her den?" She turned toward the entrance, flanked by Dappletail and Smallear.

"I'll come with you," Frostfur offered, springing to her paws.

Alarm shot through Fireheart. He had hoped to give Mistyfoot and Stonefur as much time as possible with their dead mother, but he suddenly realized that apart from Graystripe and Sandstorm, no cats even knew that the two RiverClan warriors were in the camp.

"Wait—" he began, shouldering his way through the circle.

It was too late. Speckletail and Frostfur were already standing in the entrance to Bluestar's den, their fur bristling and their tails fluffed out to twice their normal size as they confronted the strange cats. A menacing snarl came from Frostfur. "What are *you* doing here?"

# CHAPTER 2

*As Fireheart bounded across to Bluestar's* den, Speckletail spun around to face him. Her eyes were burning with anger. "There are two RiverClan cats here," she growled. "Mauling our leader's body!"

"No—no, they're not." Fireheart gasped. "They've a right to be here."

He realized that the rest of the Clan had gathered anxiously behind him and he heard Cloudtail yowling a challenge, with snarls of rage breaking out all around.

Fireheart whirled to face them. "Keep back!" he ordered. "It's all right. Mistyfoot and Stonefur—"

"You *know* they're here?" The voice was Darkstripe's; the dark tabby thrust his way through the crowd to stand nose-to-nose with Fireheart. "You let enemy cats into our camp—into our leader's den?"

Fireheart took a breath, forcing himself to stay calm. He deeply mistrusted the black-striped tabby. When the Clan had been preparing to escape the dog pack, Darkstripe had tried to slip away with Tigerstar's kits. He had sworn that he knew nothing of Tigerstar's plot to destroy ThunderClan with the dogs, but Fireheart was not sure he believed him.

"Have you forgotten what I told you?" he asked. "Mistyfoot and Stonefur helped me to pull Bluestar out of the river."

"So you say!" Darkstripe spat. "How do we know you're telling the truth? Why should RiverClan cats help ThunderClan?"

"They've helped us often enough in the past," Fireheart reminded him. "More of us would have died after the fire if RiverClan hadn't given us shelter."

"That's true," meowed Mousefur. She had returned with Cinderpelt from the medicine cat's den in time to hear the confrontation, and now she pushed forward to stand beside Darkstripe. "But it's no excuse to leave them alone in the den with Bluestar's body. What are they doing in there?"

"We are giving honor to Bluestar."

Stonefur spoke defiantly, and Fireheart turned his head to see that the RiverClan deputy and Mistyfoot had appeared in the mouth of the den. They both looked taken aback at the reaction of the ThunderClan cats, their fur beginning to bristle as they realized they were being treated as intruders.

"We wanted to say good-bye to her," Mistyfoot meowed.

"Why?" Mousefur demanded.

Fireheart's stomach clenched as Mistyfoot faced the light brown she-cat and answered, "She was our mother."

Silence fell, broken only by the call of a blackbird from the edge of the camp. Fireheart's mind raced as he faced the shocked, hostile stares of his Clan. His gaze met Sandstorm's; she looked dismayed, as if she guessed that Fireheart would never have chosen for ThunderClan to discover their leader's secret like this.

"Your mother?" growled Speckletail. "I don't believe it. Bluestar would never have allowed her kits to be raised in another Clan."

"Believe it or not, it's true," Stonefur retorted.

Fireheart stepped forward, warning Stonefur to stay silent with a flick of his tail. "I'll deal with this now. You and Mistyfoot had better go."

Stonefur gave him a curt nod and took the lead as he and Mistyfoot made their way toward the gorse tunnel. Fireheart heard one or two furious hisses as the ThunderClan cats parted to let them pass.

"The thanks of the Clan go with you," Fireheart called out after them, his voice echoing thinly off the Highrock.

Mistyfoot and Stonefur didn't respond. They didn't even turn to look back before they vanished into the tunnel.

Every hair on Fireheart's pelt prickled with the desire to turn and run from his new responsibilities. The secret that had been so heavy to keep—that Bluestar had given up her kits to another Clan—would be heavier still in the sharing. He wished that he had been given more time to think of what to say, but he knew that it was better for his Clan to hear the truth from him now, instead of from Tigerstar at the next Gathering. As Clan leader he had to face the task, however little he liked it.

Dipping his head to Cinderpelt, he bounded up onto the Highrock. There was no need to summon the Clan;

they were already turning to look up at him. For a heartbeat Fireheart was breathless, unable to speak.

He could see their anger and confusion, and smell their fear scent. Darkstripe was watching him with narrowed eyes, as if he were already planning what to tell Tigerstar. Bleakly Fireheart reflected that Tigerstar already knew; he had heard what Bluestar said to her kits as she lay dying by the river. But the ShadowClan leader would certainly be pleased to hear about ThunderClan's confusion and Fireheart's own difficulties. Tigerstar was sure to find a way to twist it to his advantage in his quest for revenge against ThunderClan and his efforts to recover his kits, Bramblepaw and Tawnypaw.

Fireheart took a deep breath and began: "It's true that Mistyfoot and Stonefur are Bluestar's kits." He struggled to keep his voice steady, and prayed to StarClan to give him the right words so that the cats would not turn against Bluestar. "Oakheart of RiverClan was their father. When her kits were born, Bluestar gave them to him to be brought up in his Clan."

"How do you know?" snarled Frostfur. "Bluestar would never have done that! If the RiverClan cats said so, they're lying."

"Bluestar told me herself," Fireheart replied.

He met the white cat's gaze; her eyes blazed with fury, her teeth were bared, but she did not quite dare to accuse *him* of lying. "Are you telling us she was a traitor?" she hissed.

One or two cats yowled a protest. Frostfur spun around, fur bristling, and Whitestorm rose to face her. Though the senior warrior looked stunned with shock, his voice was steady as he meowed, "Bluestar was *always* loyal to her Clan."

"If she was so loyal," Darkstripe put in, "why did she let a cat from another Clan father her kits?"

Fireheart found that question hard to answer. Not long ago, Graystripe had taken a mate from RiverClan, and his kits were growing up there now. The ThunderClan cats had been so horrified that Graystripe had felt he couldn't stay in his birth Clan any longer. Although he had returned, some cats still felt hostile to him and doubted his loyalty.

"Things happen," Fireheart replied. "When the kits were born, Bluestar would have brought them up to be loyal ThunderClan warriors, but—"

"I remember those kits." This time the interruption was from Smallear. "They disappeared out of the nursery. We all thought a fox or a badger had gotten them. Bluestar was distraught. Are you saying that was all a lie?"

Fireheart looked down at the old gray tom-cat. "No," he promised. "Bluestar was devastated at the loss of her kits. But she had to give them up in order to become Clan deputy."

"You're telling us her ambition meant more to her than her kits?" asked Dustpelt. The brown warrior sounded puzzled rather than angry, as if he couldn't reconcile this image with the wise leader he had always known.

"No," Fireheart told him. "She did it because the Clan needed her. She put the Clan first—just as she always did."

"That's true," Whitestorm agreed quietly. "Nothing meant more to Bluestar than ThunderClan."

"Mistyfoot and Stonefur are proud of her courage—both then and now," Fireheart went on. "As we should be."

He was relieved when there were no more open challenges, though the tension among the Clan cats did not die away completely. Mousefur and Frostfur were muttering together, casting suspicious glances up at him. Speckletail, tail-tip twitching, stalked across to join them. But Whitestorm moved from one cat to another, clearly backing up what he had said, and Smallear was nodding wisely, as if he respected the hard decision Bluestar had made.

Then a single voice rose clearly out of the hum of conversation. "Fireheart," Tawnypaw piped up, "are you going to be our leader now?"

Before Fireheart could reply, Darkstripe sprang to his paws. "Accept a kittypet as Clan leader? Are we all mad?"

"It's not a question, Darkstripe," Whitestorm pointed out, raising his voice above shocked exclamations from Sandstorm and Graystripe. "Fireheart is Clan deputy; he succeeds Bluestar. That's all there is to it."

Fireheart flashed him a grateful glance. The fur on his shoulders had begun to bristle and he deliberately relaxed so that it lay flat again. He would not let Darkstripe see that his challenging words had provoked him. Yet he could not stifle a moment of doubt. Bluestar had appointed him deputy, but her mind had been clouded by the shock of Tigerstar's treachery, and the whole Clan had been shocked because the ceremony had been late. Could that possibly mean he was not the right cat to lead ThunderClan?

"But a *kittypet*!" Darkstripe protested. His yellow eyes glared balefully up at Fireheart. "Stinking of Twolegs and their nests! Is that what we want as our leader?"

Fireheart felt the familiar rage burn in his belly. Even though he had lived with the Clan since he was six moons old, Darkstripe never let him forget that he was not forest-born.

As he struggled with the desire to leap down and sink his claws into Darkstripe's fur, Goldenflower rose to her paws and stepped forward to face the dark warrior. "You're wrong, Darkstripe," she growled. "Fireheart has proved his loyalty to the Clan a thousand times over. No Clan-born cat could have done more."

Fireheart blinked his thanks to her, surprised that Goldenflower of all cats should have supported him so determinedly. She knew of Fireheart's suspicions that her kit Bramblepaw would end up as dangerous as his father, Tigerstar. Though he had taken Bramblepaw as his own apprentice, he never felt comfortable around the young cat, and Goldenflower knew it. She had defended her kits fiercely against what she thought was Fireheart's unreasonable hostility. It was all the more surprising now that she should stand up for him against Darkstripe.

"Fireheart, don't listen to Darkstripe," Brackenfur added his voice to Goldenflower's. "Every cat here wants you as leader, apart from him. You're obviously the best cat for the job."

A murmur of agreement rose from the cats around the Highrock, and Fireheart's heart swelled with gratitude.

"And who are we to go against the decrees of StarClan?"

Mousefur added. "The deputy *always* becomes Clan leader. That is the tradition of the warrior code."

"Which Fireheart seems to know rather better than *you* do," Graystripe hissed, flicking his tail contemptuously at Darkstripe. He knew as well as Fireheart that the dark warrior had plotted with Tigerstar before the dog attack.

Fireheart gestured with one paw to his friend for silence before addressing the whole Clan. "I promise you that I will spend the rest of my life striving to become the leader that ThunderClan deserves. And with StarClan's help I will succeed."

His gaze was drawn instinctively to Sandstorm, and he felt warmth spread into his paws and the tip of his tail when he saw how proud she looked.

"As for you, Darkstripe," Fireheart spat, unable to hide his anger, "if you don't like the thought of being led by a kittypet, you can always leave."

The dark warrior lashed his tail; there was pure hatred in the look he threw Fireheart. *If I had never come to the forest,* Fireheart realized, *Tigerstar would be leader now, and you would be deputy.*

He had never intended to provoke a public confrontation with Darkstripe, but the dark tabby had driven him to it. Though ThunderClan could not afford to lose any warriors, a large part of Fireheart wanted Darkstripe to take him at his word and leave the Clan for good. Yet at the same time he knew that Darkstripe would go straight to ShadowClan and Tigerstar. It was better, Fireheart admitted to himself, to keep his enemies apart. Darkstripe would be less of a threat in ThunderClan, where Fireheart could keep an eye on him.

The black-striped warrior went on staring at him for a few heartbeats more, before whipping around to stalk away. But he did not head for the gorse tunnel; instead he vanished into the warriors' den.

"Right." Fireheart raised his voice as he turned back to the rest of the Clan. "Tonight we will hold the mourning rituals for Bluestar."

"Hang on!" Cloudtail sprang to his paws, tail fluffed up. "Aren't we going to attack ShadowClan? They slaughtered Brindleface and they led the dog pack to our camp! Don't you want revenge?"

His fur was bristling with hostility. Brindleface had been Cloudtail's foster mother when he first came to Thunder-Clan as a helpless kit. But Fireheart knew that attacking ShadowClan right now was not the answer.

He signaled with his tail to silence the yowls of agreement that had broken out as soon as Cloudtail spoke. "No," he meowed. "This is not the time to attack ShadowClan."

"*What?*" Cloudtail stared at him disbelievingly. "You'd let them get away with it?"

Fireheart took a deep breath. "ShadowClan didn't kill Brindleface, or lay the trail for the dogs. Tigerstar did. Every rabbit on the trail had his scent on it and no other cat's. We can't be sure that ShadowClan even knew what their leader was planning."

Cloudtail let out a snort of contempt. Fireheart fixed his former apprentice with a hard stare, willing him not to argue about this now. He knew that what had happened was due to the moons-old enmity between himself and Tigerstar. The ShadowClan leader would have been pleased to wipe out ThunderClan and take their territory for his own, but that was not his real motive for bringing the pack of dogs to the camp. What Tigerstar wanted more than anything else was to destroy Fireheart. Only then would he have his full revenge for the time when Fireheart had revealed his plot to kill Bluestar and driven him into exile.

Sooner or later, Fireheart now knew, he would have to come face-to-face with Tigerstar in a final confrontation that only one of them could survive. He prayed to StarClan that when the time came he would have the courage and strength to rid the forest of this bloodthirsty cat.

"Believe me," he meowed out loud, addressing the whole Clan, "Tigerstar will pay. But ThunderClan has no quarrel with ShadowClan."

To Fireheart's relief, Cloudtail sat down again, his blue eyes blazing with anger, and muttered something to Lostface. Nearby, Goldenflower was crouched with her tail wrapped protectively around Bramblepaw and Tawnypaw, as if they were still young kits. She had made Fireheart himself tell the young cats what Tigerstar had done, and she was always afraid that the Clan would judge them harshly because of their father's crimes. As Fireheart gave his decision not to attack, she visibly relaxed, and the two apprentices eased away from her. Bramblepaw flashed a look at Firestar from narrowed amber eyes, and Fireheart wondered if he saw hostility there.

He pushed the problem of Bramblepaw to the back of his mind as he looked out over the assembled cats. Long shadows were stretching across the camp, and Fireheart realized that the time had come for the Clan to make its last farewells to their beloved leader. "We must pay our respects to Bluestar," he announced. "Are you ready, Cinderpelt?" The medicine cat nodded. "Graystripe, Sandstorm," Fireheart went on, "can you bring Bluestar's body out into the clearing so that we may share tongues with her in the sight of StarClan?"

The two warriors got up and vanished into Bluestar's den, reappearing a moment later with their leader's body supported between them. They carried her to the center of the clearing and laid her gently onto the hard-packed sand.

"Sandstorm, round up a hunting patrol," Fireheart ordered. "When you've said good-bye to Bluestar I'd like you to stock up the fresh-kill pile. And Mousefur, when you have finished, could you lead a patrol out toward Snakerocks and the ShadowClan border? I want to be sure that all the dogs have gone, and that there are no ShadowClan cats on our territory. Be careful, though—don't take risks."

"Sure, Fireheart." The wiry brown tabby got to her paws. "Goldenflower, Longtail, are you coming?"

The cats she had named went to join her, and all three moved into the center of the clearing to share tongues with their leader for the last time. Sandstorm followed with Dustpelt and Cloudtail. Cinderpelt stood at Bluestar's head and gazed into the indigo sky, where the first stars of Silverpelt were beginning to appear. According to the ancient traditions of the Clans, each star represented the spirit of a warrior ancestor. Fireheart wondered if there were one more star tonight, for Bluestar.

Cinderpelt's blue eyes shone with the secrets of StarClan. "Bluestar was a noble leader," she meowed. "Let us give thanks to StarClan for her life. She was dedicated to her Clan, and her memory will never fade from the forest. Now we commend her spirit to StarClan; may she watch over us in death as she always did in life."

A soft murmuring spread throughout the Clan as the medicine cat finished speaking and stood with her head bowed. The warriors Fireheart had chosen to go out on patrol crouched beside Bluestar's body, grooming her fur and pressing their noses to her flank. After a while they backed away and other cats took their place, until all the Clan had shared tongues with their leader in the sorrowful ritual.

The patrols left, and the other cats retreated silently to their dens. Fireheart stood watching near the base of the Highrock, and as Brackenfur moved away from his leader's body he stepped forward to intercept the young warrior. "I've got a job for you," he murmured. "I want you to keep an eye on Darkstripe for me. If he so much as looks across the border to ShadowClan, I want to know about it."

The young ginger tom gazed at him, alarm battling with loyalty to his new Clan leader. "I'll do my best, Fireheart, but he won't like it."

"With any luck, he won't know about it. Don't make it too obvious, and ask one or two of the others to help you . . . Mousefur, maybe, and Frostfur." Seeing that Brackenfur was still doubtful, Fireheart added, "Darkstripe may not have known about the dogs, but he knew that Tigerstar was planning something. We can't trust him."

"I can see that," Brackenfur meowed, his eyes troubled. "But we can't watch him forever."

"It won't be forever," Fireheart assured him. "Just until Darkstripe proves where his loyalties lie—one way or the other."

Brackenfur nodded, then slipped silently into the warriors' den. With no more problems clamoring for his attention, Fireheart was able to cross the clearing to Bluestar's body. Cinderpelt still sat near her head and Whitestorm was crouched beside her, his head bowed in grief.

Fireheart dipped his head to the medicine cat. He settled himself beside Bluestar, searching her face for signs of the leader he had loved so much. But her eyes were closed, never again to burn with the fire that had commanded respect from all the Clans. Her spirit had gone to race joyously through the sky with her warrior ancestors', keeping watch over the forest.

He felt the soft caress of his leader's fur and felt a sense of security flood over him, almost as if he were a kit again, curling up close to his mother. For a moment he could almost forget the horror of her dying and the loneliness of his new responsibilities.

*Receive her with honor*, Fireheart prayed silently to StarClan, closing his eyes and pressing his nose to Bluestar's fur. *And help me keep her Clan safe.*

## CHAPTER 3

*Something was prodding Fireheart in the* side. With a muffled mew of protest he opened his eyes to see Cinderpelt stooping over him.

"You dozed off," she murmured. "But you'll have to wake up now. It's time to bury Bluestar."

Fireheart staggered to his paws. He flexed each stiff leg in turn and passed his dry tongue over his lips. He felt as if he had been crouching in the clearing for a moon at least. The sense of comfort he had felt as he slept was replaced by a wave of guilt.

"Did any cat see?" he muttered to Cinderpelt.

The medicine cat's blue eyes glimmered with sympathy. "Only me. Don't worry about it, Fireheart. No cat would blame you after what happened yesterday."

Fireheart glanced around the clearing. The pale light of dawn was just beginning to seep through the trees. A few tail-lengths away the elders had assembled to carry out their duty of bearing Bluestar's body to the burial place. The rest of the Clan were slowly emerging from their dens, forming two lines between Bluestar's body and the entrance to the gorse tunnel.

At a nod from Cinderpelt, the elders took up the body and carried Bluestar between the rows of her grieving warriors. Every cat bowed his head as their leader was borne past.

"Good-bye, Bluestar," Fireheart murmured. "I'll never forget you." Sharp thorns of pain pierced his heart when he saw the tip of her tail scoring a furrow in the blackened leaves that still lay on the ground after the recent fire.

When Bluestar had vanished with her escort, the rest of the cats began to disperse. Fireheart checked the camp, noticing with approval that the pile of fresh-kill had been stocked up. All he needed to do was send out the dawn patrol; then he could eat and rest. He felt as if a moon of sleep would not be enough to banish the exhaustion from his paws.

"Well, Fireheart," meowed Cinderpelt. "Are you ready?"

Fireheart turned, puzzled. "Ready?"

"To go to the Moonstone to receive your nine lives from StarClan." The tip of Cinderpelt's tail twitched. "Fireheart, surely you hadn't forgotten?"

Fireheart shuffled his paws uneasily. Of course he hadn't forgotten the ancient ceremony to initiate all new Clan leaders, but somehow he hadn't realized that it would take place right away. He felt dazed by the speed with which everything was happening, bearing him forward relentlessly like the swift waters of the gorge that had almost drowned him.

Fear rose in his throat and he had to swallow quickly. No leader ever spoke of the mystic rite, so no other cat, except for the medicine cats, knew what happened there. Fireheart had visited the Moonstone before and watched

Bluestar share tongues with StarClan in her sleep. That experience had been awe-inspiring enough. He could not imagine what would happen when he had to lie beside the sacred stone himself and share dreams with his warrior ancestors.

On top of this, he knew that Highstones, where the Moonstone lay in a cavern far underground, was a whole day's journey away, and the ritual demanded that he not eat beforehand, not even the strengthening herbs that other cats took for the journey.

"StarClan will give you strength," meowed Cinderpelt, as if she had read his thoughts.

Fireheart muttered in vague agreement. Glancing around, he spotted Whitestorm on his way to the warriors' den and summoned the older warrior with a flick of his tail.

"I've got to go to Highstones," he meowed. "Will you take charge of the camp? We'll need a dawn patrol."

"Consider it done," promised Whitestorm, and added, "StarClan go with you, Fireheart."

Fireheart took a last look around the camp as he followed Cinderpelt toward the gorse tunnel. He felt as if he were going on a long journey, farther than he had ever traveled before, where the prospect of return looked doubtful. And in a way he never would return, for the cat who came back would have a new name, new responsibilities, and a new relationship with StarClan.

As he turned away, a yowl sounded behind him. Graystripe and Sandstorm were racing across the clearing.

"You weren't sneaking off without saying good-bye?" Graystripe panted, skidding to a halt.

Sandstorm said nothing, but she twined her tail with Fireheart's and pressed close to his side.

"I'll be back tomorrow," Fireheart meowed. "Listen," he added awkwardly, "I know things will be different now, but I'll never stop needing you—both of you. No cat ever had such good friends."

Graystripe butted him in the shoulder. "We know that, you stupid furball," he mewed.

Sandstorm's green eyes shone as she gazed into Fireheart's. "We'll always need you too, Fireheart," she murmured. "And you'd better not forget that."

"Fireheart, come on!" Cinderpelt called from where she was waiting at the entrance to the gorse tunnel. "We have to reach Highstones by nightfall—and remember I can't move as fast as you."

"Coming!" Fireheart gave each of his friends a quick lick before plunging into the gorse tunnel after the medicine cat. His heart felt full of hope as he caught up to her and made his way to the top of the ravine. He might have been leaving his old life behind, but he could take with him everything that was important.

The sun was up in a clear blue sky and the frost had melted from the grass by the time the two cats reached Fourtrees, where the Gatherings were held between all four Clans every full moon.

"I hope we don't meet a WindClan patrol," Fireheart remarked as they crossed the border onto the high, exposed moorland, leaving the shelter of the forest behind them.

Not long before, Bluestar had tried to launch an attack on WindClan, accusing them of stealing prey from ThunderClan. Fireheart had disobeyed his leader and risked accusations of treachery to avoid a battle. Although Tallstar, the WindClan leader, had been prepared to make peace, Fireheart could imagine that the WindClan cats might still bear a grudge.

"They won't stop us," Cinderpelt replied calmly.

"They might try," Fireheart argued. "I'd rather avoid them altogether."

His hopes were dashed as he and Cinderpelt reached the crest of a stretch of moorland and saw a WindClan patrol picking their way through the heather a few foxlengths below. They were downwind, so Fireheart had not detected their scent as a warning.

The leader of the patrol raised his head, and Fireheart recognized the warrior Tornear. His heart sank when he saw that his old enemy Mudclaw was just behind him, with an apprentice Fireheart didn't know. He and Cinderpelt waited as the WindClan cats bounded through the heather toward them; there was no point in trying to avoid them now.

Mudclaw curled his lip in a snarl, but Tornear dipped his head as he halted in front of Fireheart. "Greetings, Fireheart, Cinderpelt," he meowed. "Why are you here on our territory?"

"We're on our way to Highstones," Cinderpelt replied, taking a step forward.

Fireheart felt a surge of pride to see the respectful nod the WindClan warrior gave to his medicine cat.

"No bad news, I hope?" Tornear asked; cats did not usually travel to Highstones unless a crisis in their Clan demanded direct communication with StarClan.

"The worst," Cinderpelt meowed steadily. "Bluestar died yesterday."

All three WindClan cats bowed their heads; even Mudclaw looked solemn. "She was a great and noble cat," Tornear meowed at last. "Every Clan will honor her memory."

Raising his head again, he turned to Fireheart with a look of curiosity and respect in his eyes. "So you're to be leader now?" he asked.

"Yes," Fireheart admitted. "I'm going to receive my nine lives from StarClan."

Tornear nodded, his gaze traveling slowly over the warrior's flame-colored pelt. "You're young," he commented. "But something tells me you'll make a fine leader."

"Th-thank you," Fireheart stammered, taken by surprise.

Cinderpelt rescued him. "We mustn't stay," she meowed. "It's a long way to Highstones."

"Of course." Tornear stepped back. "We'll tell Tallstar your news. May StarClan be with you!" he called as the two ThunderClan cats bounded away.

On the edge of the uplands they paused again and looked down over a very different landscape. Instead of bare hillside broken by outcrops of rock and patches of heather, Fireheart saw a scattering of Twoleg nests among fields and hedgerows.

In the distance the Thunderpath cut a swath across the land, while beyond that jagged hills reared up, their barren slopes looking gray and threatening. Fireheart swallowed; that desolate region was where they were heading.

He realized that Cinderpelt was looking at him with understanding in her blue eyes.

"Everything's different," Fireheart confessed. "You saw those WindClan cats. Even they don't treat me in the same way anymore." He knew he could never say these things to anyone except the medicine cat—not even to Sandstorm. "It's as if every cat expects me to be noble and wise. But I'm not. I'll make mistakes, just like I did before. Cinderpelt, I'm not sure I can do this."

"Mouse-brain." Fireheart was both shocked and comforted by the teasing note in Cinderpelt's voice. "When you make mistakes—not *if*, Fireheart, *when*—I'll tell you about them, believe me." More seriously, she added, "And I'll still be your friend, no matter what. No cat that ever lived was perfect all the time. Bluestar wasn't! The trick is to learn from your mistakes, and have the courage to be true to your heart." She turned her head and rasped her tongue over his ear. "You'll be fine, Fireheart. Now let's go."

Fireheart let her take the lead down the slope and across the Twoleg farmland. The two cats picked their way over the sticky earth of a plowed field and skirted the Twoleg nest where the two loners, Barley and Ravenpaw, lived. Fireheart kept a lookout, but there was no sign of them. He was sorry not to see them, for both cats were good friends to

ThunderClan, and Ravenpaw had once trained alongside Fireheart as an apprentice. The distant barking of a dog sent shivers through Fireheart's fur as he remembered the horror of being chased by the pack.

Keeping to the shadows of the hedges, they eventually reached the Thunderpath and crouched beside it, their fur ruffled by the wind of monsters racing past them. The strong reek of their fumes flooded Fireheart's nose and throat, and his eyes stung.

Cinderpelt braced herself beside him, waiting for a space between the monsters when it would be safe to cross. Fireheart felt anxious for his friend. Her leg had been permanently injured in an accident at the edge of the Thunderpath many moons ago, when she had been his apprentice; the old injury would slow her down.

"We'll go together," he meowed, feeling the familiar guilt that he had not prevented her accident. "Whenever you're ready."

Cinderpelt gave a tiny nod; Fireheart guessed she was afraid, but she wouldn't admit it. A moment later, after a brightly colored monster flashed past, she mewed, "Now!" and limped rapidly out onto the hard black surface.

Fireheart bounded at her side, forcing himself not to leave her behind even though his heart was hammering and every instinct screamed at him to run across as quickly as he could. He heard the roar of a monster in the distance, but before it arrived he and the medicine cat were safe in the hedgerow on the other side.

The medicine cat let out a gusty sigh. "Thank StarClan that's over!"

Fireheart murmured agreement, though he knew they still had to face the return journey.

Already the sun was sliding down the sky. The land on this side of the Thunderpath was less familiar to Fireheart, and every sense was alert for danger as they began to climb toward Highstones. But all he could hear was prey scuffling in the scanty grass; the tempting scent flooded his mouth, and he wished he were allowed to stop and hunt.

As Fireheart and Cinderpelt reached the foot of the final slope, the sun was setting behind the peak. The evening shadows were lengthening and a chill crept over the ground. Above his head, Fireheart could make out a square opening beneath an overhang of stone.

"We've reached Mothermouth," Cinderpelt meowed. "Let's rest for a moment."

She and Fireheart lay down together on a flat rock while the last of the light died from the sky and the stars of Silverpelt began to appear. The moon flooded all the landscape in a cold, frosty light.

"It's time," mewed Cinderpelt.

All his misgivings coursed through Fireheart once again, and at first he thought his paws would not carry him. But he rose and began walking forward, the sharp stones biting into his pads, until he stood beneath the arch known to the Clans as Mothermouth.

A black tunnel yawned into darkness. From his previous

visit Fireheart knew that there was no point in straining his eyes to see what lay ahead; the blackness was unbroken all the way to the cavern where the Moonstone lay. As he hesitated, Cinderpelt stepped forward confidently.

"Follow my scent," she told him. "I will lead you to the Moonstone. And from now on, until the ritual is over, neither of us must speak."

"But I don't know what to do," Fireheart protested.

"When we reach the Moonstone, lie down and press your nose to it." Her blue eyes gleamed in the moonlight. "StarClan will send you sleep so you may meet with them in dreams."

There was a forest full of questions that Fireheart wanted to ask her, but none whose answers would help him overcome the creeping dread he felt. He bowed his head in silence and followed Cinderpelt as she made her way into the darkness.

The tunnel sloped steadily downward, and Fireheart soon lost his sense of direction as it wound back and forth. Sometimes the walls were so close together that his fur and whiskers brushed the sides. His heart thumped wildly and he opened his mouth to draw in Cinderpelt's comforting scent, terrified at the thought that he might lose her.

At last he realized that he could see Cinderpelt's ears outlined against a faint light ahead. Other scents began to reach him, and his whiskers twitched in a flow of cold, fresh air. A heartbeat later he rounded a bend in the tunnel and the light grew suddenly stronger. Fireheart narrowed his eyes as he padded forward, sensing that the tunnel had opened out into a cave.

High above his head, a hole in the roof showed a chink of night sky. A shaft of moonlight shone through it, falling directly onto a rock in the center of the cavern. Fireheart drew in his breath sharply. He had seen the Moonstone once before, but he had forgotten just how startling it was. About three tail-lengths high, tapering toward its top, it reflected the moonlight in its dazzling crystal as if a star had fallen to the earth. The white light lit up the whole cave, turning Cinderpelt's gray fur to silver.

She turned toward Fireheart and signaled to him with her tail to take his place beside the Moonstone.

Unable to speak, even if he could think of anything to say, Fireheart obeyed. He lay down in front of the stone, settling his head on his paws so that his nose touched the smooth surface. The cold was a shock, so that he almost drew back, and for a moment he blinked at the light of stars sparkling in the depths of the stone.

Then he closed his eyes, and waited for StarClan to send him to sleep.

# CHAPTER 4

*All was darkness and cold. Fireheart* had never been so cold. He felt as if every scrap of warmth and life were being sucked out of his body. His legs twitched as painful cramps clutched at them. He imagined that he was made of ice, and if he tried to move he would shatter into a thousand brittle fragments.

But no dreams came. No sight or sound of StarClan. Only the cold and the darkness. *Something must be wrong,* Fireheart thought, beginning to panic.

He dared to open his eyes a narrow slit. At once they flew wide with shock. Instead of the shining Moonstone in a cavern far below the ground, he saw short, well-trodden grass stretching away. Night scents flooded over him, of green, growing things moist with dew. A warm breeze ruffled his fur.

Scrambling into a sitting position, Fireheart realized he was in the hollow at Fourtrees, near the base of the Great Rock. The towering oaks, in full leaf, rustled over his head, and Silverpelt glittered beyond them in the night sky.

*How did I come here?* he wondered. *Is this the dream that Cinderpelt promised?*

He raised his head and looked up at the sky. He could

not remember its being so clear; Silverpelt looked closer than he had ever seen before, scarcely higher than the topmost branches of the oaks. As Fireheart gazed at it, he realized something that sent the blood thrilling through his veins like liquid fire.

*The stars were moving.*

They swirled before his disbelieving eyes and began to spiral downward, toward the forest, toward Fourtrees, toward him. Fireheart waited, his heart pounding.

And the cats of StarClan came stalking down the sky. Frost sparkled at their paws and glittered in their eyes. Their pelts were white flame. They carried the scent of ice and fire and the wild places of the night.

Fireheart crouched before them. He could scarcely bear to go on looking, and yet he could not bear to look away. He wanted to absorb this moment into every hair on his pelt so it would be his forever.

After a time that might have lasted a hundred seasons or a single heartbeat, all the cats of StarClan had come down to earth. All around Fireheart the hollow of Fourtrees was lined with their shimmering bodies and blazing eyes. Fireheart crouched in the center, surrounded on all sides. He began to realize that some of the starry cats, those sitting closest to him, were achingly familiar.

*Bluestar!* Joy pierced him like a thorn in his heart. *And Yellowfang!* Then he drew in a familiar, sweet scent, and turned his head to see the tortoiseshell fur and gentle face that he had dreamed of so often.

*Spottedleaf—oh, Spottedleaf!* His beloved medicine cat had come back to him. Fireheart wanted to spring to his paws and yowl his joy to the whole forest, but awe kept him silent, still crouching.

"Welcome, Fireheart." The sound seemed to belong to all the cats Fireheart had ever known, and yet at the same time it was one clear voice. "Are you ready to receive your nine lives?"

Fireheart glanced around, but he couldn't see any cat speaking. "Yes," he replied, forcing his voice not to shake. "I'm ready."

A golden tabby cat rose to his paws and strode toward him, his head and tail high. Fireheart recognized Lionheart, who had become Bluestar's deputy when Fireheart was still an apprentice and who had died soon after in a battle with ShadowClan. He had been an old cat when Fireheart knew him, but now he looked young and strong again, his coat shining with pale fire.

"Lionheart!" Fireheart gasped. "Is it really you?"

Lionheart did not reply. When he was close enough, he stooped and touched his nose to Fireheart's head. It burned against him like the hottest flame and the coldest ice. Fireheart's instinct was to shrink away, but he could not move.

"With this life I give you courage," Lionheart murmured. "Use it well in defense of your Clan."

At once a bolt of energy seared through Fireheart like lightning, setting his fur on end and filling his senses with a deafening roar. His eyes grew dark, and his mind filled with a chaotic swirl of battles and hunts, the feeling of claws raking across fur and teeth meeting in the flesh of prey.

The pain ebbed, leaving Fireheart weak and trembling. The darkness faded and he found himself in the unearthly clearing again. If that was one life received, he had eight more to go. *How will I bear it?* he thought in dismay.

Lionheart was already turning away, moving back to his place in the ranks of StarClan. Another cat rose and came toward Fireheart. At first Fireheart did not recognize him, but then he glimpsed a dark, dappled coat and bushy red tail and realized this must be Redtail. Fireheart had never met the ThunderClan deputy, who was murdered by Tigerstar on the very day Fireheart came to the forest as a kittypet, but he had sought out the truth about his death and used it to prove Tigerstar's treachery.

Like Lionheart, Redtail bowed his head and touched his nose to Fireheart's. "With this life I give you justice," he mewed. "Use it well as you judge the actions of others."

Once more an agonizing spasm rushed through Fireheart, and he had to grit his teeth to stop himself from yowling. When he recovered, panting as if he had raced all the way back to camp, he saw Redtail watching him. "Thank you," the former deputy meowed solemnly. "You revealed the truth when no other cat could."

Fireheart managed to nod in acknowledgment as Redtail went back to sit beside Lionheart again, and a third cat emerged from the ranks.

This time Fireheart's jaws dropped open when he recognized the beautiful tabby, her coat glimmering with a silvery sheen. It was Graystripe's lost love Silverstream, the RiverClan queen who had died bearing his kits. Her paws scarcely skimmed the ground as she bent down to him.

"With this life I give you loyalty to what you know to be right," she meowed. Fireheart wondered if she was referring to the way he had helped Graystripe to see his forbidden love, trusting to the strength of their relationship even though it went against the warrior code. "Use it well to guide your Clan in times of trouble," Silverstream urged him.

Fireheart braced himself for another agonizing pang, but this time there was less pain as the new life rushed through him. He was aware of a warm glow of love, and realized dimly that that was what had marked out Silverstream's life—love for her Clan, for Graystripe, and for the kits she had died to give life to.

"Silverstream!" he whispered as the silver-gray she-cat turned away again. "Don't go yet. Haven't you any message for Graystripe?"

But Silverstream said nothing more, only glancing back over her shoulder, her eyes filled with love and sorrow that told Fireheart more than all the words she could ever say.

He closed his eyes, preparing himself for the next life-giving. When he looked up again, a fourth cat was approaching him. This time it was Runningwind, the ThunderClan warrior who had been killed by Tigerstar in a fight near the Thunderpath.

"With this life I give you tireless energy," he meowed as he bowed his head to touch Fireheart. "Use it well to carry out the duties of a leader."

As the life coursed through Fireheart he felt as if he were racing through the forest, his paws skimming the ground, his fur flattened by the wind. He knew the exhilaration of the hunt and the sheer joy of speed, and he had the feeling that he could outrun any enemy forever.

His gaze followed Runningwind as he returned to his place. When the fifth cat appeared his heart gave a leap of joy. It was Brindleface, Cloudtail's foster mother, who had been cruelly slaughtered by Tigerstar to give the dog pack a taste for cat blood.

"With this life I give you protection," she told him. "Use it well to care for your Clan as a mother cares for her kits."

Fireheart expected this life to be gentle and loving like Silverstream's, and he wasn't ready for the bolt of ferocity that transfixed him. He felt as though all the fury of their ancient ancestors TigerClan and LionClan were pulsing through him, challenging any cat to harm the weaker, faceless shadows that crouched by his paws. Shocked and trembling, Fireheart recognized a mother's desire to protect her kits, and realized how much Brindleface had loved them all—even Cloudtail, who was not her own.

*I must tell him*, Fireheart thought as the fury ebbed, before he remembered that he was bound to say nothing to any cat about what he had experienced in the ritual.

Brindleface drew back to sit with the other cats of StarClan again, and another familiar figure took her place. Guilt washed over Fireheart as he recognized Swiftpaw.

"I'm sorry," he murmured as he looked into the apprentice's eyes. "It was my fault you died."

Angry at Bluestar's refusal to make him a warrior, and desperate to prove himself, Swiftpaw had gone out to track down whatever was preying on the cats in the forest. The dog pack had killed him, and Fireheart knew he would blame himself forever for not trying harder to make Bluestar change her mind.

But Swiftpaw showed no anger now. His eyes shone with a wisdom far beyond his age as he touched his nose to Fireheart's. "With this life I give you mentoring. Use it well to train the young cats of your Clan."

The life Swiftpaw gave him was a pang of anguish so great Fireheart thought it would stop his heart. It ended in a jolt of pure terror, and a flash of light red as blood. Fireheart knew he was experiencing what Swiftpaw had felt in the last moments of his life.

As it ebbed away, leaving Fireheart gasping, he began to feel like a hollow in the ground as rain falls into it and spills over. He thought that his strength would hardly sustain him to receive lives from the three cats that were still to come.

The first was Yellowfang. The old medicine cat had the same air of obstinate independence and courage that had impressed and frustrated Fireheart in equal measure when she was alive. He remembered the last time he had seen her, dying in her den after the fire. Then she had been in despair, wondering if StarClan would receive her even though she had killed her own son, Brokentail, to put an end to his bloodthirsty plotting. Now the gleam of humor was back in her yellow eyes as she stooped to touch Fireheart.

"With this life I give you compassion," she announced. "Use it well for the elders of your Clan, and the sick, and all those weaker than yourself."

This time, even knowing the pain he would have to bear, Fireheart closed his eyes and drank in the life hungrily, wanting all of Yellowfang's spirit, all her courage and her loyalty to the Clan that was not hers by birth. He received it like a tide of light surging through him: her humor, her sharp tongue, her warmheartedness, and her sense of honor. He felt closer to her than ever before.

"Oh, Yellowfang . . ." Fireheart whispered, his eyes blinking open again. "I've missed you so much."

The medicine cat was already moving away. The cat who took her place was younger, stepping lightly, the sparkle of stars in her fur and in her eyes: Spottedleaf, the beautiful tortoiseshell who had been Fireheart's first love. She had come to him in dreams, but he had never seen her as plainly as this since she had been alive. He breathed in her sweet scent as she bent over him. This cat, more than any, was the one with whom he wanted to speak, because the time they had had together had been too short to let them share their true feelings.

"Spottedleaf . . ."

"With this life I give you love," she murmured in her soft

voice. "Use it well, for all the cats in your care—and especially for Sandstorm."

There was no pain in the life that poured into Fireheart now. It held the warmth of the high sun in greenleaf, burning to the tips of his paws. It was pure love; at the same time he experienced the sense of security he had known as a tiny kit, nuzzling his mother. He gazed up at Spottedleaf, wrapped in a contentment he had never known before.

He thought he caught a proud gleam in her eyes as she turned away, and his disappointment that she had not stayed to talk to him was mixed with relief that she approved of his new choice. Now he had no reason to fear that he was being unfaithful to Spottedleaf in his love for Sandstorm.

At last Bluestar approached Fireheart. She was not the old, defeated cat Fireheart had known recently, her mind giving way under the stress of her Clan's troubles. This was Bluestar at the height of her strength and power, prowling toward him across the clearing like a lion. Fireheart was almost dazzled by the glory of starlight around her, but he forced himself to meet her blue gaze squarely.

"Welcome, Fireheart, my apprentice, my warrior, and my deputy," she greeted him. "I always knew you would make a great leader one day."

As Fireheart bowed his head, Bluestar touched him with her nose and went on; "With this life I give you nobility and certainty and faith. Use it well as you lead your Clan in the ways of StarClan and the warrior code."

The warmth of Spottedleaf's life had lulled Fireheart, and

he was unprepared for the agony that shook him as he received Bluestar's. He shared the fierceness of her ambition, the anguish she had suffered when she gave up her kits, the ferocity of battle after battle in the service of her Clan. He felt her terror as her mind fragmented and she lost her trust in StarClan. The rush of power grew stronger and stronger, until Fireheart thought his pelt would never contain it. Just as he thought he must yowl his pain or die, it began to ebb, ending in a sense of calm acceptance and joy.

A long, soft sigh passed through the clearing. All the StarClan warriors had risen to their paws. Bluestar stayed in the center of the clearing and signaled with her tail that Fireheart should rise too. He obeyed her shakily, feeling as if the fullness of life inside him would spill over when he moved. His body felt as battered as if he had fought the hardest battle of his life, and yet his spirit soared with the strength of the lives he had been granted.

"I hail you by your new name, Firestar," Bluestar announced. "Your old life is no more. You have now received the nine lives of a leader, and StarClan grants to you the guardianship of ThunderClan. Defend it well; care for young and old; honor your ancestors and the traditions of the warrior code; live each life with pride and dignity."

"Firestar! Firestar!" Just as the forest Clans would acclaim a new warrior by name, so the cats of StarClan acclaimed Firestar, in rich voices that tingled in the air. "Firestar! Firestar!"

Suddenly the chanting broke off with a startled hiss.

Firestar tensed, aware that something was wrong. Bluestar's glowing eyes were fixed on something behind him. He spun around and let out a choking cry.

A massive hill of bones had appeared at the other side of the clearing, many tail-lengths high. It shone with an unnatural light, so that Firestar could see each separate bone edged as if with fire—the bones of cats and the bones of prey, all jumbled together. A hot wind swept over him, bearing the reek of carrion, even though the bones gleamed white and clean.

Firestar gazed wildly around him, seeking help or answers from the other cats. But the clearing was dark. The cats of StarClan had vanished, leaving him alone with the terrible hill of bones. As Firestar felt panic welling up inside him, he sensed the familiar presence of Bluestar by his side, warm fur pressed against his flank. He could not see her in the darkness, but her voice whispered in his ear.

"Something terrible is coming, Firestar. Four will become two. Lion and tiger will meet in battle, and blood will rule the forest."

Her scent and the warmth of her fur faded away as she finished speaking.

"Wait!" Firestar yowled. "Don't leave me! Tell me what you mean!"

But there was no reply, no explanation of the dreadful prophecy. Instead, the red light that gleamed from the hill of bones glowed brighter. Firestar stared at it in horror. Blood had begun to ooze out between the bones. The trickles merged into a river that flowed steadily toward him, until the stench of blood clung to his fur. He tried to flee, and found his paws were fixed in place. A heartbeat later, the sticky red tide was washing around him, gurgling and reeking of death.

"No!" Firestar yowled, but there was no response from the forest, just the steady whisper of blood lapping hungrily at his fur.

# CHAPTER 5

*Firestar jolted awake in terror. He* was lying in the cavern beneath Highstones with his nose pressed against the Moonstone. The shaft of moonlight had vanished, and only the faintest glimmer of starshine lit the cave. But there was no relief in waking up, for the stench of blood was still all around him and his fur felt hot and sticky.

Heart thudding wildly, Firestar scrambled to his paws. Across the cave he could just make out Cinderpelt. She had risen too, and was signaling urgently to him with her tail. Firestar's first impulse was to pour out to her all that he had seen, but he remembered her instructions to keep silent until they had left Mothermouth. Paws skidding on the cave floor in his haste, he pushed past the medicine cat and bolted into the tunnel.

As he stumbled upward toward the open air, following his own scent trail along the dark passage, the way seemed twice as long as before. Firestar's fur scraped against the tunnel walls and he was filled with horror at the thought of being buried alive. The air felt too thick to breathe, and as his panic grew in the unbroken blackness of the tunnel he began to imagine that it would never end, that he would be trapped forever in blood and darkness.

Then he saw the pale outline of the tunnel entrance, and burst out into the still night air, where the moon was sinking behind thin clouds. Firestar dug his claws into the loose earth of the hillside while shudders passed through his body from nose to tail.

A few moments later, Cinderpelt emerged behind him and pressed herself against his side until he managed to control his dreadful shivering and his breathing steadied.

"What happened?" she asked quietly.

"Don't you know?"

Cinderpelt shook her head. "I know that the ritual was interrupted—the scent of blood told me that. But I don't know why." She looked deep into his eyes; her own were burning with concern. "Tell me . . . did you receive your nine lives and your name?"

Firestar nodded, and the medicine cat relaxed slightly. "Then the rest can wait. Let's go."

For a moment Firestar felt too exhausted to move. But he did not want to stay anywhere near Mothermouth and the terrible things that he had seen in the cave. Shakily, pawstep by pawstep, he began to descend the hill. Cinderpelt padded beside him, sometimes nudging him toward an easier route, and Firestar was grateful for her unquestioning presence.

As they drew farther away from the tunnel, the stench of blood faded from his mouth and nostrils. Still, Firestar felt that even if he washed for a moon he would never get rid of the last traces from his fur. He began to feel stronger, but he was still very tired, and as soon as the rocky hillside gave way to grass he flopped down in the shelter of a hawthorn bush.

"I've got to rest," he meowed.

Cinderpelt tucked herself into the grass beside him and for a few moments the two cats shared tongues in silence. Firestar wanted to tell the medicine cat what he had seen, but something kept him silent. Partly he wanted to protect her from the dreadful fear he had felt—even if she could explain what Bluestar's prophecy meant, would it help to have another cat look forward to the future with the dread that he now felt? And partly he hoped that if he never spoke of the dreadful vision, it might not come true. Or was there a curse on his leadership that nothing could avert? Bluestar had told him before she died that he was the fire who would save the Clan. How could that be true, if the fire was quenched by the tidal wave of blood he had just seen? Firestar had experienced prophetic dreams before, and he had learned to take them seriously. He could not ignore this, especially when it came at such a significant moment, while he was receiving his nine lives and his new name.

Cinderpelt broke into his reverie. "It's okay if you don't want to talk about it yet, you know."

Firestar pushed his muzzle into her fur, grateful for her warmth. "I'll think about it first," he mewed slowly. "Right now . . . it's too close." He shivered again at the memory. "Cinderpelt," he went on, "I've never told any cat this before, but . . . sometimes I have dreams that tell me about the future."

Cinderpelt's ears twitched in surprise. "That's unusual. Clan leaders and medicine cats commune with StarClan, but I never heard of ordinary warriors having prophetic dreams. How long has this been going on?"

"Since I was a kittypet," Firestar admitted, remembering the dream of hunting a mouse that had first driven him into the forest. "But I . . . I don't know if the dreams come from StarClan." After all, before he came to the forest, he hadn't even known about StarClan. Could they have been watching over him even then?

The medicine cat's eyes were thoughtful. "In the end, all dreams come from StarClan," she murmured. "Do they always come true?"

"Yes," Firestar replied. "But not always in the way I expect. Some are easier to understand than others."

"Then you should bear that in mind when you're trying to understand this latest dream." Cinderpelt gave him a comforting lick. "Remember, Firestar, you're not alone. Now that you're Clan leader, StarClan will share many things with you. But I'm here to help you interpret the signs. Tell me as much or as little as you want."

Though Firestar was grateful for her understanding, Cinderpelt's words chilled him. His new relationship with StarClan was driving him along new paths where he might not want to go. For a few heartbeats he longed to be no more than a warrior again, hunting with Graystripe or sharing tongues with Sandstorm in the den.

"Thank you, Cinderpelt," he meowed, forcing himself

to his paws. "I promise I'll talk to you whenever I feel the need." But even though he meant what he said, deep down he wondered how helpful she would be. Firestar couldn't help feeling that this was something he had to face alone. He let out a long sigh. "Let's keep going."

However much Firestar longed to get home, his strength was failing. Since the discovery of the dog pack and the heart-stopping dash through the forest to lead them to the gorge, he had eaten little, and scarcely slept except to dream. The long journey to Highstones and the agony of receiving his nine lives, followed by the terrible vision, had taken all he had to give.

His steps became slower and more uncertain. They were passing Barley's farm when the medicine cat gave his shoulder a sharp nudge. "That's enough, Firestar," she meowed firmly. "As your medicine cat I'm telling you that you need to rest. Let's see if Barley and Ravenpaw are at home."

"Good idea." Firestar felt too relieved at the prospect of resting to argue.

Cautiously the two cats approached the Twoleg barn. Firestar was worried that the dogs might be unchained, but their scent was faint and distant. Much stronger was the scent of cats, and as they drew closer Firestar spotted a muscular black-and-white tom squeezing himself through a gap in the door.

"Barley!" he meowed in greeting. "It's good to see you. You know Cinderpelt, our medicine cat?"

Barley gave both cats a brisk nod. "It's good to see you, too, Fireheart."

"Fire*star*," Cinderpelt corrected him. "He's Clan leader now."

Barley's eyes widened in astonishment. "Congratulations! But that means that Bluestar must be dead. I'm sorry."

"She died as she lived, protecting her Clan," Firestar told him.

"I can see there's a story to tell," meowed Barley, turning back to the barn, "and Ravenpaw will want to hear it. Come on in."

Inside the barn was warm and dark, full of the scent of hay and mice. Firestar listened to the telltale scuttering noises and his head spun with hunger.

"A soft place to sleep, and all the prey you can eat," he remarked, trying not to let his desperate hunger show. "Better not tell ThunderClan or they'll all be out here, wanting to be loners."

Barley chuckled softly. "Ravenpaw," he called, "come and see who's here."

A dark shape sprang down from a nearby stack of hay with a welcoming purr. As an apprentice, Ravenpaw had been the only cat in ThunderClan who knew the truth about the death of Redtail—that he had been murdered by Ravenpaw's mentor, Tigerstar. When Tigerstar tried to kill his apprentice to prevent him from reporting what he had seen, Firestar had found this new home for him. The life of a loner suited Ravenpaw much better than that of a warrior, yet he had never forgotten his birth Clan, and remained a loyal friend to his former Clan mates.

"So Bluestar is dead," he murmured when Barley had passed on the news. His eyes clouded with grief. "I'll never forget her."

Barley gave a comforting rumble in his throat, and Firestar sensed how welcoming he must have been to the scared young apprentice who had come to him so many moons ago.

Straightening up, Ravenpaw flashed the black-and-white cat a grateful glance. "So you're Clan leader now," he continued to Firestar. "StarClan made a good choice." He led the way to the other side of the barn. "Would you like to hunt?"

"That would be great," replied Cinderpelt. She gave Firestar a questioning look, and murmured, "Shall I catch something for you?"

In spite of his exhaustion, Firestar shook his head. A fine Clan leader he would make if he couldn't catch his own prey! He stood alert, listening, and dropped into the hunter's crouch when he heard a soft scuffling deep within the hay. Pinpointing the mouse by hearing rather than sight, he sprang, and dispatched the creature with a swift bite.

Ravenpaw was lucky, Firestar reflected as he picked up the prey in his jaws and padded back to the others to eat. This was twice the size of the leaf-bare-thin mice in the forest, and easier to catch in the shadows of the barn. He gulped it down in a few famished mouthfuls and felt his strength beginning to return.

"Have some more," Ravenpaw urged. "There are plenty here."

When Firestar and Cinderpelt had eaten as much as they

could manage they lay in the soft hay, sharing tongues with their friends and bringing them up-to-date with Clan news. Ravenpaw and Barley listened, their eyes huge with shock, as Firestar told them about the dog pack.

"I always knew Tigerstar was bloodthirsty," Ravenpaw meowed, "but I didn't think even he would try to destroy a whole Clan like that."

"Thank StarClan he didn't succeed," Firestar replied. "But he came pretty close. I don't want to go through anything like that again."

"You'll have to do something to stop Tigerstar now, before he tries something else," Barley pointed out.

Firestar nodded. He hesitated, then confessed, "But I don't know how I'm going to do anything without Bluestar. Everything seems dark and . . . and overwhelming." He said nothing about the interruption of his leadership ritual, or the horror of his dream, but he saw from the sympathetic look in Cinderpelt's eyes that she knew what he was thinking.

"Remember the whole Clan is behind you," she mewed. "No cat will ever forget that you and Bluestar saved us from the pack."

"Maybe they expect too much of me."

"Nonsense!" Cinderpelt's tone was bracing. "They know you're going to be a great leader, and they'll all stand by you to the last breath."

"So will I," Ravenpaw offered, startling Firestar. The sleek black tom looked slightly embarrassed as Firestar turned to look at him, but he went on: "I know I'm not a warrior, but if you want my help you have only to ask."

Firestar blinked his gratitude. "Thank you, Ravenpaw."

"May I come to the camp soon?" Ravenpaw asked. "I'd like to pay my last respects to Bluestar at her burial place."

"Yes, of course," Firestar replied. "Bluestar gave you the right to go where you like on ThunderClan territory. There's no reason to change that now."

Ravenpaw dipped his head. "Thank you." As he looked up again, Firestar saw a glow of respect in his eyes. "You saved my life once, Firestar. I'll never be able to repay you for that. But if trouble with Tigerstar comes, I'll be proud to stand with the warriors of ThunderClan and fight him to the death."

# CHAPTER 6

*Twilight was thickening the shadows under* the trees by the time Firestar and Cinderpelt slipped down the ravine toward the camp entrance. They had slept in the barn with Barley and Ravenpaw until the sun was well above the horizon, and feasted again on plump mice before they set off for their own territory. Though Firestar was tired, some of the horror of his dream was fading, and he was looking forward to seeing his Clan mates again.

At first the new leader emerged unnoticed from the gorse tunnel with Cinderpelt. Whitestorm and Brackenfur were sitting together near the nettle patch, finishing off some fresh-kill, while three of the apprentices wrestled playfully outside their den. Firestar picked out the dark tabby pelt of his own apprentice, Bramblepaw, and reminded himself to get him back onto a strict training schedule as soon as he could. There was no reason why leadership duties should prevent him from mentoring the young cat—after all, Bluestar had been a diligent mentor to him.

He was padding over to Whitestorm when he heard his name yowled loudly, and turned to see Ashpaw racing across the clearing from the elders' den. The apprentice's gray fur was bristling with excitement. "Fireheart—no, Firestar! You're back!"

His noisy greeting alerted the rest of the Clan and soon they were pressing around Firestar, calling him by his new name and welcoming him home. Firestar wanted to give himself up to the uncomplicated enjoyment of their warm fur pressed against his, but he could not ignore the awe in their eyes as they gazed at him. He felt a sharp pang in his heart as he was reminded yet again of the new distance between himself and the rest of his Clan.

"Did you really see StarClan?" asked Fernpaw, her eyes wide.

"I really did," Firestar replied. "But I'm not allowed to say anything about the ceremony."

Fernpaw didn't look disappointed. Her eyes brimming with admiration, she turned to Dustpelt and meowed, "I bet he's going to be a great leader!"

"He'd better be," replied Dustpelt; his love for Fernpaw wouldn't let him argue with her, even though Firestar was well aware that he had never been Dustpelt's favorite cat. But the brown-coated warrior gave him a nod of respect, and Firestar knew that Dustpelt's loyalty to the warrior code would ensure his support.

"It's good to see you back," meowed Graystripe, shouldering through the warriors to reach Firestar's side. At least he seemed to have recovered from the awe he'd felt when Bluestar had named Firestar leader as she lay dying. Now his yellow eyes were filled with friendship and sympathy. "You look like a fox that's been dead for a moon. Was it tough?"

"It was," Firestar murmured, just for Graystripe's ears, but Cloudtail caught what he had said.

"It's only your belief in ancient traditions that makes you think you can't be leader without dragging all the way up to Highstones and back. As far as I'm concerned, you've already proved yourself to be the true leader of this Clan, Firestar."

Firestar gave his kin a hard stare; he was grateful for Cloudtail's loyalty and respect, but felt as frustrated as ever that the younger cat did not share his beliefs. He wished he could tell the white warrior exactly what he had experienced, if only to shock him into respect for StarClan, but he knew that was impossible.

"Shh! The ancient traditions still matter." The quiet rebuke came from Lostface, who had come to join Cloudtail. She licked his ear and added, "StarClan watch over us all."

Cloudtail returned the lick, his tongue passing gently over the injured side of Lostface's face. Firestar's annoyance faded. He couldn't help admiring Cloudtail's unwavering devotion to Lostface in spite of her terrible injuries. His kin might be difficult and hotheaded, with little respect for the warrior code, but he had brought this young cat back from the brink of death and given her a reason to live.

As the welcoming cats began to disperse, Firestar caught the eye of Whitestorm, who had greeted him and then backed off a pace or two, waiting to speak.

"How are things in camp?" Firestar asked. "Was there any trouble while I was away?"

"Not a thing," the senior warrior reported. "We've patrolled the whole territory, and there's no sign of dogs or of ShadowClan."

"Good," Firestar mewed. Glancing at the well-stocked fresh-kill pile, he added, "I see some cats have been hunting."

"Sandstorm took a patrol out, and Mousefur and Brackenfur put the apprentices to work," replied Whitestorm. "Bramblepaw is a skillful hunter. I lost count of how much prey he brought in."

"Good," Firestar repeated. His pleasure in hearing his apprentice praised was tempered by the uneasiness he always felt when Tigerstar's son was mentioned. Tigerstar had been a good hunter too, but that had not stopped him from becoming a murderer and a traitor.

Cinderpelt came up to him again. "I'm off to my den," she meowed. "Call me if you want anything. Have you remembered that you need to appoint a deputy before moonhigh?"

Firestar nodded. Other duties had been more urgent, but now he needed to give this decision serious thought. Because she had been so shocked by Tigerstar's treachery and exile, Bluestar had made Firestar's own appointment a day late, without the proper ceremony. The Clan had been terrified that StarClan would be angry, and that had made things very difficult for Firestar. He was determined not to make the same mistake with his own deputy.

Watching Cinderpelt limping across the clearing to her

den, Firestar realized that so far two cats had not come to greet him. One was Darkstripe; that did not surprise him. The other was Sandstorm, and that disturbed him. Had he done something to make her angry?

Then Firestar spotted her a few tail-lengths away, watching him with an uncharacteristically diffident air. Her green eyes flickered toward him and away again as he padded over to her.

"Sandstorm," he mewed. "Are you okay?"

"I'm fine, Firestar." She didn't meet his gaze, but looked down at her paws. "It's good to have you back."

Now Firestar was certain something was wrong. He had been looking forward all the long journey home to lying beside Sandstorm in the warriors' den, to sharing tongues with her and catching up on her news. But he would not be able to do that again. From now on he would sleep alone in Bluestar's old den—his den now—underneath the Highrock.

And with that realization came understanding of what was troubling Sandstorm. For all her confidence when he left the camp, she was not at ease with him now. "Mouse-brain," he purred affectionately, pressing his muzzle against hers. "I'm still the same cat. Nothing has changed."

"Everything's changed!" Sandstorm insisted. "You're Clan leader now."

"And you're still the best hunter and the most beautiful cat in the Clan," Firestar assured her. "You'll always be special to me."

"But you . . . you're so far away," meowed Sandstorm,

unconsciously echoing Firestar's own fears. "You're closer to Cinderpelt now than anyone else. You both know secrets about StarClan that ordinary warriors don't."

"Cinderpelt's our medicine cat," Firestar replied. "And she's one of the best friends I have. But she's not you, Sandstorm. I know things are difficult right now. There's so much I have to do to take over the Clan . . . especially after what Tigerstar tried to do with the pack of dogs. But in a few days we'll be able to go out on patrol together, just like we used to."

To his relief he felt Sandstorm relax, and some of the uncertainty faded from her eyes. "You'll need an evening patrol," she mewed. Her voice was crisp, more like the old Sandstorm, though Firestar guessed she was covering up her unhappiness. "Shall I round up some cats and go?"

"Good idea." Firestar tried to match her businesslike manner. "Go and have a sniff around Sunningrocks. Make sure RiverClan haven't been up to their old tricks." It would be just like Leopardstar, the ambitious leader of RiverClan, to try to claim the long-disputed territory while ThunderClan was shaken by the loss of Bluestar.

"Right." Sandstorm hurried off toward the nettle patch, where Brackenfur and Longtail were eating. Brackenfur called to his apprentice, Tawnypaw, and all four cats headed for the gorse tunnel.

Firestar made his way toward the leader's den. He still couldn't think of it as his own, and he found himself missing his comfy patch of moss in the warriors' den even more sharply. Before he reached it, he heard his name being called and turned to see Graystripe hurrying after him.

"Firestar, I wanted to tell you—" He broke off as if he were embarrassed.

"What's the problem?"

"Well . . ." Graystripe hesitated and then went on in a rush: "I don't know if you were thinking of choosing me to be your deputy, but I wanted to say that you don't have to. I know I haven't been back in the Clan long enough, and some cats still don't trust me. I won't be hurt if you pick another cat."

Firestar felt a pang of regret. He would have chosen Graystripe above all other cats to hunt and fight by his side, and to give him the special support that a deputy gave the Clan leader. But it was true that he could not choose Graystripe so soon after his friend's return from RiverClan. Though Firestar himself had no doubt of his friend's loyalty to ThunderClan, Graystripe still had to prove himself before the rest of the Clan would accept him.

Leaning forward, Firestar touched noses with his friend. "Thank you, Graystripe," he mewed. "I'm glad you understand."

Graystripe shrugged, more embarrassed than ever. "I just wanted to say." He turned and vanished through the branches of the warrior's den.

Firestar felt choked with emotion and shook himself briskly. Padding around the Highrock to the den entrance, he heard movement inside. Thornpaw, the oldest apprentice, whirled around as Firestar went in.

"Oh Firestar!" he exclaimed. "Whitestorm told me to fetch you some new bedding—and some fresh-kill." He flicked his tail to the far side of the den, where a rabbit lay beside a thick pile of moss and heather.

"That looks great, Thornpaw," Firestar meowed. "Thank you—and thank Whitestorm for me."

The ginger apprentice dipped his head and started to leave, only to halt as Firestar called him back.

"Remind Mousefur to have a word with me tomorrow," Firestar mewed, naming Thornpaw's mentor. "It's about time we started thinking about your warrior ceremony." *It's long overdue*, he reflected. Thornpaw had proved himself an able apprentice, and would have been a warrior moons ago but for Bluestar's reluctance to trust any of her Clan. He was the only one left of the group that had included Swiftpaw and Lostface, neither of whom would ever experience a warrior ceremony.

Thornpaw's eyes lit up with excitement. "Yes, Firestar! Thanks!" he meowed, and dashed off.

Firestar settled himself in the mossy nest and took a few mouthfuls of the rabbit. It had been thoughtful of Whitestorm to have the bedding changed, though Firestar still felt that Bluestar's scent lingered in the very walls of the den. Perhaps it always would, and that was no bad thing. There was pain in his memories of her, but comfort too, when he thought of her wisdom and her courage in leading her Clan.

Shadows gathered around him as the last of the light died.

Firestar was acutely conscious of being completely alone for the first time since joining the Clan: no warmth of other cats sleeping close by, no soft meows and purrs as his friends shared tongues, no gentle snoring or the sound of cats shifting in their dreams. For a few heartbeats he felt lonelier than ever.

Then he told himself to stop being so mouse-brained. He had an important decision to make, and it was vital for ThunderClan that he get it right. His choice of deputy would affect the life of the Clan for seasons to come.

Settling deeper into the moss, he wondered whether he ought to sleep now, and ask Spottedleaf in a dream which cat would be the right deputy. He closed his eyes and almost at once he caught a trace of Spottedleaf's sweet scent. But no vision came; he could see only darkness.

Then he heard a whisper in his ear, filled with Spottedleaf's gentle teasing. "Oh, no, Firestar. This is *your* decision."

Sighing, Firestar opened his eyes again. "All right, Spottedleaf," he mewed aloud. "I'll decide."

The deputy could not be Graystripe, that was clear, and Firestar was grateful to his friend for making that part of his choice easy for him. He let his mind drift over the other possible cats. The new deputy would have to be experienced, and a cat whose loyalty had never been questioned. Sandstorm was brave and intelligent, and choosing her would reassure her more than anything else that Firestar still valued her and wanted her at his side.

But that was not the right reason to choose a deputy.

Besides, the warrior code dictated that no cat could be deputy without having been a mentor first. Sandstorm had never had an apprentice, so Firestar could not choose her. With a prickle of shame, he recognized that that was his own fault, because he had given Tawnypaw to Brackenfur to mentor, even though Sandstorm had been the obvious choice. He had done it to protect her, afraid that the mentors of Tigerstar's kits would be in danger from their bloodthirsty father. It had taken Sandstorm a long time to forgive him, and Firestar hoped she would never realize that his previous mistake had prevented her from being deputy now.

But was Sandstorm really the right choice anyway? Surely there was one cat who towered over all the other possibilities? Whitestorm was experienced, wise, and brave. When Firestar had been made deputy, he had shown not a scrap of the resentment that a lesser cat might have felt. He had supported him from the beginning, and he was the cat Firestar naturally turned to when he needed advice. He was old, yes, but still strong and active. There were a good few moons left before he would be joining the elders in their den.

Bluestar would approve, too, for the white warrior's friendship had meant a great deal to her in her last moons.

*Yes,* Firestar thought. *Whitestorm will be the new deputy.* He stretched in satisfaction. All that remained was to announce the decision to the Clan.

Firestar waited for a while, finishing the rabbit, drowsing but not letting himself fall into deep sleep in case he missed moonhigh. Silver light seeped into the den as the moon rose.

Eventually he got to his paws, shook the scraps of moss from his fur, and padded out into the clearing.

Several of the Clan were pacing among the ferns at the edge, obviously waiting for the announcement. Sandstorm and the evening patrol had returned and were eating their share of the fresh-kill. Firestar flicked his tail in greeting to the ginger she-cat, but did not go over to speak to her. Instead he sprang up onto the Highrock and yowled, "Let all cats old enough to catch their own prey join here beneath the Highrock for a Clan meeting."

His summons was still ringing in the air when more cats began to appear, slipping from the shelter of their dens or padding into the moonlight from the shadows around the edges of the camp. Firestar saw Darkstripe stalk into the open and sit a few tail-lengths away from the rock, his tail wrapped around his paws and a scornful look in his eyes. Unobtrusively, Brackenfur followed him and took up a position close by.

Bramblepaw emerged from the apprentices' den; Firestar couldn't help wondering if he would go over to Darkstripe, but he stayed with his sister, Tawnypaw, near the edge of the gathering crowd. The eyes of both apprentices were watchful, flicking back and forth. As Mousefur walked past them she snapped at Tawnypaw, and the younger she-cat turned her head away sharply, as if she and Mousefur had disagreed over something. Tawnypaw was bright and very confident, Firestar reflected; he wouldn't be surprised if she offended the experienced warriors now and then.

Sandstorm and Graystripe were sitting together near the rock, close to Cloudtail and Lostface, and the elders all came out in a group and settled down in the center of the clearing.

Firestar saw Whitestorm strolling over from the nettle patch with Cinderpelt. There was no air of anticipation about him as he stopped for a quick word with Fernpaw and Ashpaw before taking his own place beside the Highrock.

Swallowing his nervousness, Firestar began. "The time has come to appoint a new deputy." Pausing, he felt the presence of Bluestar very close to him as he remembered the ritual words she used to speak. "I say these words before StarClan," he continued, "that the spirits of our ancestors may hear and approve my choice."

By now all the cats had turned their faces up to him; he looked down at their eyes gleaming in the moonlight and could almost taste their excitement.

"Whitestorm will be the new deputy of ThunderClan," he announced.

For a heartbeat there was silence. Whitestorm was blinking up at Firestar, a look of pleasure and surprise spreading over his face. Firestar realized that the surprise was part of what he liked so much about the old warrior; Whitestorm had never assumed that he would be the one chosen.

Slowly he rose to his paws. "Firestar, cats of ThunderClan," he meowed, "I never expected to be given this honor. I swear by StarClan that I will do all I can to serve you."

As he finished speaking, sound gradually swelled from the assembled cats, a mixture of yowls and purrs and voices calling, "Whitestorm!" All the Clan began to press around the white warrior, congratulating him. Firestar knew that he had made a very popular choice.

For a few moments he remained on the Highrock and watched. A new feeling of optimism surged through his paws, filling him with confidence and warmth. He had his nine lives; he had the best deputy a cat could wish for; and he had a team of warriors who were ready to face anything. The threat of the pack was over: Firestar had to believe that soon they would be able to drive Tigerstar out of the forest for good.

Then, just as he was poised to leap down and offer his own good wishes to Whitestorm, he caught sight of Darkstripe. He alone of all the cats had not moved or spoken. He was staring up at Firestar, and his eyes burned with cold fire.

Firestar was instantly reminded of the dreadful vision in the ceremony, the hill of bones and the tide of blood that had flowed from it. Bluestar's words rang in his ears again: *Four will become two. Lion and tiger will meet in battle, and blood will rule the forest.*

Firestar still did not know what the prophecy meant, but the words were laden with doom. There would be battle and bloodshed. And in Darkstripe's malignant stare, Firestar seemed to see the first cloud that would eventually unleash the storm of war.

# CHAPTER 7

*A raw, damp cold pushed its* way through Firestar's fur as he padded through Tallpines. The sky was heavy with gray cloud and seemed undecided between sending rain or snow onto the forest. Here, where the ravages of the fire had been worst, ash still covered the ground, and the few plants that had begun to grow back had shriveled again with the coming of leaf-bare.

It was the day after his announcement to the Clan, and Firestar had left his new deputy in charge of the camp while he patrolled the border alone. He wanted some time by himself, to get used to being leader and to think about what lay ahead. Sometimes he felt he would burst with the pride of being chosen by StarClan to lead ThunderClan, but he also knew it would not be easy. Grief for Bluestar was a dull ache that would stay with him forever. And he was afraid of what Tigerstar might do next. Firestar could not be comforted, as the other cats were, by the absence of any traces of ShadowClan in their territory. He knew Tigerstar would not rest until he had brought his enemy down—and news that Firestar was now the leader of ThunderClan would only fuel the fires of his revenge.

Firestar emerged from the trees near Twolegplace and looked up at Princess's fence to see if his sister had ventured out of her Twoleg nest. But there was no sign of her, and when he drank in the air he caught only a faint scent. Padding along the edge of the trees, Firestar came to a part of the forest he rarely visited, and recognized the Twoleg nest where he himself had lived as a kittypet, so many moons ago. Overcome by curiosity, he darted across the stretch of open ground at the edge of the trees and leaped to the top of the fence.

Memories of playing there as a kit flooded over him as he looked down at the stretch of grass bordered by Twoleg plants. There was a more recent memory, too, of coming here to find catnip when Bluestar was ill with greencough. Firestar could see the clump of catnip now from where he was sitting, and smell its tempting scent.

A flicker of movement from the nest caught his gaze, and he saw one of his old Twolegs pass by the window and disappear again. Firestar suddenly wondered how his Twolegs had felt when he left them to live in the forest. He hoped they hadn't worried about him. They had cared for him well, in the way that Twolegs tried to, and Firestar knew he would always be grateful. He would have liked to tell them how happy he was in the forest, and how he was fulfilling the destiny StarClan had laid out for him, but he knew there was no way he could make Twolegs understand.

He was bunching his muscles, ready to leap down into the forest, when something black and white moved in the next garden. Glancing down, he saw Smudge, his old friend from his kittypet days. He looked as plump as ever, with a contented expression on his broad face. He was talking to a pretty brown tabby she-cat, a stranger to Firestar; their mews reached him but they were too far away for him to make out the words.

He almost jumped down to say hello, until he remembered that they would probably be frightened by the sight of a ruffian like himself. Not long after coming to the forest, Firestar had met Smudge in the woods, and nearly scared the life out of him before his friend recognized him. The life he led now was worlds away from theirs.

The sound of a door opening roused Firestar from his thoughts, and he edged along the fence into the shelter of a holly bush as one of his old Twolegs came out of the house and called. At once the pretty brown tabby meowed good-bye to Smudge and scrambled under the fence that divided the gardens. She ran up to the Twoleg, who scooped her up and stroked her before carrying her indoors, purring loudly.

*She's their new kittypet!* Firestar thought. The closing of the door stirred a pang of envy in him, just for a heartbeat. The little tabby would have no need to catch her prey before she could eat; she would have a warm place to sleep, and no risk of dying in battle or from one of the many dangers that beset the forest cats. She would have the friendship of Smudge and other kittypets, and the care of her Twolegs—everything that Firestar had turned his back on to live as a Clan cat in the forest.

But at the same time she would never know the satisfaction of learning warrior skills, or of racing into battle beside her friends. She would never understand what it meant to live by the warrior code, and to follow the will of StarClan.

*If I could relive my life*, Firestar thought, *I wouldn't change a thing.*

Suddenly claws scrabbled on the fence below him and from the corner of his eye he caught a glimpse of quick, brown movement. Turning his head, he found himself face-to-face with Bramblepaw.

It was a moment before Firestar recovered himself enough to speak. "What are *you* doing here?"

"I followed you from camp, Firestar. I . . . I was curious about where you were going, and I wanted to practice my tracking skills."

"Well, they seem good enough, if you got this far." Firestar wasn't sure whether he was angry with his apprentice or not. Bramblepaw shouldn't have followed him without permission, but it *was* impressive to have tracked him all the way from the camp. He felt a twinge of guilt, too, that Bramblepaw should have caught him looking over a Twoleg fence at a pair of kittypets. Once before, when Firestar was an apprentice, Tigerstar had spied on him and caught him talking to Smudge. The huge tabby had reported straight back to Bluestar, deliberately calling into question Firestar's loyalty to Clan life.

Meeting Bramblepaw's eyes, Firestar saw the young cat's nervousness fading, to be replaced by a steady gaze, as if he were weighing his mentor up. It was a long, intelligent look, and Firestar realized that he could see respect in the amber depths. He was aware yet again of his certainty that Bramblepaw could be an outstanding warrior, if only he could escape his father's dark heritage. But would Bramblepaw ever be truly loyal to his birth Clan, with his father still in the forest?

"Can I trust you?" Firestar blurted out suddenly.

The young cat didn't rush to defend himself. Instead Bramblepaw held him with that serious gaze for a moment more. "Can *I* trust *you*?" he responded, twitching his ears in the direction of the Twoleg garden.

Bristling, Firestar initially had no intention of justifying himself to his apprentice; it was not Bramblepaw's place to question the actions of his mentor—who also happened to be Clan leader. But in spite of the guilt Bramblepaw's question had provoked, Firestar couldn't help admiring the spirit that had dared to ask.

He took a deep breath. "You *can* trust me," he promised solemnly. "I chose to leave my life as a kittypet. Whatever happens, I'll always put the Clan first." It was time, he decided, to be more open with Bramblepaw. "But I do come here now and again," he continued. "I see my sister sometimes, and I wonder how things would have been if I'd stayed. Yet I always leave knowing that my heart lies with ThunderClan."

Bramblepaw gave a little nod, as if the answer satisfied him. "I know what it's like to have loyalties questioned," he meowed.

Another pang of guilt stabbed Firestar, even though he knew he was not the only cat to have suspicions about Bramblepaw. "How do you get on with the other apprentices?" he asked.

"They're okay. But I know some of the warriors don't like me and Tawnypaw, because Tigerstar's our father."

The words were spoken with such understanding that Firestar was even more ashamed of himself. *We're more alike than I ever realized,* Firestar thought. *Constantly having to prove our loyalties by fighting twice as hard, defending ourselves twice as much to our enemies—and to our Clan mates.*

"Can you cope with that?" he meowed cautiously.

Bramblepaw blinked. "I know where my loyalties lie. I'll prove that someday."

There was no boasting in the way he spoke, just calm determination. Firestar realized that he believed him. His apprentice had rewarded him for his honesty about visiting Twolegplace by being honest with him in return. Now, Firestar knew he owed it to Bramblepaw to trust his word.

"What about Tawnypaw?" he asked.

"Well . . ." Her brother hesitated, a troubled look in his eyes. "She can be a bit difficult at times—but it's just her way. She's a loyal cat at heart."

"I'm sure she is," Firestar mewed, though he noticed that Bramblepaw wasn't entirely at ease discussing his sister with the Clan leader. He would need to keep a closer eye on Tawnypaw in future, and make sure she had all the support she needed to become a reliable ThunderClan warrior. A word with her mentor, Brackenfur, would be a good idea.

Struck by a sudden warmth toward his apprentice, Firestar added, "I've got to get on if I'm to finish patrolling the border before dark. Do you want to come with me?"

Bramblepaw's amber eyes lit up. "Can I?"

"Sure." Firestar leaped down from the fence and waited for the young cat to scramble down behind him. "We'll do some training on the way."

"Great!" Bramblepaw meowed enthusiastically.

He padded close to his mentor's shoulder as Firestar led the way back into the trees.

Firestar halted on the edge of the Thunderpath and drew in the scent that flowed across from ShadowClan territory. *Tigerstar is out there*, he thought. *What is he planning? What will he do next?*

As he stood wrapped in silent apprehension, he noticed scraps of white drifting down from the sky. *Snow!* Firestar thought, glancing up at a sky where the clouds were darker than ever. Hearing a surprised squeak from Bramblepaw, he turned around. A snowflake had landed on Bramblepaw's nose and was slowly melting. The apprentice flicked out a pink tongue and licked it off, his yellow eyes round with wonder.

"What is it, Firestar?" he asked. "It's *cold*!"

Firestar let out a purr of amusement. "It's snow," he replied. "It comes in leaf-bare. If it goes on like this, the flakes will cover all the ground and the trees."

"Really? But they're so tiny!"

"There will be lots of them, though."

The flakes were already growing larger and falling more thickly, almost hiding the trees on the other side of the Thunderpath and smothering the ShadowClan scent. Even the roar of the monsters was muffled and they moved slowly, as if their glowing eyes couldn't see well through the snow.

Firestar knew that snowfall would bring more problems to the forest. Prey would die in the cold, or huddle deep in holes where hunters could not follow. It would be harder than ever to feed the Clan.

His apprentice was watching the falling flakes with wide eyes. Firestar saw him reach out one paw tentatively to dab at one of them. A heartbeat later he was leaping and whirling with high-pitched mews of excitement, as if he were trying to catch every single flake before it reached the ground.

Firestar was surprised by a rush of affection. It was good to see the young cat playing like a kit again. Surely the dark-hearted Tigerstar had never chased snowflakes just for the joy of it? Or if he had, when had he lost the joy, and begun to care only for his own power?

There was no answer to that question, and Firestar knew that for Tigerstar, just as much as for himself, there was no going back. Their paws were firmly on the path StarClan had decided they should follow, and sooner or later the two leaders must meet to decide who should remain in the forest.

# CHAPTER 8

*The snow had stopped by the* time Firestar and Bramblepaw returned to camp. The clouds had cleared away and the setting sun cast long blue shadows over the thin coating of white that powdered the ground. Both cats were carrying fresh-kill; Firestar had watched his apprentice's hunting skills and been impressed by the young cat's concentration and skillful stalking.

They had just reached the top of the ravine when they heard a yowl behind them. Firestar turned to see Graystripe bounding through the undergrowth.

"Hi," panted the gray warrior as he caught up with them. His eyes widened when he saw their catch. "You've had better luck than me. I couldn't find so much as a mouse."

Firestar grunted sympathetically as he led the way toward the gorse tunnel. He noticed that Sorrelkit, the most adventurous of Willowpelt's three kits, had left the camp and climbed halfway up the steep slope farther along the ravine. To Firestar's surprise, she was with Darkstripe; the warrior was bending over her, saying something to her.

"Odd," Firestar muttered through a mouthful of squirrel fur, half to himself. "Darkstripe has never shown much interest in kits before. And what's he doing out here on his own?"

Suddenly Firestar heard a sharp exclamation from Graystripe and his friend flashed past him, hurtling along the side of the ravine, his paws scrabbling against the loose snow-covered stones. At the same moment Sorrelkit's legs crumpled underneath her sturdy tortoiseshell body and she started writhing in the snow. Firestar dropped his fresh-kill in amazement as Graystripe yowled, "No!" and flung himself on the dark warrior. Darkstripe clawed and flailed at him with his hind legs, but Graystripe's teeth were sunk in his throat and would not let go.

"What—?" Firestar dashed down the slope with Bramblepaw right behind him. He dodged the fighting cats, still locked together in a whirlwind of teeth and claws, and reached Sorrelkit's side.

The little kit twisted and turned on the ground, her eyes wide and glazed. She was letting out high-pitched moans of pain, and there was foam on her lips.

"Get Cinderpelt!" Firestar ordered Bramblepaw.

His apprentice shot off, his paws sending up puffs of snow. Firestar bent over the young kit and placed a paw gently on her belly. "It's all right," he murmured. "Cinderpelt is coming."

Sorrelkit's jaws gaped wide and Firestar caught a glimpse of half-chewed berries in her mouth, scarlet against her white teeth.

"Deathberries!" He gasped.

There was a dark-leaved shrub growing from a crack in the rock just above his head, with more of the lethal scarlet berries clustered among the leaves. He remembered a time many moons ago when Cinderpelt had appeared just in time to stop Cloudtail from eating the deathberries, and warned him of how poisonous they were. Later, Yellowfang had used them to kill her son, Brokentail; Firestar had seen for himself how quickly and fatally they worked.

Crouching over Sorrelkit, Firestar did his best to scoop the crushed berries out of her mouth, but the kit was in too much terror and pain to keep still and make his task easier. Her head thrashed from side to side, and her body was convulsing in regular spasms that to Fireheart's horror seemed to be growing weaker. He could still hear Graystripe and Darkstripe screeching in the throes of their fight, but they seemed oddly far away. All his attention was concentrated on the kit.

Then to his relief he felt Cinderpelt arrive beside him. "Deathberries!" he told her quickly. "I've tried to get them out, but . . ."

Cinderpelt took his place by the kit's side. She had a bundle of leaves in her mouth; setting them down, she mewed, "Good. Keep holding her, Firestar, while I take a look."

With two of them to help, and the kit's struggles definitely growing weaker, Cinderpelt was soon able to paw out the remains of the deathberries. Then she rapidly chewed up one of her leaves and stuffed the pulp into Sorrelkit's mouth. "Swallow it," she ordered. To Firestar she added, "It's yarrow. It'll make her sick."

The kit's throat convulsed. A moment later she vomited; Firestar could see more scarlet specks among the pulp of leaves.

"Good," Cinderpelt mewed soothingly. "That's very good. You're going to be fine, Sorrelkit."

The little kit lay gasping and trembling; then Firestar watched in dismay as she went limp and her eyes closed.

"Is she dead?" he whispered.

Before Cinderpelt could reply, a yowl came from the entrance to the camp. "My kit! Where's my kit?" It was Willowpelt, racing up the ravine with Bramblepaw. She crouched beside Sorrelkit, her blue eyes wide and distraught. "What happened?"

"She ate deathberries," Cinderpelt explained. "But I think I've gotten rid of them all. We'll carry her back to my den and I'll keep an eye on her."

Willowpelt began licking Sorrelkit's tortoiseshell fur. By now Firestar had seen the faint rise and fall of the kit's flank as she breathed. She was not dead, but he could see from Cinderpelt's anxious look that she was still in danger from the effects of the poison.

For the first time Firestar had a chance to draw breath and look for Graystripe. The gray warrior had pinned Darkstripe down a few tail-lengths away with one paw on his neck and another on his belly. Darkstripe was bleeding from one ear, and he spat in fury as he fought vainly to free himself.

"What's going on?" Firestar demanded.

"Don't ask me," snarled Graystripe. Firestar could hardly

remember seeing his friend look so savage. "Ask this . . . this piece of fox dung why he tried to murder a kit!"

"Murder?" Firestar echoed. The accusation was so unexpected that for a heartbeat he could do nothing but stare stupidly.

"Murder," repeated Graystripe. "Go on, ask him why he was feeding deathberries to Sorrelkit."

"You mouse-brained fool." Darkstripe's voice was cold as he gazed up at his attacker. "I wasn't feeding her the berries. I was trying to stop her from eating them."

"I know what I saw," Graystripe insisted through gritted teeth.

Firestar tried to recall the image of the warrior and the kit that he had seen when he paused at the top of the ravine. "Let him get up," he meowed reluctantly to his friend. "Darkstripe, tell me what happened."

The warrior rose and shook himself. Firestar could see bare patches on his flank where Graystripe had clawed out lumps of fur.

"I was coming back to camp," he began. "I found the stupid kit stuffing herself with deathberries, and I was trying to stop her when this idiot jumped on me." He stared resentfully at Graystripe. "Why would I want to murder a kit?"

"That's what I want to know!" spat Graystripe.

"Of course, we know who the noble Firestar will believe!" Darkstripe sneered. "There's no use expecting justice in ThunderClan these days."

The accusation stung Firestar, all the more so because he

recognized that there was a core of truth in it. He would take Graystripe's word over Darkstripe's any day, but he had to be absolutely certain that his friend wasn't making a mistake.

"I don't have to decide now," Firestar meowed. "As soon as Sorrelkit wakes up, she'll be able to tell us what happened."

As he spoke he thought he saw a flicker of unease in Darkstripe's eyes, but it was gone so quickly he could not be sure. The dark warrior twitched his ears contemptuously. "Fine," he meowed. "Then you'll see which of us is telling the truth." He stalked off toward the camp entrance with tail held high.

"I did see it, Firestar," Graystripe assured him, his sides heaving from the fight. "I can't understand why he'd want to hurt Sorrelkit, but I'm quite sure that's what he was doing."

Firestar sighed. "I believe you, but we have to let every cat see that justice is done. I can't punish Darkstripe until Sorrelkit tells us what happened."

*If she ever does,* he added silently to himself. He watched Cinderpelt and Willowpelt gently picking up the kit and carrying her toward the gorse tunnel. Sorrelkit's head lolled limply and her tail brushed the ground. Firestar's belly clenched as he remembered the kit bouncing around the camp. If Darkstripe had really tried to kill her, he would pay.

"Graystripe," he murmured, "go with Cinderpelt. I want you or another warrior on guard in her den until Sorrelkit wakes up. Ask Sandstorm and Goldenflower if they'll help. I don't want anything else to happen to Sorrelkit before she's fit to talk."

Graystripe's eyes gleamed with understanding. "Okay, Firestar," he meowed. "I'm on my way." He bounded down the slope and caught up with the other cats as they disappeared into the tunnel.

Firestar was left in the ravine with Bramblepaw. "I've left a squirrel up there," he meowed to his apprentice, jerking his head toward the top of the ravine. "Could you collect it for me, please? And then you can rest and eat. You've had a long day."

"Thanks," Bramblepaw mewed. He took a few steps up the ravine and glanced back. "Sorrelkit will be okay, won't she?"

Firestar let out a long breath. "I don't know, Bramblepaw," he admitted. "I just don't know."

## CHAPTER 9

♣

*Firestar made his way thoughtfully back* into the camp. Glancing around, he caught sight of Darkstripe gulping down a piece of fresh-kill beside the nettle patch. Mousefur, Goldenflower, and Frostfur were eating close by, but Firestar noticed that they had all turned their backs on Darkstripe and were not looking at him.

Graystripe must have already begun to spread the news of what had happened in the ravine. Frostfur and Goldenflower in particular, who had both raised kits of their own, would be horrified by the very suspicion that a Clan warrior would murder a kit. It was a good sign, Firestar realized, if they seemed to believe Graystripe's version of events. It showed that his friend was becoming accepted by the Clan again, beginning to recover the popularity he had once had.

Firestar was heading toward Graystripe when movement by the warriors' den caught his eye. Brackenfur was just emerging from between the branches, gazing wildly around. He spotted Darkstripe, took a step toward him, and then veered away to join Firestar.

"I've just heard!" he gasped. "Firestar, I'm sorry. He got

away from me. This is all my fault!"

"Steady." Firestar let his tail rest a moment on the agitated young warrior's shoulder, gesturing for calm. "Tell me what happened."

Brackenfur took a couple of gulping breaths, struggling for self-control. "Darkstripe said he was going out to hunt," he began. "I went with him, but when we got into the forest he said he had to make dirt. He went behind a bush and I waited for him. He was taking a long time, so I went to look—and he'd gone!" His eyes stretched wide with dismay. "If Sorrelkit dies, I'll never forgive myself."

"Sorrelkit won't die," Firestar reassured him, though he was not certain that it was the truth. The kit was still very ill.

And now there was something else to worry about. Brackenfur's story showed that Darkstripe had realized he was being watched. He had gotten rid of his guard very neatly. *He must have had a reason*, Firestar reflected. What had the dark tabby meant to do, and why had he tried to kill Sorrelkit?

"What do you want me to do now?" Brackenfur asked miserably.

"Stop blaming yourself, to begin with," Firestar replied. "Darkstripe was bound to let us know where his loyalties lie sooner or later."

Except for his anxiety over Sorrelkit, Firestar wasn't sorry that Darkstripe had shown his true self in a way that no cat could ignore. Although he had hoped to keep the dark warrior in the Clan, where he could watch him for signs of treachery, now he knew that Darkstripe would never be loyal, to him or to ThunderClan, and there could be no place for a cat who would poison a defenseless kit. *Let him go to Tigerstar, where he belongs,* Firestar thought.

"Carry on guarding Darkstripe," he went on to Brackenfur. "You can let him know you're doing it now. Tell him from me he's not to leave camp until Sorrelkit can tell her story."

Brackenfur gave a tense nod and hurried across to the nettle patch, where he crouched beside Darkstripe and spoke to him. The warrior snarled something in reply and went back to tearing apart his piece of fresh-kill.

As Firestar watched, a pawstep sounded behind him and he turned to see Sandstorm; the ginger she-cat pressed her muzzle against his, a purr deep in her throat. Firestar drew in her scent, comforted for a moment just by being close to her.

"Are you coming to eat?" she asked. "I waited for you. Graystripe told me what happened," she continued as they padded together over to the nettle patch. "I said I'd relieve him later, to guard Cinderpelt's den."

"Thanks," Firestar mewed.

He shot a glance at the black-striped warrior as they walked past him to the pile of fresh-kill. Darkstripe had finished his meal; he rose to his paws and stalked toward the warriors' den without acknowledging Firestar's presence. Brackenfur followed with a determined look on his face.

Dustpelt emerged from the den just as Darkstripe reached it; Firestar couldn't help noticing that the brown tabby veered sharply away as he went to join Fernpaw outside the apprentices' den. The cats of ThunderClan were making their feelings very clear. Dustpelt had been Darkstripe's apprentice, and now he didn't even want to speak to his former mentor.

Firestar picked out a magpie from the fresh-kill pile and took it over to the nettle patch.

"Hey, Firestar," meowed Mousefur as he approached. "Thornpaw said you were going to have a word with me about his warrior ceremony. It's about time."

"It certainly is," Firestar agreed. Bluestar's refusal to make the three oldest apprentices into warriors had led to Swiftpaw's death and Lostface's injuries, and there wouldn't be a cat in the Clan who didn't remember that when Thornpaw finally received his warrior name. "Why don't the three of us take the dawn patrol tomorrow? That should give me a chance to see how he's shaping up—not that I have any doubts," he added hastily.

"I should think not!" Mousefur mewed. "Will you tell Thornpaw about the patrol or shall I?"

"I will," Firestar replied, taking a quick bite of his magpie. "I want a word with Fernpaw and Ashpaw, too."

When he and Sandstorm had finished eating, the ginger she-cat went off to Cinderpelt's den, while Firestar padded over toward the tree stump where the apprentices ate. Dustpelt and Fernpaw were already there with Thornpaw and Ashpaw, and Cloudtail was just strolling over from the elders' den, Lostface close beside him.

"Thornpaw." Firestar gave the apprentice a nod as he settled down beside him. "Are your claws sharp? All your warrior skills ready?"

Thornpaw sat up straight, his eyes suddenly gleaming. "Yes, Firestar!"

"Dawn patrol tomorrow, then," Firestar told him. "If it goes well, we'll hold your ceremony at sunhigh."

Thornpaw's ears quivered with anticipation, but then the light in his eyes slowly died and he looked away.

"What's the matter?" Firestar asked.

"Swiftpaw . . . and Lostface." Thornpaw spoke in a low voice, with a flick of the tail toward the injured she-cat. "They should both be with me."

"I know." Firestar closed his eyes briefly at the memory of so much pain. "But you mustn't let that spoil it for you. You've deserved this for moons."

"I *will* be with you, Thornpaw." Lostface spoke up from where she was sitting beside Cloudtail. "I'll be the first cat to call you by your new name."

"Thanks, Lostface," Thornpaw mewed with a grateful dip of his head.

"And while we're on the subject of names," Cloudtail broke in, "what about *hers*?" He tilted his head toward Lostface; he always refused to use the cruel name Bluestar had bestowed on the injured cat. "What about getting it changed?"

"*Can* you change a warrior's name?" Firestar asked. "It's given in the sight of StarClan."

Cloudtail let out a sigh of exasperation. "I never thought I'd call my Clan leader a mouse-brain, but *honestly*! Do you think One-eye or Halftail started off with those names? They had other warrior names first, you can be sure of that.

There must be a ceremony of some sort. And I know the rest of the Clan won't accept a new name until you've said the right words."

"Please, Firestar." Lostface was looking at him with a hopeful expression. "I'm sure the other cats wouldn't feel so awkward talking to me if I didn't have this awful name."

"Of course." Firestar felt a stir of distress that he hadn't noticed the burden the young cat was carrying. "I'll talk to the elders right away. One-eye is bound to know what to do."

He rose to his paws and suddenly remembered what else he had meant to say. "Ashpaw, Fernpaw, don't think that you've been forgotten. You were brilliant in the race with the dog pack, but you're still a bit young to be made warriors." That was true, but at the same time Firestar wanted Thornpaw to keep his seniority by being made warrior first. "I promise it won't be long," he told them.

"We understand," Ashpaw mewed. "There's still stuff we need to learn."

"Firestar," Fernpaw asked nervously, "what's going to happen about . . . about Darkstripe? If he did that to Sorrelkit, I don't want him for my mentor."

"If he did that to Sorrelkit, he won't *be* your mentor," Firestar promised.

"Sorrelkit?" Cloudtail demanded. "What's all this about Sorrelkit? Did something happen while we were out hunting?"

Immediately Thornpaw and Ashpaw shifted position to crouch beside him and Lostface, and began passing on the news in hushed voices.

"So who's going to mentor Fernpaw then?" Dustpelt asked Firestar, taking it for granted that Darkstripe was guilty. "I could manage her as well as Ashpaw," he suggested hopefully.

Fernpaw brightened but Firestar shook his head. "Not a chance, Dustpelt. You wouldn't be nearly tough enough with her."

Dustpelt's eyes sparked with annoyance; then he nodded sheepishly. "I suppose you're right."

"Don't worry," Firestar promised as he headed for the elders' den. "I'll make sure she gets a good mentor."

Inside their den beside the fallen tree trunk, the elders were settling down for the night.

"What's the matter *now*?" Smallear grumbled, raising his head from his mossy nest. "Can't a cat get a wink of sleep around here?"

Dappletail let out a drowsy purr. "Don't listen to him, Firestar. You're always welcome."

"Thanks, Dappletail," Firestar meowed. "But it's One-eye I want to talk to."

One-eye was curled up in a clump of ferns in the shelter of the trunk. She blinked her single eye and opened her jaws in a huge yawn. "I'm listening, Firestar. But make it quick."

"I need to ask you about names," Firestar began, and he explained how Cloudtail wanted a new name for Lostface.

At the sound of the young cat's name, Speckletail padded over and sat listening. She had cared for Lostface when she was newly injured, and a strong bond had developed between them.

"I can't say I blame Cloudtail," she commented when Firestar had finished. "No cat wants a name like that."

One-eye yawned. "I was already old when they changed my name to One-eye," she mewed, "and to be honest I don't care *what* they call me so long as they bring the fresh-kill on time. But it's different for a young cat."

"So can you tell me what to do?" Firestar prompted.

"Of course I can." One-eye raised her tail and beckoned him closer. "Come here, and listen carefully. . . ."

Heavy rain fell during the night. When Firestar led Mousefur and Thornpaw out of the camp at dawn, he saw that the light snowfall had vanished. Every fern and clump of grass was loaded with drops of water that shone as daylight seeped into the sky. Shivering, Firestar set a brisk pace.

He could see from the gleam in Thornpaw's eyes that the young cat was wildly excited, but he kept calm, determined to show his leader that he was fit to be a warrior. The three cats paused at the top of the ravine, where the breeze was carrying a strong scent of mouse. Thornpaw flashed an inquiring look at Firestar, who nodded.

"We're not hunting," he mewed quietly, "but we won't say no to a bit of prey. Let's see your action."

Thornpaw froze for a moment, pinpointing the mouse scuffling among the leaves under a bush. Stealthily he crept up on it, his body falling smoothly into the hunter's crouch. Firestar noticed approvingly that he remembered how sensitive the mouse would be to the vibration of his pawsteps; he almost seemed to float over the ground. Then he sprang, and turned back to Firestar and his mentor with triumph in his eyes and the limp body of the mouse in his jaws.

"Well done!" meowed Mousefur.

"That was great," Firestar agreed. "Bury it now, and we'll pick it up on the way back."

When Thornpaw had scraped earth over his catch, Firestar led the patrol toward Snakerocks. He had not been this way since that dreadful morning when he had discovered the trail of dead rabbits laid by Tigerstar to lead the dog pack to the ThunderClan camp. He swallowed bile in his throat as he remembered the reek of blood, but this morning he could detect nothing but the ordinary forest scents. When they reached Snakerocks everything was silent. The howls and barking that he had heard coming from the cave were now no more than a memory.

"Right, Thornpaw," Firestar meowed, trying not to reveal the clinging horror that he still felt about this place. "What can you smell?"

The apprentice lifted his head and opened his jaws to draw air past his scent glands. Firestar could see that he was concentrating fiercely.

"Fox," he announced at last. "It's stale, though . . . two days old, I'd guess. Squirrel. And . . . and just a trace of dog." He shot a glance at Firestar, who could see that the young cat shared his own misgivings. Thornpaw knew as well as any of them that this was where Swiftpaw had died and Lostface had been attacked.

"Anything else?"

"The Thunderpath," Thornpaw replied. "And there's something . . ." He tasted the air again. "Firestar, I don't understand. I think I can smell cats, but it's not the scent of any of the Clans. Coming from over there." He flicked his tail. "What do you think?"

Firestar took a deep breath and realized that Thornpaw was right. The breeze was blowing a faint trace of unfamiliar cat scent toward them.

"Let's take a look," Firestar murmured. "And be careful. It might only be a lost kittypet, but you can never tell."

As the three cats padded warily through the undergrowth, the scent grew stronger. Firestar felt more certain now about the scent. "Rogues or loners," he meowed. "Three of them, I'd guess. And the scent is fresh. We must have just missed them."

"But what are they doing on our territory?" Thornpaw asked. "Are they Tigerstar's rogues, do you think?" He was referring to the band of Clanless cats who had helped Tigerstar to attack ThunderClan during his exile, before he had joined ShadowClan.

"No," replied Mousefur. "Tigerstar's rogues took on ShadowClan scent long ago. This must be a new lot."

"As for what they're doing," Firestar added, "I'd like to know that, too. Let's follow them. Thornpaw, you lead."

Thornpaw was serious now, his excitement at his upcoming warrior ceremony lost in the possible threat from the group of rogues. He did his best to follow the scent but lost it in a marshy stretch of ground, where not even Firestar could pick it up again.

"I'm sorry, Firestar," mewed Thornpaw, crestfallen.

"It's not your fault," Firestar reassured him. "If the scent's gone, it's gone." He raised his head, staring in the direction the trail had led them. It looked as if the strange cats were heading for the Thunderpath, or perhaps for Twolegplace. In either case, they were on their way out of the territory. He shrugged. "I'll tell the patrols to keep a lookout, but hopefully there's nothing to worry about. That was well scented, Thornpaw." Turning to the young cat, he added with a purr of approval, "Let's head back to camp. We have a warrior ceremony to arrange."

"Let all cats old enough to catch their own prey join here beneath the Highrock for a Clan meeting!"

Almost at once Firestar saw Thornpaw approaching from the apprentices' den with Mousefur beside him. Both cats had groomed themselves for the ceremony; Thornpaw's golden-brown fur shone in the gray light of leaf-bare, and he looked as if he would burst with pride.

As he waited for the rest of the Clan to emerge, Firestar spotted Cinderpelt coming from her den. Graystripe was with her, and the two cats had their heads together, talking in low voices. Firestar wondered how Sorrelkit was getting on. He had briefly looked into the medicine cat's den before he left with the dawn patrol. The kit had been sleeping then, and Cinderpelt had still not been prepared to say whether she thought the poison was out of her system. Firestar decided to check on Sorrelkit again as soon as the ceremony was over.

He could not help noticing Darkstripe emerging from the warriors' den with Brackenfur right behind him. When they sat down in front of the Highrock, a space cleared itself all around them. None of the other cats wanted to be anywhere near Darkstripe. The warrior stared straight ahead with a sneer on his face, but Firestar guessed he would be as anxious as the rest of them to know if Sorrelkit would recover.

Firestar looked at the rest of the Clan for a moment. This was a day that Thornpaw would remember for the rest of his life, but it was special for Firestar too, because Thornpaw was the first warrior he would make as Clan leader.

His voice rang out clearly as he began the ceremony with the words that were familiar to him from his own ceremony and all the others he had seen. "I, Firestar, leader of Thunder-Clan, call upon my warrior ancestors to look down on this apprentice. He has trained hard to understand the ways of your noble code, and I commend him to you as a warrior in his turn." Turning to the apprentice, Firestar continued, "Thornpaw, do you promise to uphold the warrior code and to protect and defend this Clan, even at the cost of your life?"

Thornpaw's reply was firm and confident. "I do."

"Then by the powers of StarClan," Firestar declared, "I give you your warrior name: Thornpaw, from this moment you will be known as Thornclaw. StarClan honors your loyalty and your intelligence, and we welcome you as a full warrior of ThunderClan."

Stepping forward, Firestar rested his muzzle on the top of Thornclaw's head, feeling the new warrior quiver with excitement. Thornclaw licked his shoulder in return, and met his gaze with a long look in which happiness and sorrow were mingled. Firestar knew he was remembering his den mate Swiftpaw, dead before he could know the fulfilment of being a warrior.

As Thornclaw stepped back to join the warriors, Lostface slipped over to him. "Thornclaw!" she purred, swiping her tongue over his ear. She had kept her promise to be the first cat to greet him with his new warrior name, and her voice held warmth and pride in his achievement.

Cloudtail pressed up behind her, greeting Thornclaw in his turn, and flashed a questioning look at Firestar.

Firestar gave him a nod. For a few moments he allowed the Clan to welcome the new warrior by chanting his name, and then he signaled with his tail for silence. When the cats had settled down, he meowed, "Before you go, I've something more to say. First, I want to honor the apprentice who should have been here, receiving his warrior name along with Thornclaw. You all know how Swiftpaw met his death trying to hunt down the dog pack who threatened us. His Clan will always remember that."

There was a murmur of agreement from the assembled cats. Firestar glanced at Longtail, who had been the dead apprentice's mentor, and saw a look of pride and grief cross his face.

"In addition," Firestar continued, "I want to give thanks from the Clan to Fernpaw and Ashpaw. They showed the bravery of warriors in the race against the dogs, and although they are still too young to receive their warrior names, we honor them."

"Fernpaw! Ashpaw!" The two apprentices looked overwhelmed to hear themselves praised by their Clan mates, and Dustpelt's eyes shone with delight. Only Darkstripe, Fernpaw's mentor, remained silent, staring coldly in front of him without even turning to look at his apprentice.

Firestar waited until the noise died down. "There's one more ceremony to perform." He flicked his tail to beckon Lostface out of the crowd. Nervously she stepped forward to stand in front of him; Cloudtail followed her, remaining a tail-length or so away.

A murmur of surprise went through the watching cats. Many of them, Firestar realized, would not know what was about to happen. The name-changing ceremony for a warrior who had already been given a new name had not been held for many seasons.

Remembering what One-eye had told him, he began to speak. "Spirits of StarClan, you know every cat by name. I ask you now to take away the name from the cat you see before you, for it no longer stands for what she is."

He paused and saw the young ginger-and-white she-cat shiver, as she waited, nameless, before StarClan. Firestar hoped she would like the name he had chosen for her; he had thought hard before he was sure he had gotten it right.

"By my authority as Clan leader," Firestar announced, "and with the approval of our warrior ancestors, I give this cat a new name. From this moment she will be known as Brightheart, for though her body has been gravely injured, we honor her brave spirit and the light that shines on within her."

He stepped close to the newly named Brightheart, and as he had done in the warrior ceremony, rested his muzzle on her head. She responded like any newly named warrior by licking his shoulder.

"Brightheart! Brightheart!" The yowl rose from the assembled cats. Brightheart had been popular when she was an apprentice, and the whole Clan had grieved over her injuries. She would never be a warrior in the truest sense of the word, but there would always be a place for her in ThunderClan.

Firestar led Brightheart to where Cloudtail was waiting. "Well?" he asked. "Is that fair enough for you?"

Cloudtail could barely reply; he was too busy pressing his muzzle against Brightheart's and winding his tail with hers. "It's perfect, Firestar," he murmured.

Brightheart's good eye brimmed with happiness and she was purring too hard to speak, but she blinked her gratitude at Firestar. She had carried the burden of Bluestar's anger against StarClan for too long, and even if she could never become a full warrior, she had a name to be proud of now.

Firestar swallowed, his throat choked with emotion. It was moments like this that made being a leader worthwhile.

"Listen, Firestar," meowed Cloudtail after a moment,

"Brightheart and I are going to train together. We're going to work on a fighting technique she can manage with just one eye and ear. When she's able to fight again, can she leave the elders and come to live in the warriors' den with the rest of us?"

"Well . . ." Firestar was uncertain. Brightheart could never be a full warrior because she couldn't hunt alone, and she would be at a serious disadvantage in a fight. But it was hard to resist her determination; besides, Firestar wanted her to be able to defend herself and her Clan mates as best she could. "You haven't got an apprentice yet, Cloudtail," he agreed, "so you do have the time to spend with Brightheart."

"Does that mean we can train together?" Cloudtail urged.

"Please, Firestar," meowed Brightheart. "I want to be some use to the Clan."

"All right," Firestar agreed. With a sudden thought he added, "If you work out some new moves, we can teach them to the others. Brightheart isn't the first warrior to be injured like this, and she won't be the last."

Cloudtail meowed agreement. The two young cats were moving away when Whitestorm, who had been Brightheart's mentor, came up to congratulate her. To Firestar, he added, "I looked in on Sorrelkit just before the ceremony. She was starting to wake up. Cinderpelt thinks she'll recover."

"That's great news!" Firestar purred. Whitestorm, he remembered, was Sorrelkit's father. "Do you think she's fit yet to tell us what happened?"

"You'll have to ask Cinderpelt," the white warrior replied.

"Go now—I'll see to the patrols."

Firestar thanked him and hurried toward the medicine cat's den.

Cinderpelt met him at the mouth of the fern tunnel. "I was coming to look for you," she meowed. After hearing Whitestorm's good news, Firestar was surprised to see the depth of anxiety in her eyes. "Sorrelkit is awake," she went on. "She's going to be fine. But you need to hear the story she has to tell."

# CHAPTER 10

*Sorrelkit was curled up in a* mossy nest near the entrance to Cinderpelt's den. She raised her head as Firestar approached with the medicine cat, but her eyes were heavy and it looked as though she was finding it difficult to move.

Sandstorm was crouched close beside her on guard duty. "Poor little scrap," she murmured to Firestar. "She nearly died. We've got to do something about Darkstripe."

The pale ginger she-cat was looking as anxious as Cinderpelt; she would have heard Sorrelkit's story too, Firestar realized. He nodded. "You can leave Darkstripe to me." Settling down beside Sorrelkit, he mewed gently, "I'm glad to see you're awake, Sorrelkit. Can you tell me what happened to you?"

The tiny tortoiseshell kit blinked up at him. "Sootkit and Rainkit were asleep in the nursery," she began in a faint voice. "But I wasn't sleepy. My mother wasn't watching, so I went to play in the ravine. I wanted to catch a mouse. And then I saw Darkstripe." Her voice shook and she hesitated.

"Go on," Firestar encouraged her.

"He was coming up the ravine by himself. I knew he should have had Brackenfur with him, and I . . . I wondered where he was going. I followed him—I remembered the time he took Bramblepaw and Tawnypaw out of the camp, and I thought I might have an adventure like that, too."

Firestar felt a pang of sadness as he remembered how Sorrelkit was always so bright and curious, getting into trouble because of her misguided courage. This limp scrap of fur didn't look at all adventurous now, and Firestar could only hope that with Cinderpelt's care she would soon be her lively self again.

"I followed him a long way," Sorrelkit went on, sounding rather proud of herself. "I'd never been so far from the camp. I hid from Darkstripe too—he didn't know I was there. And then he met another cat—a cat I'd never seen before."

"What other cat? What did it look like? What scent did it have?" Firestar questioned her urgently.

Sorrelkit looked bewildered. "I didn't recognize the scent," she mewed. Her nose wrinkled. "But it was yucky. He was a big white cat—bigger than you, Firestar. And he had black paws."

Firestar stared at her as he realized whom she had seen. "Blackfoot!" he exclaimed. "Tigerstar's deputy. That was ShadowClan scent you smelled, Sorrelkit."

"And what's Darkstripe doing, meeting the ShadowClan deputy on *our* territory?" Sandstorm growled. "That's what I'd like to know."

"So what happened then?" Firestar prompted the kit.

"I got scared," Sorrelkit admitted, looking down at her paws. "I ran back to camp, but I think Darkstripe must have heard me, because he caught up with me in the ravine. I thought he would be angry because I spied on him, but he told me how clever I was. He gave me some red berries for a special treat. They looked tasty, but when I ate them I started to feel really ill. . . . And I don't remember anything else, except waking up here."

She sank her head on her paws again as she finished, as if telling the long story had exhausted her.

Cinderpelt nosed her gently, checking her breathing. "Those were deathberries," she mewed. "You must never, ever touch them again."

"I won't, Cinderpelt, I promise," murmured the tiny kit.

"Thank you, Sorrelkit," Firestar meowed. He was angry but not surprised to discover that Graystripe had been right all along. The real shock was the news that Blackfoot had been seen on ThunderClan territory, and that Darkstripe had obviously arranged to meet him.

"What are you going to do about Darkstripe?" asked Sandstorm.

"I'll have to question him," Firestar replied. "But I don't expect he'll tell me anything."

"He can't stay in ThunderClan after this," Sandstorm pointed out, her voice hard as flint. "There's more than one cat who would rip his throat out for a couple of mouse tails."

"Leave him to me," Firestar mewed grimly.

Cinderpelt stayed with Sorrelkit, who was drifting off to sleep again, while Firestar returned to the main clearing with Sandstorm. Many of the cats were still there, sharing tongues after the earlier meeting. Whitestorm was heading for the gorse tunnel with Goldenflower and Longtail.

The patrol turned back and all the cats looked up, startled, as Firestar bounded to the top of the Highrock and yowled the summons to another meeting. His gaze sought out Darkstripe, but there was no sign of him.

"Where's Darkstripe?" he meowed at Graystripe as his friend made his way to the base of the rock.

"In the den," Graystripe replied.

"Fetch him."

Graystripe disappeared into the warriors' den, and emerged a moment later with Darkstripe and Brackenfur by his side. All three cats returned to the base of the Highrock, where Darkstripe sat and looked up at Firestar with a sneer on his face.

"Well?" he asked. "What does our noble leader want now?"

Firestar met his eyes steadily. "Sorrelkit is awake."

For a few heartbeats Darkstripe held his gaze, and then he looked away. "Have you called a Clan meeting to tell us that?" His tone was scoffing, but his fur had bristled uneasily at the news.

"Cats of ThunderClan." Firestar raised his voice. "I've called you together so that you can witness what Darkstripe has to say. You all heard what happened to Sorrelkit yesterday. She's awake now, and Cinderpelt says she'll be fine. I've talked to her and she confirms what Graystripe said. Darkstripe did feed her the deathberries. So, Darkstripe"—his gaze went back to the dark warrior below—"what have you to say for yourself?"

"She's lying," Darkstripe retorted. An angry hiss came from more than one of the cats around him, and he added, blustering, "Or she made a mistake. Kits never listen to what any cat says. She obviously didn't hear me properly when I told her not to eat them."

"She's not lying or mistaken," Firestar meowed. "And she told me something even more interesting: your reason for feeding her the deathberries. She saw you meeting Blackfoot, the deputy of ShadowClan, on our territory. Would you like to tell us what that was all about?"

More furious snarls came from the Clan, and a cat at the back of the crowd yowled, "Traitor!" Firestar had to signal with his tail for silence, and it was several moments before the angry cats quieted down again.

Darkstripe waited until he could make himself heard. "I don't have to justify myself to a kittypet," he growled.

Firestar's claws scraped against the rock beneath his paws, and he felt reassured by their sharpness. "That's exactly what you have to do. I want to know what you and Tigerstar are planning." Panic suddenly flooded over him, and he forced it back. "Darkstripe, you *know* what Tigerstar tried to do to us. The dog pack would have torn the whole Clan to pieces. How can you even think of following him after that?"

Darkstripe met his eyes resentfully and did not reply. Firestar remembered how he had caught him on the morning the pack attacked, trying to slip away from the camp with Tigerstar's kits. Darkstripe had known that Tigerstar was planning something; he would have abandoned the rest of the

Clan to a ghastly death without even trying to warn them. That was what his loyalty to ThunderClan was worth.

Firestar wanted to be fair, so that no cat, not even Darkstripe himself, could accuse him of persecuting Tigerstar's former allies. Even more than that, Firestar was still afraid of what Darkstripe might do if he left ThunderClan and was free to go to Tigerstar. But he was left with no choice. Exile was the only possible sentence for a cat guilty of Darkstripe's crimes.

"You could have been a valuable warrior," he went on to Darkstripe. "I gave you one chance after another to prove yourself. I wanted to trust you, and—"

"Trust me?" Darkstripe interrupted. "You've never trusted me. Do you think I didn't know you told that ginger fool to watch me?" He spat the last words toward Brackenfur, still seated beside him. "Did you expect me to live the rest of my days with a shadow?"

"No. I was waiting for you to show your loyalty." Firestar crouched on the rock and held Darkstripe's furious gaze without flinching. "This is the Clan where you were born; these are the cats you grew up with. Doesn't that mean anything to you? The warrior code says you should protect them with your life!"

As Darkstripe rose to his paws Firestar thought he could see fear flickering in his eyes, as if the dark warrior had never intended to make a final break with ThunderClan. He could not be sure, after all, that Tigerstar would welcome him; he had refused to follow the former deputy into exile, and he had failed in his attempt to take Bramblepaw and Tawnypaw to their father before the attack from the dogs. Tigerstar was not a cat who forgave easily.

But there was no trace of fear or regret in Darkstripe's voice as he spoke. "This is *not* my Clan," he hissed scornfully, to gasps of shock from the warriors around him. "Not any longer. ThunderClan is led by a kittypet, and there's nothing left to fight for. I feel no loyalty to ThunderClan. In the whole forest, the only cat worth following is Tigerstar."

"Then follow him," Firestar retorted. "You are no longer a warrior of ThunderClan. If you are found in our territory after sunset today, we shall treat you as we would any enemy. Go now."

Darkstripe's burning gaze held Firestar's for a moment longer, but he did not reply. Unhurriedly, he turned his back on Firestar and stalked toward the camp entrance. The cats nearby drew back as he passed them.

"You know what will be waiting for you if you try to come back," Cloudtail snarled, curling his lip. Willowpelt said nothing, but spat, her fur bristling.

As soon as the tip of Darkstripe's tail had vanished into the tunnel, a murmur of speculation broke out among the crowd of cats. One voice rose up clearly. "Has Darkstripe gone to ShadowClan?" asked Tawnypaw.

She had not joined in the Clan's protests when Firestar had tried to force Darkstripe to admit his guilt. Instead she had watched everything in silent fascination, her eyes following the dark warrior every pawstep of the way to the tunnel.

She looked shocked and sickened, but there was something else in her expression that Firestar could not read.

He froze as she asked her question. This apprentice knew that her father was the leader of ShadowClan. Did she understand the full extent of Darkstripe's treachery?

"I don't know," he admitted. "Darkstripe can go where he likes. From now on he is not a member of ThunderClan."

"Does that mean we can chase him out of the territory if we see him?" Whitestorm called.

"Yes, it does," Firestar replied. Addressing all the cats, he added, "If you scent him, or any ShadowClan cats, tell me or Whitestorm. And that reminds me—this morning Thornclaw scented rogue cats on our territory. Keep a lookout for them, too, and report anything you find."

Giving the orders helped him calm down. He could not help feeling the first creeping sensations of relief that at last he had Darkstripe out of his fur. There would be no more kittypet taunts, no more worries about whether all the Clan's business was being relayed straight to Tigerstar. Even though Firestar was worried about what Darkstripe would do now, there was more gain than loss in the dark warrior's departure. Yet still Firestar could not help wishing that he could have earned his loyalty.

"Hey, Firestar!" Dustpelt's voice startled him out of his thoughts. "What about Fernpaw? She hasn't got a mentor now."

"Thanks, Dustpelt, I'll deal with that right away. Fernpaw, come up to the rock."

Fernpaw obeyed, leaving Dustpelt's side to step delicately around the cats in her way until she stood at the foot of the Highrock.

Firestar glanced around to make sure the warrior he wanted was present, and hastily summoned the right words. "Longtail, you are without an apprentice since Swiftpaw died. You were an excellent mentor to him, and I expect you to pass on your skills to Fernpaw for the rest of her apprenticeship."

Longtail sprang to his paws, his eyes wide with surprise and gratitude. Firestar beckoned him with his tail, hoping that with Darkstripe gone the last of the hostility between himself and Longtail could be buried. The pale tabby warrior could easily be a fine member of the Clan.

Still looking stunned, Longtail padded up to Fernpaw and touched noses with her. Fernpaw dipped her head and both cats withdrew to where Dustpelt and Ashpaw were sitting.

Firestar leaped down from the Highrock. Now that everything was over exhaustion hit him like a blow from a badger's paw. What he wanted more than anything was to curl up with his friends in the warriors' den, to share tongues and sleep. But as leader of the Clan, he couldn't do that.

Darkstripe's treachery and the knowledge that ShadowClan cats were on his territory had revived all the memories of his nine-lives ceremony. Why had the hill of bones appeared in his dream, and the river of blood that had flowed from it? What did Bluestar's prophecy mean?

Desperate for answers, Firestar decided he would go to

Cinderpelt's den to see if the medicine cat had received any guidance from StarClan.

To his relief, Sandstorm was no longer on guard; he did not want the ginger she-cat to see him like this. Sorrelkit was asleep in her nest, and from the mouth of the split rock came faint sounds of Cinderpelt moving around inside. Firestar went closer and saw her rearranging the piles of healing herbs and berries that she kept there.

"Nearly out of juniper . . ." she muttered, then saw Firestar. "What's the matter? What's happened now?"

She limped out of the den and came up to him, nosing him anxiously as she smelled his fear-scent. "Firestar, what's wrong?"

Firestar shook his head to clear it of apprehension. It was a relief to go right back to the beginning, and tell Cinderpelt about the dream that had come to him as he lay beside the Moonstone.

Cinderpelt sat beside him and listened in silence, her steady gaze never leaving his face.

"Bluestar told me, 'Four will become two. Lion and tiger will meet in battle, and blood will rule the forest,'" Firestar finished. "And then blood oozed out of the hill of bones and started to fill the hollow. Blood everywhere . . . Cinderpelt, what does it all mean?"

"I don't know," Cinderpelt confessed. "StarClan have not shown me any of this. Just as they have the power to show me what will happen, so they can choose not to share with me. I'm sorry, Firestar—but I'll keep thinking about it, and maybe something will happen to make it clearer soon."

She pushed her nose against Firestar's fur to comfort him, but though Firestar was grateful for her sympathy, he could not forget the horror of his dream. What dreadful fate lay in store for him? And if even Cinderpelt could not answer that question, what hope was there for ThunderClan?

## CHAPTER 11

*Firestar emerged from the forest near* Sunningrocks and paused to taste the air. The sun was rising behind him, sending long shadows from the forest toward the river. Several days had passed since Darkstripe had left ThunderClan, and so far the patrols had not brought any news of him, nor of ShadowClan cats in the territory. But the memory of Firestar's dream was still too sharp for him to believe that the threat from the territory beyond the Thunderpath was over.

Graystripe and Thornclaw padded out of the trees behind him. "Smell anything?" Graystripe asked.

Firestar shrugged. "Only RiverClan cats. No more than I'd expect, this close to the border. But I want to make sure that they haven't been near Sunningrocks."

"We'll renew the scent markings," meowed Graystripe. "Come on, Thornclaw."

While his friends disappeared into the gullies among the rocks, Firestar remained where he was, carefully drawing the air over his scent glands. Though he was worried about ShadowClan, he had not forgotten RiverClan or their ambitious leader, Leopardstar. She had tried to retake Sunningrocks not long before, and Firestar would not be surprised if she decided to try again.

Not many moments passed before he detected fresh RiverClan scent. Instantly suspicious, he padded around the base of the rocks, only to relax a few moments later as he caught sight of Mistyfoot. She was alone, crouched at the very edge of the river, and as Firestar watched she scooped a fish out of the water and killed it with one blow of her paw.

"Well done!" Firestar called.

Mistyfoot turned, saw him, and padded up the gently sloping bank as far as the border. Firestar went to meet her there, glad to see that she still looked friendly in spite of the way she had left the ThunderClan camp. But he noticed with alarm that Mistyfoot was much thinner than when he had last seen her, and he wondered if something bad had happened following the revelation that Bluestar had been her mother.

"How are you, Mistyfoot?" he meowed. "I hope there hasn't been any trouble."

"About me and Stonefur?" Mistyfoot replied, guessing his thoughts. She hesitated. "Stonefur told the Clan the truth about Bluestar," she meowed at last. "Some of them didn't like it. One or two of them won't talk to us at all now, and most of them are a bit uneasy with us."

"I'm sorry to hear that," Firestar mewed. "What about Leopardstar? Has she said anything?"

"I could tell she wasn't pleased. She supported us in front of the Clan, but I think she has an eye on us all the same, to make sure we're still loyal."

"Of course you're loyal!" Firestar exclaimed.

"Yes, and the rest of the Clan will realize it sooner or later. Besides . . ." Mistyfoot paused again, and then went on. "That isn't the worst of our problems."

"What do you mean?"

"Tigerstar." Mistyfoot shivered. "He visits Leopardstar regularly, and I can't work out why. I'm sure they're planning something."

A jolt of fear shot through Firestar. "Planning what?"

Mistyfoot twitched her ears. "I've no idea. Leopardstar hasn't told Stonefur, even though he's her deputy. But there are a couple of ShadowClan warriors stationed permanently in our camp."

"*What?* That shouldn't happen! It must be against the warrior code!"

Mistyfoot shrugged, looking defeated. "Try telling that to Leopardstar."

"But what are they doing there?"

"Leopardstar *says* that they're staying with us so the Clans can exchange training methods and fighting techniques, but I don't see much sign of it. All they do is watch. . . . It's like they're learning all about us, all our secrets and weaknesses." Mistyfoot's fur bristled as if she saw her enemies in front of her. "That's why I came over here, to get away from them for a bit."

"That's terrible," Firestar meowed. "What is Leopardstar thinking?"

"You want my opinion? She wants to do the best for her

Clan and she thinks Tigerstar is the strongest leader in the forest, so she's set out to be his ally."

"I'm not sure Tigerstar has allies," Firestar warned her. "Only followers."

Mistyfoot nodded. "I know." She sat down, licked one paw, and drew it two or three times over her ear.

Firestar wondered if she was regretting saying so much to a warrior of another Clan. "How is the prey running?" he asked, hoping to distract her. "At least the river hasn't frozen yet."

"Not yet. Prey's scarce, but that's nothing new." Mistyfoot flicked her ears dismissively. "It's leaf-bare, after all. And those two warriors of Tigerclaw's don't help," she added. "They sit there in camp stuffing their faces, but they never bring back much fresh-kill."

She broke off at the sound of Graystripe's voice yowling her name. Firestar turned to see his friend bounding down the bank toward them with Thornclaw just behind him.

"Hi, Mistyfoot," panted Graystripe as he came up. "How are Featherpaw and Stormpaw?"

"They're fine, Graystripe," replied Mistyfoot, with a purr of welcome for her former Clan mate. Though Graystripe's stay in RiverClan had been short, the two cats had become good friends, and Mistyfoot was always willing to give Graystripe news of his kits. "Featherpaw is turning into a great fighter. ThunderClan will have to watch out when she's made a warrior."

Graystripe let out a purr. "Well, she couldn't have a better mentor."

Firestar backed away while Graystripe and Mistyfoot discussed the two apprentices. Thornclaw padded up to him and meowed, "We've renewed the scent markings, Firestar. There's no fresh RiverClan scent around the rocks."

"That's good," Firestar responded, though his thoughts were only half on what the young warrior was telling him. Mistyfoot's news deeply disturbed him. It sounded as if RiverClan and ShadowClan were allied more closely than ever before. And if Tigerstar decided to go to war, ThunderClan would be trapped between them.

*Oh, StarClan,* Firestar murmured to himself. *Show me what I should do now.*

After his talk with Mistyfoot, Firestar ordered extra patrols, but no cat reported anything unusual. The days slipped past peacefully until the time of the next Gathering approached.

As the sun went down behind the thorn hedge, Firestar sat with Whitestorm beside the nettle patch, sharing fresh-kill before the journey.

"Who will you take to the Gathering?" the white warrior asked.

Firestar swallowed a mouthful of squirrel. "Not you, I think," he replied. "I'm certain Tigerstar is going to make a move of some sort, and I want you to guard the camp. I'll leave you some strong warriors, too."

"I think you're right." Whitestorm swiped his tongue around his mouth as he finished his vole. "Tigerstar may have failed with the dog pack but he's bound to try something else."

"I'll take Fernpaw and Ashpaw," Firestar decided. "And Thornclaw. He'll be looking forward to his first Gathering as a warrior. And Sandstorm, Graystripe, and Frostfur. That should leave you with enough fighting strength if Tigerstar sends warriors to attack."

"You think he'll break the truce?" inquired Whitestorm.

Firestar flicked his ears. "What do you think? He led the dog pack to us—do you think he'd bother about a little thing like ignoring the will of StarClan?"

"StarClan?" Whitestorm snorted. "Tigerstar behaves as if he's never heard of StarClan." He paused, and then asked, "What about the two young apprentices—Tigerstar's kits? Do you want to take them with you?"

Firestar shook his head. "Not in a hundred moons. You know what's going to happen, don't you? Tigerstar wants those kits. At the last Gathering, he gave Bluestar one moon to decide whether to hand them over. That time's up now. If Bramblepaw and Tawnypaw are there, I wouldn't put it past Tigerstar to try taking them from the Gathering."

"Nor would I." Whitestorm rumbled in agreement. "You think we should keep them, then?"

Firestar was startled. "Don't you?" He had assumed that ThunderClan would insist on their right to keep the two apprentices, but if his deputy thought that they should give the young cats to their father, Firestar would consider his opinion carefully.

But Whitestorm was nodding. "There's no question that they're ThunderClan kits. Their mother is ThunderClan, and so was their father at the time they were born. Tigerstar going to ShadowClan doesn't alter that. But if we want to keep them, we'll have to fight for them."

"Then we fight," Firestar meowed determinedly. "Besides," he added, "if we meekly hand them over, Tigerstar will see that as a sign of weakness. He'd be making more demands before you could say 'mouse.'"

"True."

Firestar took another bite of squirrel, his eyes narrowing as his thoughts moved to the approaching Gathering. "You know, Whitestorm," he began, "Tigerstar won't have it all his own way. I've got news for the Gathering, too. How do you think the other Clans will react when I tell them how Tigerstar tried to use the dog pack to destroy us? Not even Brokentail was as ruthless as that. Even Tigerstar's *own* Clan will turn against him. They might even drive him from the forest, and then we'll be rid of him."

Whitestorm's ears twitched; to Firestar's surprise the white warrior didn't look as optimistic as he had expected. "Maybe," he meowed, "but don't be surprised if it doesn't work out like that."

Firestar stared at him. "You think the warrior code allows a cat to have another Clan torn apart by dogs?"

"No, of course not. But Tigerstar could always deny it. What proof do we have?"

Firestar thought seriously about what his deputy was saying. One cat—Longtail—had seen Tigerstar feed a rabbit to the pack. Several of the Clan had detected Tigerstar's scent on the trail of rabbits. And Tigerstar had attacked Firestar himself close to the gorge, to make sure that the dog pack caught him and pulled him down. Only Bluestar's sudden appearance had saved him.

True, Mistyfoot and Stonefur had witnessed Tigerstar's presence by the river that day, but they were already having problems within their own Clan. If they spoke up against Tigerstar their Clan mates might not believe them. It would be wrong, Firestar realized, to add to their troubles.

And all the rest of his evidence rested on the word of ThunderClan cats alone. Both WindClan and RiverClan knew there had been a serious rift between Tigerstar and his birth Clan that had driven the former deputy to leave. Tigerstar could try to make it seem as if the ThunderClan cats were lying.

"Then we'll see who they believe," Firestar insisted angrily. "Not every cat thinks that Tigerstar is StarClan's gift to the forest. He won't have it all his own way."

"Let's hope not." Whitestorm got to his paws and stretched. "You're going to have a lively time tonight, Firestar. I'll go and tell the warriors you've chosen to be ready."

As he padded away, Firestar crouched down beside the nettles and finished his squirrel. There was going to be trouble at this Gathering. Tigerstar was certain to claim his kits again, and Firestar suspected that he would take this opportunity to reveal Bluestar's secret as well and denounce Mistyfoot and Stonefur as half-Clan cats.

*But I've got plenty to say, too,* he thought, pushing aside the doubts Whitestorm had raised. *When I've finished, no cat in the forest—not even his own Clan—will trust Tigerstar again.*

## CHAPTER 12

*Firestar paused at the top of* the hollow before leading his cats down to the Gathering. The night was still. Clouds were building up on the horizon, so that Firestar had begun to wonder if StarClan was going to hide the moon to show that it was not their will for the Gathering to take place.

But for now the moon rose high above the clouds, and the scent of cats drifted up to Firestar from the hollow below.

"Only WindClan so far," murmured Graystripe, who was crouched at Firestar's shoulder. "What's keeping the others?"

Firestar shrugged. "StarClan knows. Personally, I wouldn't care if Tigerstar never showed up."

He signaled with his tail and led his warriors as they raced down through the bushes and into the clearing at the center of the hollow. As Graystripe had said, only WindClan cats were there. Firestar spotted their leader, Tallstar, seated with his deputy, Deadfoot, near the base of the Great Rock.

"Greetings, Firestar," Tallstar mewed, dipping his head courteously as Firestar approached. "Tornear told me he met you on your way to Highstones. We grieve for Bluestar."

"So do her own Clan," Firestar responded, bowing his

head in turn. "She was a noble leader."

"But you will be a worthy successor," meowed the black-and-white tom, surprising Firestar by the warmth of his tone. "You've served your Clan well."

"I-I hope to serve it even better in future," Firestar stammered.

Tallstar nodded once more in response, and sprang up to the top of the rock. Before following him, Firestar glanced around at his own cats. They were already circling among the WindClan warriors and beginning to exchange their news. Firestar was pleased to see that the two Clans seemed friendly toward each other, in spite of the recent clash over missing prey. Worried as he was about ShadowClan and RiverClan, it was good to think that he might find allies in WindClan.

Waving with his tail toward Onewhisker and his apprentice, Gorsepaw, who were settling down to talk with Sandstorm, Firestar jumped up to stand beside Tallstar on the top of the Great Rock.

He had stood here once before, when he took Bluestar's place while she was ill after the fire, but he was still not used to looking down on his cats from such a great height, nor seeing their eyes gleam pale from reflected moonlight as they stared up at him. Firestar's tension increased as he thought about what was to come, and the confrontation with Tigerstar that would surely happen before moonset.

"ShadowClan and RiverClan are late," he remarked.

Tallstar twitched his ears in agreement. "Clouds threaten

the moon," he pointed out. A trace of anxiety crossed his face. "Perhaps StarClan is angry."

Looking up, Firestar saw that the clouds he had noticed earlier were spreading farther across the sky.

The air tasted damp, and his fur prickled with expectation. What would it mean, Firestar wondered, if StarClan veiled the moon and Tigerstar was left to plot in secret until the next Gathering?

"Tallstar," he began, deciding that the time had come to confide in the WindClan leader and ask for his advice. "I'm worried about what Tigerstar might be planning—"

He never finished. A triumphant yowling from the top of the hollow interrupted him, and a heartbeat later more cats raced into the clearing as ShadowClan and RiverClan arrived together, their cats fanning out below him. Tigerstar reached the top of the Great Rock in a single bound, and Leopardstar scrambled up beside him.

"Cats of all Clans!" Tigerstar declared, not waiting to greet Tallstar and Firestar or discuss which of the leaders should speak first. "I have news for you. Listen well, for great change is coming to the forest."

Firestar stared at the ShadowClan leader in confusion. When Tigerstar first mentioned news, he had thought for a moment he was referring to Mistyfoot and Stonefur's half-Clan heritage. Yet that would not merit such a spectacular arrival or make Tigerstar talk about great change.

Below them in the clearing there was dead silence. All the cats stared up at the Great Rock, their eyes wide as they waited for Tigerstar to explain. Every hair on Firestar's pelt began to bristle, and he did not know whether it was due to the tension of the assembled warriors or the threatening rain clouds.

"Great change," Tigerstar repeated. "And StarClan has shown me that it is ShadowClan's task to prepare every cat in the forest to meet it."

"Every cat?" Firestar heard the quiet mutter from Tallstar. The WindClan leader took a step forward. "Tigerstar—"

"ShadowClan has the favor of StarClan," Tigerstar swept on, ignoring the interruption. "We are blessed because we survived the sickness, and I have received the blessing of our warrior ancestors most of all because it was my task to restore the Clan and make it great again."

*Oh, yes?* Firestar thought. He refused to believe that StarClan were showing favor to Tigerstar after all that he had done to his birth Clan. Glancing down into the clearing, he looked for Runningnose. The ShadowClan medicine cat had done his best to support his Clan during Nightstar's ill-fated leadership, and Firestar had an idea that he was not entirely happy with Tigerstar as the old tom's replacement. He wondered what Runningnose thought of the announcement Tigerstar had just made, but though his gaze searched the clearing carefully he could see no sign of the medicine cat.

*Left at home,* Firestar asked himself, *so he can't deny what Tigerstar claims?*

At the same time, he couldn't help noticing that Stonefur was also missing, and he wondered if the RiverClan deputy was in more trouble because of his half-Clan parentage, and what he thought about his leader's decision to ally her Clan with Tigerstar.

One cat Firestar did spot in the clearing below was Darkstripe. The former ThunderClan warrior was sitting beside Blackfoot, the ShadowClan deputy, and his eyes shone with admiration as he looked up at Tigerstar. It was clear that he had gone straight to his old ally after being driven out of ThunderClan.

"All of you know," Tigerstar went on, "that changes have already come to us—unwelcome changes beyond our control. Last leaf-bare much of the forest was covered by floods. A fire swept through ThunderClan territory." As he mentioned the fire he flashed a look at Firestar, who would have liked to claw the arrogance off his enemy's battle-scarred face. "Twolegs are moving into our territory in ever greater numbers. Life is growing harder, and as the forest changes around us, we must change to meet the crisis."

Yowls of support rose from below, though Firestar noticed that they came only from ShadowClan and RiverClan cats. The warriors of ThunderClan and WindClan were exchanging stunned glances, as if they couldn't work out what Tigerstar was trying to say. Firestar felt just as shocked. He had been so certain that Tigerstar would reveal Mistyfoot and Stonefur's secret at this Gathering, and demand his own kits, Bramblepaw and Tawnypaw, from ThunderClan. Firestar had braced himself, but now he was left to face a completely different challenge.

"StarClan have shown me the way," Tigerstar meowed with a glance at the sky, where the storm clouds were massing more thickly still. "To survive the hardship ahead of us, we must join together. As four Clans, we waste our energies in striving against each other. As one, we would be strong. We must unite!"

Total silence met his words. Firestar could hear a faint breeze stirring the leafless branches of the four oak trees, and in the distance a mutter of thunder. He gaped at Tigerstar. A single Clan in the forest? When StarClan had always decreed that there should be four?

"Leopardstar has already agreed to join RiverClan with ShadowClan," Tigerstar told them. "We shall be joint leaders of a greater Clan, to be known as TigerClan."

*Joint leaders?* Firestar didn't believe that for a moment. Tigerstar would never share his leadership with any cat.

Now Tigerstar turned to Firestar and Tallstar. "We have come to invite you to join the new Clan," he meowed, his amber eyes glittering. "Let us rule the forest together in friendship and peace."

Before he had finished speaking, Tallstar stepped forward, his fur bristling aggressively. But it was not to Tigerstar that he spoke; instead he addressed all the cats in the clearing below.

"TigerClan was the name of one of the great Clans of ancient times." Tallstar's voice rang out as strong and clear as if he were still a young cat. "Tigerstar has no right to use it now. Nor does he have the right to change the number of

Clans in the forest. We have lived as four Clans for innumerable seasons, following the warrior code laid down for us by StarClan. To throw aside our ancient ways would bring disaster." Turning to Tigerstar, he hissed, "I'll die before I join my Clan to yours!"

Tigerstar blinked slowly. Firestar could see a dangerous gleam in his eyes, but his voice was calm as he replied, "Tallstar, I understand. These are important matters, and an older cat like yourself will need time to see that what I'm suggesting is for the good of all our Clans."

"I'm not so old that I've lost my wits, you piece of fox dung!" Tallstar snarled.

Tigerstar flattened his ears, but he kept his temper. "And what does the new leader of ThunderClan think?" he sneered. All the hatred he had ever felt toward the flame-colored warrior was contained in those words, and even the air felt scorched.

Firestar's veins throbbed as though they were filled with ice as he imagined the future. His territory and Tallstar's lay between Tigerstar's and Leopardstar's. With ShadowClan and RiverClan in alliance, the two remaining Clans could be crushed between them.

Glancing down, Firestar saw unease spread among the ThunderClan and WindClan warriors. Sandstorm was on her paws, yowling, "Never, Firestar, never!" but some of the WindClan cats were talking urgently to each other, as if they were considering Tigerstar's proposition. The dark tabby warrior had been clever, Firestar realized. Much of what he had said was true—times were growing harder, for all the reasons he had given. Maybe some cats would believe their problems could be solved by joining together as one Clan. But Firestar was convinced that the cats of the forest could fulfill their destiny only if there were four Clans. And even if he had considered for one moment the idea of joining together as one, he would have rejected it if Tigerstar was to be the new Clan's leader.

"Well, Firestar," Tigerstar rumbled, with another swift glance at the storm-dark sky. "Have you lost your tongue?"

Firestar took a couple of paces that brought him to Tallstar's side. "I'll never let you take over my Clan," he spat at Tigerstar.

"Make us," Tallstar invited. "If you can."

"Make you?" Tigerstar's amber eyes widened; for a heartbeat he looked almost genuinely hurt. "I came here in peace with a plan to help us all. Tallstar, Firestar, I want you to recognize that this is the right decision and come to me willingly. But don't delay too long," he added, a hint of menace in his voice. "StarClan will not wait forever."

Fury blazed up in Firestar. How dared Tigerstar claim that his attempt to take over the whole forest was the will of StarClan?

Spinning around, he turned his back on the ShadowClan leader and paced to the front of the rock, where he could look down on all the assembled cats. The time had come for him to speak. When he had finished, Tigerstar would be revealed for what he was—a murderer who would wade through the blood of countless cats to get what he wanted. Let Leopardstar see the kind of cat she had trusted!

"Cats of WindClan, RiverClan, and ShadowClan!" Firestar yowled. "I can stay silent no longer. You cannot trust Tigerstar any more than you would trust a cornered badger."

Out of the corner of his eye he saw a swift movement from Tigerstar, a bunching of muscles under the rippling tabby pelt, but then the ShadowClan leader glanced at the sky again, controlled himself, and went on listening with a look of deliberate indifference.

"I know many of you must have wondered why Tigerstar left ThunderClan," Firestar went on. "You want to know the truth? This cat is power-hungry and dangerous, and he is willing to murder other cats to get what he wants."

He broke off as lightning stabbed down from the sky, a blazing claw of white fire that raked the forest. Thunder crashed overhead, drowning Firestar's words; it sounded as if the Great Rock itself were being torn up.

"A sign! A sign!" Tigerstar yowled. He gazed up at the sky, his yellow eyes glowing in the light of the moon that still shone between the gathering clouds. "I thank you, StarClan, for showing us your will. This Gathering is over."

Calling a command to his cats to follow him, he bunched his muscles to leap down from the Great Rock. Before he sprang he turned his head, eyes narrowed with hatred. "Bad luck, kittypet," he spat. "Think about my offer. It's your last chance to save those miserable cats."

Before Firestar had the chance to respond, the ShadowClan

leader launched himself from the Great Rock and disappeared into the bushes that lined the hollow. ShadowClan cats poured after him. Leopardstar jumped down in her turn and gathered the warriors of RiverClan.

Firestar and Tallstar faced each other, shocked and bewildered, as lightning stabbed down again. A gust of wind buffeted the rock, almost carrying Firestar off his paws, and rain poured from the sky as the storm broke.

Almost blinded by the lashing rain, Firestar half jumped, half slithered down the side of the rock and streaked across the open ground to the shelter of the bushes, calling to his warriors as he went. Moments later he found himself crouching beneath a hawthorn bush with Graystripe and Sandstorm huddled close to him. Shaking rain from his pelt, he looked around for Tallstar, but the WindClan leader had not followed him.

The rain was striking the ground so hard that the drops scattered into a mist of spray. The four oaks thrashed and groaned in the wind. Grasses and ferns were flattened in the fury of the storm. But the chaos in the clearing was no worse than the chaos in Firestar's mind.

"I can't believe this!" he meowed, raising his voice above the howling wind. "I didn't think even Tigerstar would dare to claim power over all the forest."

"But what can we do about it?" asked Graystripe. "You didn't get to tell the truth about Tigerstar."

"It's not Firestar's fault that the storm broke," Sandstorm pointed out, her hackles rising.

"Too late to worry about it," Firestar told them. "That prey's killed and eaten now. We have to decide what we do next."

"What is there to decide?" snarled Sandstorm. The light of battle shone in her green eyes. "We fight, of course—until we've driven that piece of crowfood out of the forest for good."

Firestar nodded. Though he said nothing, he couldn't help thinking of Bluestar's prophecy during his dream at the Moonstone.

*Four will become two. Lion and Tiger will meet in battle.*

*"Tiger" must mean the new TigerClan, but who or what is "Lion"?* Firestar pushed the question aside as he remembered Bluestar's ominous parting words.

*Blood will rule the forest.*

## CHAPTER 13

*The squall was soon over. Firestar* led his cats home through a forest where every twig and fern dripped water under a clearing sky. Silverpelt glittered brightly, and Firestar raised his eyes to utter a silent prayer: *Great StarClan, show me what to do.*

He began to worry about whether Tigerstar had sent warriors to attack the camp while Firestar and the others were away. It would be one way to weaken ThunderClan so that Firestar had no choice but to ally his surviving cats with TigerClan. Relief flooded over him as he emerged from the gorse tunnel to see that everything was peaceful.

Whitestorm got up from sentry duty outside the warriors' den and padded over. "You're back early. I wondered if those stormclouds would cover the moon."

"Yes, but it was worse than that," Firestar replied.

"Worse?" Whitestorm's eyes widened in astonishment as Firestar told him what had happened at the Gathering just before thunder and lightning prevented his revealing words. More cats joined them, and Firestar was aware of shocked mews as his Clan learned what Tigerstar was planning.

"When the storm broke," Firestar finished, "Tigerstar said

it was a sign from StarClan that he had their favor. He and Leopardstar left, so the Gathering broke up."

"It might well have been a sign," mewed Whitestorm thoughtfully. "But one that shows StarClan are angry with Tigerstar."

"Cinderpelt, what do you think?" Firestar asked the medicine cat, who had listened to the story with deep foreboding in her blue eyes.

"I don't know," she admitted. "If it was a sign, it would mean StarClan stopped you from telling the truth about Tigerstar, and I find that hard to believe." She shrugged. "There are times when a storm is just a storm."

"It was an unlucky one for ThunderClan, then," muttered Longtail.

"I wish I'd been there," Cloudtail growled. "I'd have torn Tigerstar's throat out. No more problem."

"In that case, it's a good thing you weren't there," Firestar retorted. "Attacking a Clan leader at a Gathering? *That* would have made StarClan angry."

Cloudtail narrowed his eyes at Firestar, the challenge clear in his blue gaze. "Why don't StarClan do something to help us, then, if they're so powerful?"

"Maybe they will," Brightheart suggested gently.

"So what are we going to do?" asked Mousefur. She was shifting from paw to paw as if she wanted to race out of camp and confront her enemies right away. "You're not thinking of joining this . . . TigerClan, are you?"

"Never," Firestar assured her. "But we need time to think,

and rest." He yawned and stretched. "For now, we'll need extra patrols. Any volunteers to go out at dawn?"

"I will," Mousefur offered instantly.

"Thanks," meowed Firestar. "Keep a lookout along the border with ShadowClan. And if you come across any of Tigerstar's warriors, you know what to do."

"Oh, *yes.*" Cloudtail lashed his tail eagerly. "I'll come with you, Mousefur. I could do with some ShadowClan fur to line my nest."

Firestar didn't try to check the young warrior's hostility. No cat could doubt Cloudtail's loyalty to ThunderClan, however scornful he was about StarClan and the warrior code.

Whitestorm named Brackenfur and Thornclaw to join the patrol as well, and all four cats padded off to get some rest before dawn. One by one, the other Clan cats headed for their dens. Firestar was aware of their shock, and the fear they did not quite succeed in hiding.

Eventually he was left alone with only Cinderpelt by his side. He let out a long sigh. "Will there ever be any end to this?" he murmured.

Cinderpelt pressed her muzzle comfortingly against his. "I don't know. It's in the paws of StarClan." She narrowed her eyes. "But sometimes I don't believe there'll be any peace in the forest until Tigerstar is dead."

"Right," Firestar meowed. "Attack me."

A few foxlengths away, Bramblepaw crouched on the floor of the hollow. Firestar waited as the apprentice began to creep toward him, his amber eyes darting from side to side as if he was choosing the best place to strike.

A heartbeat later Bramblepaw launched himself into the air. But Firestar was ready for him. Slipping rapidly to one side, he butted Bramblepaw in the flank as he came down, and the young cat lost his balance and rolled over, his paws scuffing up dust.

"You'll have to be quicker than that," Firestar told him. "Don't give your enemy time to think."

Bramblepaw scrambled up, spitting out sand, and immediately sprang again. His outstretched paws caught Firestar on the side of the head, thrusting the older cat sideways so that his paws slid out from under him. Bramblepaw held him down, his nose almost touching Firestar's.

"Like that?" he asked.

Firestar pushed him off. "Let me up, you great lump!" Shaking sand out of his pelt, he added, "Yes, just like that. You're shaping up well, Bramblepaw."

The apprentice's eyes glowed and Firestar suddenly felt as if he were looking at a young Tigerstar—but this was Tigerstar as he should have been: strong, skillful, brave and, yes, ambitious, but in Bramblepaw all the ambition seemed to be focused on becoming the best warrior that he could be in the service of his Clan.

Firestar couldn't resist letting out a purr of satisfaction. Amid all the troubles that beset ThunderClan, it was a relief to escape for a short time for a training session with his apprentice.

But Bramblepaw's next words reminded him of his weightier responsibilities. "Firestar, I wanted to ask you . . . why does every cat think it would be so bad to be part of TigerClan?"

*"What?"* Firestar felt a surge of anger; he could hardly believe his apprentice had asked the question.

Bramblepaw flinched, but he went on, steadily meeting his mentor's eyes. "Ashpaw told me what Tigerstar said. It's true that times are hard. Every cat's always complaining about the shortage of prey, and how there are more Twolegs in the forest than ever before. Besides, TigerClan will be the strongest Clan in the forest if RiverClan joins with ShadowClan. Wouldn't it make sense to join them?"

Firestar took a deep breath. After all, he had asked questions like these when he first came to the forest, not understanding why there should be rivalry and battle between the Clans. He sat down beside Bramblepaw. "It's not as simple as that," he meowed. "For one thing, there have always been four Clans in the forest. For another, it would mean the end of ThunderClan."

"Why?"

"Because we cannot believe Tigerstar when he says the four leaders would rule jointly." Firestar tried to speak gently, remembering he was talking about the young cat's father, but there was no hiding the stark truth. "Tigerstar would take control. We would lose everything that makes us ThunderClan."

For a few heartbeats Bramblepaw was silent. Then he

meowed, "I see. Thank you, Firestar. That's what I wanted to know."

"Then let's get on." Firestar sprang to his paws. "There's a move I think you might find useful. . . ."

But as he continued with the training session, he found that his optimism about Bramblepaw's loyalties had started to fade.

When the training session was over, Firestar sent Bramblepaw to hunt for the elders. He was about to return to camp when Cloudtail bounded over the top of the training hollow, closely followed by Brightheart.

"Firestar! We're going to practice Brightheart's fighting moves. Do you want to see how she's coming on?"

"Yes, of course—go ahead." Even though Brightheart's wounds were healed, Firestar found it hard to think of her as a fighting cat. He couldn't imagine she would ever be able to go into battle with her Clan. But since her change of name she looked much happier and more confident, and he wanted to encourage her as much as he could.

Cloudtail and Brightheart ran into the middle of the hollow. For a few heartbeats they prowled around each other; then Cloudtail darted in and gave Brightheart a couple of blows with sheathed paws on the blind side of her head. Brightheart rolled with the impact and Firestar tensed, imagining the damage an enemy cat might have done with his claws out and all his strength behind the blow.

But instead of rolling away from Cloudtail, Brightheart

propelled herself toward him, tangling her paws with his and throwing him off balance. Firestar pricked his ears with interest as the two cats writhed together on the ground, and suddenly Brightheart was on top, pinning Cloudtail down with one paw on his neck.

"I've never seen that before," Firestar meowed, padding over to join them as Brightheart released Cloudtail and the young white warrior jumped up and shook sand out of his pelt. "Brightheart, try it on me."

Looking nervous, Brightheart faced him. Firestar found it harder than he had expected to come up on her blind side; the young she-cat kept weaving back and forth so that he had to change his position. When at last he leaped at her, she slid under his outstretched paws and tripped him in the same way that she had surprised Cloudtail. For a few heartbeats they wrestled together until at last Firestar managed to hold her down.

"Harder than it looks, isn't it?" meowed Cloudtail, strolling up beside them with a delighted expression.

"It certainly is. Well done, Brightheart." Firestar let the she-cat get up; her uninjured eye was shining at his praise. For the first time he began to wonder if she had a future as a warrior after all. "Keep practicing," he told her. "And let me watch you again soon. I think you might have something to teach the Clan."

After the storm, the weather turned cold again. Every morning the grass and ferns were furred with frost, and there was another light fall of snow. Prey became scarcer still, and what the hunters managed to catch was thin and scrawny, scarcely a mouthful for a hungry cat.

"If I don't get a decent meal soon I'll fade away to a shadow," Graystripe complained.

He and Firestar were on patrol not far from Fourtrees, along with Longtail and Thornclaw. Firestar had hoped they would find more prey farther from the camp, where the fire had never reached, but the catch was pitifully small.

"I'm going to try down by the stream," Firestar meowed.

He headed down the slope to where a thicker growth of fern and shrubs marked the line of the stream. When he paused to taste the air the prey-scent was faint, and he could not hear any of the small sounds that would have alerted him to creatures scurrying through the grass.

With so little fresh-kill, the Clan was growing weaker by the day. Just enduring leaf-bare would be hard enough, but on top of that there was the new threat from TigerClan. Would they be strong enough to defend themselves? Firestar wondered.

His pawsteps led him by instinct down toward the stream and he crouched down to drink, prodding the thin ice at the very edge and shaking icy drops off his paw when it gave way.

As Firestar bent his head to lap from the stream, the sun came out behind him, striking through the leaves. Light dazzled on the water and surrounded Firestar's reflection with golden rays. For a moment the image of his head disappeared, to be replaced by that of a roaring lion. It was the beast

Firestar had heard described in so many elders' tales, his flame-colored pelt blazing into a luxuriant mane, his eyes shining with unlimited strength and power.

Startled, Firestar leaped backward. He let out a yowl as he collided with a tree and stumbled into the dead leaves among its roots. When he looked up, Spottedleaf was facing him from across the stream.

The beautiful tortoiseshell's eyes were brimming with amusement, and she let out a little *mrrow* of laughter.

"Spottedleaf!" Firestar gasped. She had never come to him before when he was awake, and he wondered what this might mean. He sprang to his paws, ready to splash through the stream to her side, but she signaled with her tail for him to stay where he was.

"Take heed of what you have seen, Firestar," she told him, her amusement vanishing like the frost at dawn. "Learn what you must be."

"What do you mean?" Firestar asked urgently.

But as she finished speaking, Spottedleaf began to fade. Her eyes rested on him, filled with love, and her body paled until Firestar could see the bank of the stream through it.

"Spottedleaf, don't leave me yet," he begged. "I need you."

But her eyes shone for a heartbeat longer, and then she was gone.

"Firestar!" It was Graystripe's voice. Firestar shook his head to clear it and turned to face his friend as he came padding down the bank.

"Are you okay?" Graystripe asked. "You yowled loud

enough to scare all the prey between here and Fourtrees!"

"I'm fine," Firestar replied. "Something startled me, that's all."

Graystripe examined him for a moment longer, as if he wasn't quite satisfied with his leader's explanation, and then turned away. "If you say so," he meowed, retreating up the bank. "Come and see the rabbit Longtail caught—it's as big as a fox!"

Firestar stayed where he was. He was still trembling from the shock of his vision. He had seen himself like one of the great warriors of old, a member of LionClan. Bluestar's prophecy echoed in his head again: *Lion and Tiger will meet in battle.*

Did this mean that a new Clan—LionClan—would arise to combat TigerClan? And did StarClan intend *Firestar* to lead it?

# CHAPTER 14

*"Firestar," meowed Graystripe. "I want to* ask you something."

Firestar was crouching by the nettle patch. He had just seen Brackenfur leaving at the head of the evening patrol, and now he was eating his share of fresh-kill before rounding up a patrol of his own for an extra check on the ShadowClan border.

"Sure," he replied. "What is it?"

Graystripe crouched beside him, but before he could speak Tawnypaw came stalking out of the elders' den, her head and her tail held high as she headed for the gorse tunnel. Her amber eyes blazed with anger. Bramblepaw emerged behind her, his jaws clamped on a bundle of bedding moss. He looked worried.

"Tawnypaw!" Firestar called. "What's the matter?"

For a heartbeat he thought the apprentice was going to ignore him. Then she veered sharply to stand in front of him. "Smallear!" she spat. "If ever a cat asked to have his fur clawed off—"

"You shouldn't talk like that about an elder," Firestar rebuked her. "Smallear's given good service to the Clan and we should respect that."

"What about a bit of respect for me?" Tawnypaw was so furious she seemed to have forgotten she was talking to her leader. "Just because I was a little late going to clear out the old bedding, Smallear said that Tigerstar had never wanted to serve the elders either, and he could see I was going to turn out just like my father." She scraped her claws on the sandy floor of the clearing as if she were picturing the old tom's fur. "It's not the first time he's said things, either. I don't see why I should have to put up with it!"

While she was speaking, Bramblepaw had come to join them, putting down the moss he was carrying. "You know Smallear's joints are aching because of the cold weather," he meowed.

"You're not my mentor!" Tawnypaw flared up at her brother. "Don't tell me what to do."

"Calm down, Tawnypaw," Firestar mewed. He wanted to reassure her that no cat believed she would end up a murderer and traitor like her father, but he knew that wasn't entirely true. "You're doing very well as an apprentice, and you're going to make a great warrior. Sooner or later the Clan will see that."

"That's what I've been telling her," Bramblepaw meowed, and added to his sister, "We've got to live down what Tigerstar did. That's the only way the Clan will believe in our loyalty."

"Some cats believe in it already," Graystripe put in, and Bramblepaw flashed him a grateful glance.

The worst of Tawnypaw's fury was fading, though her amber eyes still burned. With a toss of her head she turned away, flinging her parting words over her shoulder as she stalked toward the gorse tunnel. "I'm going to fetch some fresh moss."

"I'm sorry, Firestar," Bramblepaw murmured when she had gone. "But Tawnypaw's right to be upset."

"I know," Firestar reassured him. "If I can catch Smallear at a good moment, I'll have a word with him."

"Thanks, Firestar." Bramblepaw dipped his head in gratitude, picked up his moss, and hurried after his sister.

Firestar gazed worriedly after the two apprentices. He must talk to Smallear, he decided, and soon. Constantly taunting the young cats about their parentage was not the way to ensure their loyalty to ThunderClan.

Realising that Graystripe was still waiting patiently beside him, he mewed, "Okay, tell me what's on your mind."

"It's my kits," Graystripe confessed. "Ever since the Gathering, I can't get them out of my mind. Mistyfoot and Stonefur weren't there, so I couldn't ask them for news, but now that Tigerstar has essentially taken over RiverClan, I'm sure my kits are in danger."

Firestar took a bite of vole and chewed thoughtfully. "I don't see why they should be at risk more than any other cat," he replied, swallowing his mouthful. "Tigerstar will want to look after all the apprentices to guarantee a strong fighting force."

Graystripe didn't look reassured. "But Tigerstar knows who their father is," he pointed out. "He hates me, and I'm worried that he'll take it out on Featherpaw and Stormpaw."

Firestar realized that Graystripe had a fair point about Tigerstar's hostility. "What would you like to do?"

Graystripe blinked nervously. "I want you to come with me across the river and bring them back to ThunderClan."

Firestar stared at his friend. "Are you completely mouse-brained? You're asking your Clan leader to stroll into RiverClan territory and steal a couple of apprentices?"

Graystripe scraped his forepaw on the ground. "Well, if you put it like that . . ."

"How else would you put it?" Firestar tried to control his shock, but Graystripe's suggestion was too close to Brokentail's old crime of stealing kits. If Firestar agreed and RiverClan found out about it, they would be justified in attacking ThunderClan. And with ShadowClan to help them, that was a risk Firestar couldn't take.

"I knew you wouldn't listen." Graystripe turned and began to retreat, his tail drooping.

"I *am* listening. Graystripe, come back and let's think about this." As Graystripe stopped, Firestar went on: "You don't *know* that Featherpaw and Stormpaw are in danger. And they're apprentices now, not kits. They have the right to decide their own future. What if they want to stay in RiverClan?"

"I know." Graystripe sounded despairing. "Don't worry, Firestar. I understand there's nothing you can do to help."

"I didn't say that." Against all his better judgment, Firestar knew he couldn't stand by and do nothing to help his friend. Graystripe pricked his ears, half-hopeful, as Firestar went on: "Suppose we go over there quietly, just the two of us, and check on them? If they're okay, then you won't need to worry any more. If they're not, I'll tell them there's a place for them in ThunderClan, if that's what they choose."

Graystripe's yellow eyes had begun to glow as Firestar spoke. "That's great!" he meowed. "Thanks, Firestar. Can we go now?"

"If you like. Let me finish this vole first. You find Whitestorm and tell him he's in charge of the camp. But don't tell him where we're going," he added quickly.

Graystripe bounded off to the warriors' den while Firestar swallowed the last few gulps of vole and swiped his tongue over his mouth. By the time he had finished, Graystripe had reappeared and the two friends headed for the mouth of the gorse tunnel.

Reaching it, however, they stopped short as a familiar black shape slipped into the clearing.

"Ravenpaw!" Firestar exclaimed happily. "It's good to see you."

"It's good to see *you*," Ravenpaw responded, touching noses in greeting with Firestar and then with Graystripe. "Graystripe, I haven't seen you in moons! How are you?"

"I'm fine. It's easy to see you're doing well," he added, eyeing Ravenpaw's glossy black pelt.

"I came to pay my respects to Bluestar," Ravenpaw explained. "You remember, Firestar, you said I could."

"Yes, of course." Firestar glanced at Graystripe, whose paws were working urgently in his haste to be off. "Ravenpaw, can you go and find Cinderpelt? She'll show you the place where Bluestar is buried. Graystripe and I are just off on a mission."

"That sounds like the old days!" meowed Ravenpaw, half enviously. "What is it this time?"

"We're going over to RiverClan to check on my kits," Graystripe told him in a rush. "I'm worried about them, now that Tigerstar is taking over."

Ravenpaw's shocked look reminded Firestar that he knew nothing of the recent developments in the forest. Rapidly he told the black cat what Tigerstar had announced at the last Gathering.

"But that's a disaster!" Ravenpaw hissed when he had finished. "Is there anything I can do to help? I could come with you."

His eyes were gleaming. Firestar guessed Ravenpaw was excited by the prospect of adventure. How different he was now from the nervous apprentice he had once been, bullied by his fierce mentor, Tigerclaw!

"All right," he meowed, trusting his instincts that it would be good to have Ravenpaw with them. "We'll be glad to have you."

As he bounded through the forest, his two oldest friends by his side, Firestar felt his mind flood with memories of how they had trained and hunted together as apprentices. For a short time he could almost imagine that those days had returned, that he had shed his responsibilities like falling leaves and was young and carefree again.

But he knew that this was impossible. He was Clan leader

now, and he could never escape from his duty to the cats who depended on him.

The sun had gone down by the time that Firestar and his friends reached the edge of the forest. Warning Graystripe and Ravenpaw to stay back, Firestar crept through the undergrowth until he could look out over the river.

In front of him lay the stepping-stones, the easiest route into RiverClan territory. As Firestar peered at the cold, gray water, he caught a strong scent of cats—RiverClan and ShadowClan mixed. A patrol was making its way along the opposite bank. They were too far away for Firestar to be sure which cats they were, but he could not see the blue-gray pelts of Mistyfoot and Stonefur.

He felt a pang of disappointment. If either of their friends had been near the border, Graystripe could have asked them for news and the matter could have ended there. Now they would have to go right into RiverClan territory.

Firestar knew he was risking everything on slipping in and slipping out again quietly, unobserved. If it was ever found out that a Clan leader had trespassed on another Clan's territory, he would be in trouble. But he knew that he had to do it for Graystripe.

The gray warrior had crept up beside him. "What's the matter?" he whispered. "Why are we waiting here?"

Firestar angled his ears toward the patrol. A moment later they disappeared into a reed bed and their scent slowly faded.

"Okay, let's go," Firestar meowed.

Leading the way, he leaped from one stepping-stone to another across the black, swiftly flowing water. He thought back to the floods of last leaf-bare, when he and Graystripe had almost drowned saving the lives of two of Mistyfoot's kits. Leopardstar had conveniently forgotten that now, Firestar realized, as well as how the two ThunderClan warriors had helped the starving cats of RiverClan by taking them fresh-kill from their own hunting grounds.

But there was no point in thinking about that now. Reaching the far bank, Firestar slid into the shelter of a clump of reeds and checked once again that no enemy cats were near. All he could scent was the traces of the patrol, steadily growing fainter.

Treading softly, he made his way upriver toward the RiverClan camp. Graystripe and Ravenpaw followed, silent as shadows.

Suddenly a new scent drifted on the breeze. Firestar paused, his whiskers twitching. His eyes widened as he recognized the reek of carrion, crowfood that had rotted for days until its foul stench poisoned the air.

"Ugh! What's that?" growled Ravenpaw, forgetting the need for silence.

Firestar swallowed the bile that rose into his throat. "I don't know. I'd say it was a foxhole, but there's no scent of fox."

"It stinks, whatever it is," Graystripe muttered. "Come on, Firestar, we need to keep going before some cat catches us."

"No," Firestar meowed. "I know you're worried about your kits, Graystripe, but this is too strange. We have to investigate."

A few tail-lengths ahead, a tiny stream flowed sluggishly into the main river. Firestar turned to follow it through more reeds. The stench grew stronger, and beneath the smell of crowfood he began to pick up the scent of many cats, a mixture of ShadowClan and RiverClan like the patrol. He halted and signaled for his friends to do the same as he began to make out noises from somewhere ahead: movement in the reeds and the voices of cats mingling together.

"What *is* this?" Graystripe whispered. "We're nowhere near the camp."

Firestar flicked the tip of his tail for silence. At least the stench would mask their ThunderClan scent and make it easier for them to stay hidden.

More cautiously than ever Firestar crept on again until the reeds began to thin out and he came to the edge of a clearing. Flattening himself against the damp ground he crawled as far forward as he dared and looked out.

At once he had to clamp his teeth hard to keep back a yowl of shock and anger. The stream ran along one side of the clearing, its near-stagnant waters clogged by the remains of fresh-kill carelessly flung there and left to rot. Cats crouched on the bank, tearing at prey. But that was not what had roused Firestar's fury.

Opposite his hiding place, on the far side of the clearing was a vast hill of bones. They gleamed like stripped branches in the last of the watery daylight, some tiny shrew bones hardly bigger than teeth, others as big as the leg bone of a fox or a badger.

Icy trembling seized Firestar's body. For a heartbeat he thought he was back in his dream at Fourtrees. He remembered the blood that had come oozing out of that hill of bones, and longed to flee in terror. But this was far worse than the dream because Firestar knew that it was happening now, in the real world. And crouched on top of the pile, his fur black against the sun-bleached remains, was Tigerstar, leader of the new united Clan.

Firestar forced himself to stay hidden. He had to find out what Tigerstar was doing. Graystripe and Ravenpaw crept forward to crouch beside him. Ravenpaw's fur bristled, and Graystripe looked as if he were going to be sick.

After the first shock ebbed, Firestar examined the scene more closely. The hill was made up of only prey bones, not mixed with cat bones like the one in his dream. On one side of it stood the ShadowClan deputy, Blackfoot. On the other side was Leopardstar. Her gaze flicked nervously back and forth across the clearing. Firestar wondered if she regretted what had happened to her Clan, and he guessed that her ambition to make her Clan strong had blinded her to Tigerstar's real nature. But whatever the former RiverClan leader felt, it was too late for her to go back now.

"I can't see my kits," Graystripe whispered, a breath of sound close to Firestar's ear.

Mistyfoot and Stonefur weren't there either, Firestar realized. In fact, most of the cats in the clearing came from ShadowClan, though he spotted the RiverClan warriors Mudfur and Heavystep. There was no sign of either medicine cat, and Firestar wondered if that was significant.

He was still watching, too stunned to know what to do next, when Tigerstar rose to his paws. A few small bones rattled down the side of the hill. The dark tabby's eyes blazed in the fading light as he let out a triumphant yowl.

"Cats of TigerClan, gather here around the Bonehill for a Clan meeting!"

Immediately the cats in the clearing approached the hill, crouching low in respect. Others appeared from the reeds.

"He must have built that hill to look like the Highrock," Ravenpaw murmured. "So he can look down on his Clan."

The dark tabby waited until his warriors were all in place and then announced, "It is time for the trial to begin. Fetch the prisoners!"

Firestar exchanged a bewildered look with Graystripe. Where had Tigerstar found prisoners? Had he already mounted an attack on WindClan?

At Tigerstar's order, a ShadowClan warrior—Jaggedtooth, who had been one of Brokentail's rogues—vanished into the reeds. He returned a few moments later dragging another cat with him. At first Firestar did not recognize the skinny gray warrior, his fur unkempt and one ear shredded and bleeding. Then, as Jaggedtooth pushed him into the circle of cats beneath the Bonehill, Firestar realized it was Stonefur.

Firestar felt Graystripe stiffen beside him, and put out a warning paw for his friend not to give them away. Graystripe's ears twitched but he stayed still and silent, watching.

The reeds parted again. This time Firestar knew at once the cat who stepped into the clearing, his fur sleek and his head raised proudly. It was Darkstripe. *Traitor!* Firestar thought, his belly clenching in anger.

More movement in the reeds heralded the arrival of another ShadowClan warrior who was shepherding two smaller cats, one a silver-gray tabby and the other with thick, gray fur. They were as thin as Stonefur, their steps unsteady as they staggered into the clearing. Huddling together in the shadow of the Bonehill, they looked around them with wide, scared eyes.

An icy chill gripped Firestar's muscles. The two young cats were Graystripe's kits, Featherpaw and Stormpaw.

# CHAPTER 15

♣

*Graystripe growled deep in his throat* and gathered himself to spring.

"No!" Firestar gasped, leaping on his friend before he could leave the shadow of the reeds. "If Tigerstar sees us, we're crowfood!"

On Graystripe's other side Ravenpaw grabbed him by one shoulder. "Firestar's right," he hissed. "What chance would we have against all these cats?"

Graystripe writhed desperately, as if he hadn't heard. "Let me go!" he snarled. "I'll flay that piece of fox dung! I'll rip his heart out!"

"No!" Firestar repeated in an agonized whisper. "We'll be slaughtered if we show ourselves now. We won't leave your kits, Graystripe, I promise we won't, but we've got to wait for the right moment to rescue them."

Graystripe went on struggling for a moment longer, then subsided with a grunt of agreement. Firestar let him go, nodding to Ravenpaw to do the same.

"Listen," he murmured. "Let's find out what's going on."

While they had been holding Graystripe down, Tigerstar

had begun to speak, his voice drowning the noise of their scuffle among the reeds.

"Cats of TigerClan," he began, "you all know the hardships that we have to face. The cold of leaf-bare threatens us. Twolegs threaten us. The other two Clans in the forest, who have not yet realized the wisdom of joining with TigerClan, are a threat to us."

Firestar's tail-tip twitched in anger and he flashed a look at Graystripe. *Tigerstar* was the threat! All that ThunderClan and WindClan wanted was to get on with their lives in peace, according to the ancient traditions of StarClan and the warrior code.

But Graystripe's burning gaze was fixed on his two kits, cowering at the base of the Bonehill; he was unaware of Firestar's glance.

"Surrounded as we are by enemies," Tigerstar went on, "we must be sure of the loyalty of our own warriors. There is no room in TigerClan for the halfhearted. No room for cats who might waver in battle, or worse still, turn on their own Clan mates. TigerClan will not tolerate traitors!"

*Except the traitor who leads it,* Firestar thought. *Or Darkstripe, who would have watched his own Clan be devoured by dogs.*

The cats in the clearing broke out into yowls of agreement. Tigerstar allowed the clamor to continue for a moment before signaling with his tail for silence. The noise died and he began to speak again.

"Especially we will not tolerate the abomination of half-Clan cats. No loyal warrior would ever take a mate from another Clan, diluting the pure blood that our warrior ancestors decreed for us. Bluestar and Graystripe of ThunderClan both flouted the warrior code when they took mates from RiverClan. The kits of such a union, like the ones you see in front of you now, can never be trusted."

He paused, and his deputy Blackfoot yowled out, "Filth! Filth!"

Darkstripe took up the cry, and a chorus of yowls and screeches echoed his words. This time Tigerstar let them fall quiet in their own time, gazing out over the cats below him with a look of calm satisfaction.

*He and Blackfoot must have rehearsed all this,* Firestar realized in horror.

He noticed that it was the ShadowClan warriors who yowled the loudest. The RiverClan cats joined in less enthusiastically; Firestar guessed they might not all fully agree with the ShadowClan leader, but they did not dare stay silent.

The two half-Clan apprentices flattened themselves close to the ground, as if they were afraid of being swept away in the gale of the Clan's fury. Stonefur crouched over them as if he could protect them, gazing around with defiance in his eyes.

*Where is Mistyfoot?* Firestar wondered. *Tigerstar knows she's half-Clan too. What has he done with her?*

Tigerstar spoke again. "Half-Clan cats have been tolerated until now, but the time for tolerance has passed. There is no place in TigerClan for warriors who owe allegiance to two Clans. How can we trust them not to betray our secrets, or even turn on us and kill us? Can we expect StarClan to fight on our side if we allow those who are not pure in heart and blood to walk freely among us?"

"No!" Darkstripe screeched, flexing his claws and lashing his tail from side to side.

"No, my friends. We must get rid of the abominations in our midst! Then our Clan will be clean again and we can be sure of the favor of StarClan."

Stonefur sprang to his paws. He was so weak that he stumbled and almost fell, but he managed to stay upright and face Tigerstar.

"No cat has ever questioned my loyalty," he snarled. "Come down here and tell me to my face that I'm a traitor!"

Firestar wanted to wail aloud at the blue-gray warrior's hopeless courage. Tigerstar could have swatted him aside with one paw, and yet Stonefur still remained defiant.

"Mistyfoot and I never even knew that Bluestar was our mother until a couple of moons ago," Stonefur insisted. "We have been loyal RiverClan warriors all our lives. Let any cat who thinks different come out here and prove it!"

Tigerstar angrily swept his tail toward Leopardstar. "You showed poor judgment when you chose this cat as your deputy," he growled. "RiverClan is choked by the weeds of treachery, and we must root them out."

To Firestar's dismay, Leopardstar bowed her head. The gesture showed just how far Tigerstar's power extended, that the once-formidable RiverClan leader was unable or unwilling to protect her own deputy.

Yet the dark tabby's words gave Firestar hope. It sounded as if Tigerstar was about to banish Stonefur and the two apprentices. If he did, then Firestar and his friends could wait for them at the border, ready to take them back to Thunder-Clan, where they would be safe.

When Tigerstar spoke again, his voice was measured and cold. "Stonefur, I will give you a chance to show your loyalty to TigerClan. Kill these two half-Clan apprentices."

An eerie silence spread through the clearing, broken only by Graystripe's gasp of outrage. Luckily the TigerClan warriors were so intent on the scene in front of them that no cat heard him.

"Firestar!" Graystripe whispered. "We *must* do something!" His claws dug into the ground and his muscles bunched, ready to spring, yet his eyes were fixed on Firestar as if he would not attack without his leader's order.

Ravenpaw's eyes, bright with distress, turned to Firestar. "We can't just watch them die!"

Firestar could feel his fur prickling with tension. He knew he could not stay crouching here in hiding while Graystripe's kits were slaughtered a few foxlengths away. If all else failed, he was ready to give up his life in a battle to save them.

"Wait just a moment," he murmured. "Let's see what Stonefur does."

The blue-gray warrior had turned to face Leopardstar. "I take orders from *you*," he growled. "You must know this is wrong. What do you want me to do?"

For a heartbeat Leopardstar looked uncertain, and again

Firestar began to hope that she would take a stand against Tigerstar and stop the destruction of her Clan. But he had underestimated the strength of her ambition, and her misguided faith that Tigerstar offered an invincible future. "These are difficult times," she meowed at last. "As we fight for survival we must be able to count on every one of our Clan mates. There is no room for divided loyalties. Do as Tigerstar tells you."

Stonefur held her gaze for a moment more, a moment that to Firestar seemed to last for several moons. Then he faced the two apprentices and they shrank away from him, their eyes glazed with terror.

Stormpaw gave his sister a comforting lick. "We'll fight him," he promised. "I won't let him kill us."

*Brave words,* Firestar thought desperately. Stonefur was a skilled, experienced warrior, and even in his weakened state he was a formidable threat to two half-trained apprentices who had obviously been ill-treated and imprisoned as well.

The RiverClan warrior gave a little nod to Stormpaw, just like any mentor approving of his apprentice's courage. Then he turned to look up at Tigerstar again.

"You'll have to kill me first, Tigerstar!" he spat.

Narrowing his eyes, Tigerstar flicked his tail at Darkstripe. "Very well. Kill him," he ordered.

The black-striped warrior crouched low, every hair on his pelt quivering with joy that Tigerstar had given him a chance to prove his loyalty to his new Clan. With a grunt of effort, he hurled himself at Stonefur.

Pity and fear throbbed through Firestar. He could see only one end to the fight. The blue-gray warrior was so weak that he would be no match for Darkstripe. Firestar wanted to leap into the clearing and fight on Stonefur's side, but he knew it would be suicidal in the presence of so many enemy cats. He knew that he had to hold back in the hope, however slight, of saving the apprentices. Firestar had scarcely known an ordeal worse than the one he faced now, remaining hidden while his friend was slaughtered.

Yet Stonefur's skills had not deserted him. Quick as lightning, he dropped backward so that instead of landing on his shoulders Darkstripe was faced with all four paws, claws extended to rip at his fur.

Firestar felt his throat tighten. He remembered a day during his apprenticeship when Stonefur's mother, Bluestar, had taught him that very move. *Bluestar, if you can see this, help him now!* he begged.

The two warriors were a clawing, screeching knot of fur on the floor of the clearing. The rest of the cats scrambled backward to give them space, still keeping the same eerie silence. They were so intent on the battle, Firestar wondered for a moment if this might be the best time to rescue the apprentices. But Tigerstar was still crouched on top of the Bonehill, with a clear view of the whole clearing, and he would easily see them coming.

Stonefur had fastened his teeth into Darkstripe's scruff and was trying to shake the dark warrior, but Darkstripe's greater size and strength were too much. He lost his grip and the two warriors sprang apart, breathing hard. Blood was trickling from a scratch above Darkstripe's left eye, and clumps of fur were missing from his flank. Stonefur's pelt was even more ragged, and as he shook one forepaw spots of blood spattered on the ground.

"Get a move on, Darkstripe!" Blackfoot jeered. "You're fighting like a kittypet!"

With a hiss of fury Darkstripe launched another attack, but Stonefur was ready for him again. Slipping to one side, he raked his claws down Darkstripe's side, and followed up with a blow to his back leg as the dark warrior crashed past him. Stonefur staggered from the force of the impact, but by the time Darkstripe regained his paws, he had recovered. This time the RiverClan warrior went on the attack, bowling Darkstripe over and fastening teeth and claws in his neck.

Firestar heard Graystripe's intake of breath. His yellow eyes were blazing; on his other side Ravenpaw was sinking his unsheathed claws into the ground. Firestar felt hope burn in his belly. Was it possible that Stonefur could win?

But Tigerstar had no intention of letting Stonefur escape. As Darkstripe struggled vainly to break free, the massive tabby flicked his ears at Blackfoot. "Finish it," he ordered.

The ShadowClan deputy flung himself into the battle. He bit Stonefur in the shoulder and dragged him off Darkstripe, ducking to avoid his flailing paws. Darkstripe sprang on Stonefur to hold his hindquarters down, while Blackfoot scored his claws across the blue-gray warrior's throat.

Stonefur let out a gurgling cry that was cut short. Both

TigerClan cats released him and stood back. Stonefur's body convulsed as blood welled from his throat.

A thin wailing noise went up from the watching cats, strengthening into a cry of triumph. Even Leopardstar, after a brief hesitation, joined in. The two apprentices were the only cats to remain silent, their terrified eyes fixed on the warrior who had died to save them.

Firestar could only stare in horror as Stonefur went limp and the last breath left his body.

# CHAPTER 16

*"No." Graystripe's voice rasped in his* throat.

Firestar pressed closer to his friend, sharing his grief at Stonefur's death and his anger that the RiverClan warrior's courage had been worth nothing in an unfair fight.

Blackfoot looked down at Stonefur's body in satisfaction.

Darkstripe whirled to confront the two apprentices. "Tigerstar," he meowed, "let *me* kill them."

Graystripe would have sprung forward then, in spite of anything Firestar could do, but before he could move Tigerstar shook his battle-scarred head. "Really, Darkstripe? A prisoner can defeat you, but you think you could take on two apprentices?"

Darkstripe bowed his head in shame. His leader's eyes narrowed coldly as he stared at the two young cats. They were huddled together, trembling with shock. They hardly seemed to realize that their own lives were hanging by a hair.

"No," Tigerstar meowed at last. "For now I will let them live. They may be useful to me alive."

Firestar flashed a look at Graystripe, who returned his glance with mingled relief and apprehension in his eyes.

Tigerstar summoned Jaggedtooth. "Take the apprentices back to their prison."

The ShadowClan warrior dipped his head and herded the two stunned cats away through the reeds. Graystripe's hungry gaze followed them out of sight.

"The meeting is at an end," Tigerstar declared.

At once the cats in the clearing began to slip away. Tigerstar leaped down from the Bonehill and vanished into the reeds, flanked by Blackfoot and Darkstripe. Eventually only Leopardstar was left. She padded forward until she stood over the broken body of her former deputy. Slowly she bent her head and nosed Stonefur's torn gray pelt. If she meowed a last farewell, Firestar did not hear it, and after a moment she turned and followed Tigerstar through the reeds.

"Now!" Graystripe sprang to his paws. "Firestar, we've got to rescue my kits."

"Yes, but don't go rushing off," Firestar warned him. "We have to make sure all the cats have gone."

His friend's body was quivering with suppressed tension. "I don't care!" he spat. "If they try to stop us, I'll rip them all apart."

"The kits are safe for the moment," murmured Ravenpaw. "There's no need to take risks."

Firestar cautiously raised his head above the level of the reeds. By now it was quite dark; the only light came from Silverpelt and a pale glow from the moon low in the sky. The ShadowClan and RiverClan scents were rapidly fading. The only sound was the dry rustle of wind in the reeds.

Crouching down again, Firestar murmured, "They've gone for now. This is our chance. We've got to find where they're keeping the apprentices, and—"

"And get them away," Graystripe interrupted. "Whatever it takes."

Firestar nodded. "Ravenpaw, are you up for it? It will be dangerous."

The loner's eyes widened. "You think I'd leave, after we saw *that*? No way. I'm with you, Firestar."

"Good." Firestar blinked in gratitude. "I thought you would be."

Beckoning his two friends with his tail, he led the way into the clearing, his pawsteps growing hesitant as he left the shelter of the reeds. He knew what he was doing was against the warrior code, but what Tigerstar had done had left him no alternative. He did not know how his warrior ancestors could have watched the slaughter of Stonefur without doing anything to save him.

Creeping close to the ground, the three cats reached the stream where rotting fresh-kill lay strewn along the bank. In the midst of his cold fury, Firestar spared a moment to be angry at the waste of prey in such a hard season.

"Look at that!" he hissed.

"But we could roll in it," Ravenpaw suggested. "It'll disguise our scent."

Firestar gave him a brief nod, approval calming his anger. Ravenpaw was thinking like a warrior. Firestar crouched down and pressed his fur into the decaying carcass of a rabbit. Graystripe and Ravenpaw followed. The gray warrior's eyes were like chips of yellow flint.

When all three cats were thoroughly covered with the scent of crowfood, Firestar headed into the reeds where he had seen Jaggedtooth disappear with the two apprentices. There was a narrow path along the frozen mud, as if cats regularly came and went that way. All Firestar's senses were alert.

As they headed away from the river toward the farmland on the other side of RiverClan territory, the reeds thinned out and the ground rose. When Firestar and his friends came to the edge of the cover, they saw a grassy slope in front of them with an occasional clump of gorse and hawthorn. About halfway up a dark hole yawned in the hillside. Jaggedtooth was crouched outside it.

"There are pawprints leading into that hole," Firestar murmured.

Graystripe lifted his muzzle to taste the air and let out a faint sound of disgust. "Sick cats," he meowed quietly. "You're right, Firestar; this is the place." He bared his teeth. "Jaggedtooth is mine."

"No." Firestar's tail whipped out, signaling his friend to stay where he was. "We can't afford a fight. The noise would bring every cat in the territory. We have to get rid of him another way."

"I can do that." Ravenpaw's paws anxiously kneaded the ground, but his expression was determined. "He'll recognize you two, but he doesn't know me."

Firestar hesitated, then nodded. "How will you do it?"

"I've got a plan." Ravenpaw's eyes shone with anticipation, and Firestar realized that the loner was almost relishing the danger, as if he had missed having a chance to use his warrior skills. "Don't worry; it'll be fine," the black cat assured him.

Straightening up, he strolled out of the reeds and up the slope, his head and tail held high. Jaggedtooth got up and paced forward to meet him, the tabby fur on his neck bristling.

Firestar gathered himself, ready to spring if the ShadowClan warrior attacked. But though Jaggedtooth looked aggressive, he did nothing more than give Ravenpaw a suspicious sniff.

"I don't know you," he growled. "Who are you and what do you want?"

"Think you know all the RiverClan cats, do you?" Ravenpaw inquired coolly. "I've got a message from Tigerstar."

Jaggedtooth grunted and his whiskers twitched as he sniffed Ravenpaw again. "Great StarClan, you stink!"

"You don't smell so pleasant yourself," Ravenpaw retorted. "Do you want this message or don't you?"

Firestar and Graystripe exchanged a glance as Jaggedtooth hesitated. Firestar felt his heart thud painfully against his ribs.

"Go on, then," the ShadowClan warrior meowed at last.

"Tigerstar wants you to go to him at once," mewed Ravenpaw. "He sent me to take your place guarding the prisoners."

"What?" Jaggedtooth lashed his tail in disbelief. "Only

ShadowClan guards the prisoners. You RiverClan cats are all too soft. Why did Tigerstar send you and not one of our own Clan?"

Firestar flinched. Ravenpaw had made a potentially fatal mistake.

But the loner didn't seem bothered. Turning away, he meowed, "I thought we were supposed to be all one Clan now. But suit yourself. I'll tell Tigerstar you wouldn't come."

"No, wait." Jaggedtooth twitched his ears. "I didn't say that. If Tigerstar wants me . . . Where is he, then?"

"Over there." Ravenpaw pointed with his tail in the direction of the RiverClan camp. "He had Darkstripe and Blackfoot with him."

Jaggedtooth made up his mind. "Right," he muttered. "But you stay out here till I get back. If I smell your stink inside the hole I'll rip your fur off."

He headed down the slope. Ravenpaw watched him go, then padded up and sat down just outside the hole. Firestar and Graystripe crouched in the reeds as Jaggedtooth passed within a couple of tail-lengths of them. He was hurrying now, and did not even stop to scent the air as he vanished down the path.

Once he had gone, Firestar and Graystripe bounded across the open ground to join Ravenpaw. Graystripe paused briefly to sniff and meowed, "Yes! They're in there!" before he vanished inside the hole.

Firestar stopped in front of Ravenpaw. "Well done!"

Ravenpaw licked his paw and drew it over his ear two or

three times to hide his embarrassment. "It was easy. He's such a stupid furball."

"Yes, but he'll know something's up as soon as he finds Tigerstar," Firestar pointed out. "Keep watch, and call out if you see any cat." With a last glance behind him, he plunged into the hole after Graystripe.

He found himself in a long, narrow passage carved out of the sandy soil. Thick darkness engulfed him after the first few tail-lengths. There was a lingering scent of fox, but it was faint and stale, as if the original occupant of the hole were long gone. Stronger by far was the fear scent rising from the darkness, the scent of cats who had given up all hope.

The passage led steadily downward. Before he reached the end of it, Firestar heard the sound of scuffling and surprised mews. One of the apprentices called out, "Father? Is it really you?"

A moment later Firestar could no longer feel his fur brushing the passage walls on either side. His next step brought him up against a cat's haunches; he recognized Graystripe by his scent. The scent of the two apprentices was stronger than ever, and with a jolt of relief Firestar recognized another cat.

"Mistyfoot!" he exclaimed. "Thank StarClan we've found you."

"Is that Firestar?" Mistyfoot's voice was hoarse, close to his ear. "What are you doing here?"

"It's a long story," Firestar replied. "I'll tell you everything, but first we have to get out of here. Graystripe, are you ready?"

A tense mew of agreement came from his friend. Though

Firestar couldn't see him, he could picture him huddled close to Featherpaw and Stormpaw.

"Let's go," Firestar meowed, turning with difficulty in the narrow mouth of the underground den. "Mistyfoot, we're going to take you all back to ThunderClan with us." Remembering how weak Stonefur and the apprentices had looked, he added, "Can you make it that far?"

"Once I'm out of this hole I can make it anywhere," Mistyfoot mewed determinedly.

"So can we," added Featherpaw.

"That's great. Mistyfoot, I'm so sorry, but we couldn't rescue Stonefur . . ." Firestar began, looking for words to tell the she-cat about her brother's death.

"I already know," meowed Mistyfoot, her voice ragged with grief. "The apprentices told me. They say he died bravely."

"Very bravely. All StarClan will honor him." Firestar pushed his muzzle into Mistyfoot's fur, a gesture of comfort. "Come on. We'll make sure he didn't die for nothing. Tigerstar will not hurt you as well."

His heart thudding with fear, Firestar scrabbled his way back up the tunnel. At the top he paused to check that it was safe to emerge, then led the way into the open. He felt as if the rancid stench of the prison would cling to his fur forever. Ravenpaw took his place at the back of the group, keeping a lookout as they crept down the slope.

Silent as shadows, the cats followed the path through the reeds until they came to the clearing again. It was empty, the Bonehill casting its ominous shadow as far as the body of

Stonefur lying still in the moonlight.

Mistyfoot went over to her brother and bent her head to nose his fur. Outside the darkness of her prison, Firestar saw that she was as skinny and unkempt as the dead warrior, every rib showing, her fur matted and her eyes dull with suffering.

"Stonefur, Stonefur," she murmured. "What will I do without you?"

Firestar's fur bristled with tension as he listened for the sound of approaching cats, but he forced himself to give Mistyfoot time to mourn. They could not take Stonefur's body with them for the proper warrior's vigil; this was Mistyfoot's last farewell.

Stormpaw, who had been Stonefur's apprentice, approached as well. He touched his nose to his mentor's head before padding back to stand beside his father.

Firestar could not help remembering Bluestar, and how much she had loved her lost kits. Had she been here, he wondered, to lead her son to StarClan? She and Stonefur had both died bravely, their cruel deaths caused by Tigerstar's evil ambition. Every hair on Firestar's pelt pricked with his longing to confront the dark tabby warrior and make him pay for his crimes.

"Firestar, we have to go," Graystripe hissed, the whites of his eyes bright in the half-light.

His words roused Mistyfoot. Before Firestar could reply, she raised her head, gave Stonefur one last, loving look, and padded over to where the others were waiting for her.

Firestar set a brisk pace back toward the river, feeling himself relax as the stench of the Bonehill and the scattered prey began to fade. Graystripe helped the two apprentices along, encouraging them with gentle nudges and mews. Mistyfoot kept up bravely, limping on paws cracked and sore after her imprisonment, while Ravenpaw stayed at the rear, his ears tilted back for the sounds of pursuit.

The night was silent except for the murmur of water, and by the time the river came in sight they had not encountered any other cats. Turning downstream toward the stepping-stones, Firestar dared to hope that they would escape undetected.

Then a distant yowling sounded through the reeds and the six cats froze in their tracks.

"The prisoners have escaped!"

# CHAPTER 17

*"Quick—the stepping-stones!" Firestar hissed.*

Alone, the ThunderClan cats could have raced easily out of danger, but none of them would abandon the prisoners. Graystripe fell back to join Ravenpaw as rearguard, while Firestar tried to urge on the RiverClan cats.

"You'll have to leave us!" Mistyfoot gasped. "There's no sense in all of us being captured."

"Never!" snarled Graystripe. "We're all in this together."

By now they were bounding alongside the river, the RiverClan cats stumbling in their efforts to keep up. Firestar could already see the ripples in the water where the current was broken by the stepping-stones. But the yowling behind them grew louder, and when he turned his head to draw in a rapid gulp of air he could taste the scent of ShadowClan.

"Great StarClan!" he whispered. "They're catching up."

None of the pursuing cats had appeared yet by the time they reached the stepping-stones. Firestar leaped onto the first stone, then the second, and gestured with his tail for Mistyfoot to follow.

"Hurry!" he urged.

Mistyfoot bent her hind legs and leaped, staggering as her paws hit the slippery surface, but managing to keep her balance. The two apprentices came next. Firestar stopped when he was halfway across and waited, the river water lapping his paws, while the other cats leaped out behind him.

Because the RiverClan cats were so weak they were agonizingly slow, bracing themselves for each leap. Mistyfoot reached him first, and Firestar edged to the side of the stone to let her go past. The two apprentices were still some way behind. Firestar's claws scraped the rough stone in his impatience, though he tried to stay calm. When the first dark shapes of pursuing cats slipped out of the reeds he forced himself to say nothing. Stormpaw was just nerving himself to leap; Firestar locked his gaze with the younger cat's. "Come on," he mewed steadily. "You're doing fine."

But as her brother gathered himself, Featherpaw, a couple of stones behind him, spotted the ShadowClan warriors racing along the riverbank. "They're coming!" she yowled.

Caught off balance, Stormpaw misjudged the distance and fell short. His forepaws landed on the stone, but his hindquarters splashed into the river. The current bubbled around him, dragging at his thick fur as he scrabbled to pull himself to safety.

"I'm slipping!" He gasped. "I can't hold on!"

Firestar jumped back onto the previous stone, barely managing to balance in the space left by Stormpaw's clawing forepaws. He fastened his teeth in the apprentice's scruff just as the younger cat lost his grip and slid backward into the river. For a few heartbeats Firestar felt his own paws sliding on the smooth rock under Stormpaw's weight and the force of the current.

Then he spotted Graystripe swimming up behind his son, paws thrusting strongly through the icy water. The gray warrior shoved his shoulder underneath Stormpaw and heaved him upward. Firestar managed to haul the apprentice out to crouch shivering on the rock.

Glancing toward the RiverClan shore, Firestar saw Ravenpaw urging Featherpaw onto the next stone, getting his own paws wet to leave her space to stand on the driest part.

Behind them, the pursuing cats had reached the first stone. Blackfoot was in the lead, flanked by Jaggedtooth and three or four others—too many to fight, Firestar realized.

"Come on!" he yowled. "Hurry!" He nudged the shivering Stormpaw. "Keep going—follow Mistyfoot!"

Blackfoot crouched, ready to spring, his eyes fixed on the stepping-stone where Ravenpaw had put himself between Featherpaw and the ShadowClan warrior. Firestar's belly clenched. The loner was brave, but his training days were far behind him and he would be no match for a seasoned warrior like Tigerstar's deputy.

Graystripe began swimming back toward Ravenpaw. A wild screech split the air as the rest of the ShadowClan warriors spread along the bank in a menacing line.

"Keep going!" Firestar gasped to Mistyfoot. "Take Stormpaw with you. I'm going back."

But before he could move, a fierce battle yowl went up

from the forest on the ThunderClan side of the river. Firestar saw three shapes streaking out of the undergrowth: Cloudtail, with Sandstorm and Thornclaw just behind him.

"Thank StarClan—" he began, breaking off as Cloudtail leaped toward the river, eyes blazing and claws extended. He was heading straight for Mistyfoot, who was just jumping from the last stone onto the bank.

Firestar raced across the remaining stones to intercept the white warrior, barrelling into his side and knocking him off his paws. "Mouse-brain!" he snapped. "The enemy is back there."

He jerked his head toward the middle of the river, where Ravenpaw and Graystripe were tussling with Blackfoot on the central stone. Stormpaw was nerving himself for the last leap onto the bank, while Featherpaw huddled two or three stones farther back. Sandstorm and Thornclaw launched themselves across the stones to face the ShadowClan warriors, the two apprentices cowering at the edge of their stones to let them pass.

Muttering "Sorry" to Mistyfoot, Cloudtail sprang after them. Firestar bunched his muscles to follow, but before he leaped he saw Blackfoot slip off the stone to be swept away in the current. He ducked briefly below the surface of the water, then reappeared swimming clumsily back toward the RiverClan side, his ears flat against his head. The three ThunderClan warriors stood crowded together on one stone, digging in their claws and growling fiercely at the remaining pursuers.

"You'll come no farther if you want to stay alive," snarled Sandstorm.

The ShadowClan warriors milled about uncertainly on the first two or three stones. Unused to the river, they were unsteady on their paws and clearly unwilling to join battle with the furious ThunderClan cats.

"Get back!" Blackfoot yowled as he clambered onto the bank, his fur streaming. "Let them escape; they're only half-Clan crowfood."

His warriors seemed happy to obey, and within moments all the ShadowClan cats had vanished into the reeds.

Firestar concentrated on helping the two apprentices finish crossing. Graystripe and Ravenpaw followed closely behind. Checking his cats for wounds, Firestar saw that Graystripe had lost a clump of fur from one shoulder, and Ravenpaw's left ear was bleeding, but otherwise they seemed unhurt.

"Well done, all of you," he meowed, turning to the other ThunderClan warriors. "I was never so glad to see any cats as when you three came out of the forest. What brought you here?"

"You did," Cloudtail panted. "You ordered extra patrols to watch the border. Lucky for you that we came along when we did."

Firestar felt his legs go weak with relief. StarClan had sent the patrol at just the right moment. "Okay," he meowed, "we'd better get back to camp. These three cats need to rest. Ravenpaw, you'd better come too and let Cinderpelt look at that ear."

Firestar stayed at the rear in case the ShadowClan

warriors decided to cross the river after all, but behind them everything was quiet. After a few moments, Sandstorm dropped back to join him.

"What happened?" she asked. "What are these RiverClan cats doing here?"

Firestar paused to give her ear a quick lick. "They were prisoners," he explained. "If we'd left them there, Tigerstar would have killed them."

Sandstorm turned her green gaze on him, horrified. "Why?"

"Because their parents came from different Clans," Firestar explained. "Tigerstar says half-Clan cats aren't fit to live in any Clan."

"But his own kits are half-Clan!" Sandstorm protested.

Firestar shook his head. "No, because Tigerstar was a ThunderClan cat when they were born. At least, that would be his excuse. You don't think that the great Tigerstar would father anything but pure-blooded kits, do you?"

The shock and disgust in Sandstorm's eyes deepened, then turned to sympathy as she looked at the RiverClan cats. "Poor things," she murmured. "Will you let them stay in ThunderClan?"

Firestar nodded. "What else can we do?"

The moon was high and bathing the ravine in a silvery light by the time that Firestar and the others reached the camp. Firestar could hardly believe that everything could be so peaceful here, only a short distance from the bloodstained clearing of the Bonehill and all the violence unleashed by Tigerstar's ambition.

But as he emerged from the gorse tunnel into the camp, the illusion of peace was shattered. Whitestorm came hurrying toward him with Brackenfur at his heels. The younger warrior looked distraught.

"Thank StarClan you're back, Firestar!" he exclaimed. "It's Tawnypaw—she's disappeared!"

## CHAPTER 18

*"Disappeared?" Firestar echoed in alarm. "What* happened?"

"We're not sure." Whitestorm was calmer than Brackenfur, but his eyes gave away his concern. "It was Bramblepaw who first said he couldn't find her. I thought he was making a fuss about nothing, but we searched the camp. She isn't here, and no cat saw her leave."

"It's my fault!" Brackenfur broke in. "I'm her mentor."

"It's not your fault," Whitestorm assured him. "I sent you on hunting patrol. No cat expects you to be in two places at once."

Brackenfur shook his head despairingly.

"Fetch Bramblepaw," Firestar ordered; Thornclaw bounded off at once to the apprentices' den.

While he waited, Firestar sent Ravenpaw and the three RiverClan cats to see Cinderpelt; Graystripe went with them to explain what had happened, and to assure himself that his kits would be all right. Though the gray warrior was cold and drenched from the icy river, all his concern was for his kits, and as they crossed the clearing he stuck close to their side like a bulky shadow.

"I don't know what to think," meowed Whitestorm when they had gone. "Maybe Tawnypaw got some idea into her head and went off by herself. She could be trapped or injured somewhere—"

"Or she could be in ShadowClan," Brackenfur interrupted, his fur bristling. "Tigerstar could have stolen her!"

"But Tigerstar was over in RiverClan territory," Firestar told them quietly. "So were Blackfoot and Darkstripe." He saw Whitestorm's ears twitch in surprise, and he knew he would have to explain everything to his deputy as soon as possible.

"He could have sent some other cat to do his dirty work," Cloudtail put in.

"Have you scented ShadowClan cats around the camp?" Firestar asked Whitestorm. "Or RiverClan?"

The white warrior shook his head. "No cats but our own, Firestar."

"Then it sounds as if she left willingly," Firestar meowed. "Perhaps she just felt like hunting by herself for a change." But he couldn't help remembering the incident before he left the camp, when Tawnypaw had been furious with Smallear for comparing her with her father. Firestar wondered if he had misjudged how hurt she had felt.

He broke off his thoughts as Bramblepaw came up. "Tell me what Tawnypaw did before she disappeared," Firestar ordered.

"Just the usual apprentice chores." Bramblepaw sounded anxious; his amber eyes were wide and confused. "We changed the elders' bedding and brought them fresh-kill, and

I went to get some mouse bile from Cinderpelt to put on a tick in Smallear's fur. When I came back Tawnypaw had gone, and I haven't seen her since."

"Where have you looked so far?"

"I went back to where we got the moss for the bedding, but she wasn't there," his apprentice replied. "And I checked the training hollow."

Firestar nodded. "Did you ask the elders if she said anything to them?"

"I did," replied Whitestorm, "but they couldn't remember anything out of the ordinary."

"And what about Goldenflower?" Firestar went on. "Did Tawnypaw say anything to her?"

Whitestorm shook his head. "She was frantic. I sent her with Mousefur to search toward Tallpines. They aren't back yet."

"Did you try to track Tawnypaw?" Firestar asked.

"Yes, of course," Brackenfur replied. "We tracked her to the top of the ravine, but after that we lost the scent."

Firestar hesitated. More than anything he wanted to believe that there was an easy explanation for Tawnypaw's absence. StarClan forbid he should wish a young cat to be lying injured somewhere, but even that would be preferable to his worst fears, that Tawnypaw had gone willingly to join her father.

"I'll try again," he decided. "It's probably too late, but—"

"I'll come with you," Cloudtail offered.

Firestar gave him a nod of gratitude; Cloudtail was one

of the best trackers in the Clan. "Okay," he meowed. "Sandstorm, Thornclaw, you come too."

Firestar led the way out of the camp again. Exhaustion dragged at his paws; the night was half-over, and so far he had not slept. He would have liked nothing better than to settle down in his den with a piece of fresh-kill, but he guessed it would be a long time before he could do that.

It was not difficult to pick up Tawnypaw's scent in the ravine, even though it was fading by now, but toward the top he lost it, as Brackenfur had done. Firestar began to suspect that the young cat had leaped from rock to rock, where her scent would not linger, so as to confuse any cats who might try to follow her. Firestar's worst fears flooded back; had Tawnypaw really been so unhappy in ThunderClan that she felt she had to leave?

His thoughts were interrupted by a yowl from Cloudtail among the bushes at the top of the ravine. "Over here! She went this way!"

When Firestar bounded up to join him, he too could distinguish the faintest trace of Tawnypaw's scent. He and Cloudtail followed it into the trees, noses to the ground as they focused on the traces of cat among all the stronger, distracting scents of prey. No other cat's scent joined Tawnypaw's. This far, at least, she had been alone.

Then, at the edge of a clearing, they lost the scent trail again, and not even Cloudtail's sharp nose could pick it up.

A cold wind had sprung up, driving clouds across the moon and ruffling the cats' fur, and as Firestar cast back and forth across the clearing in a last effort to find the scent again, a thin, icy rain began to fall.

"Mouse dung!" Cloudtail spat. "That just about finishes us."

Reluctantly Firestar agreed. Calling Sandstorm and Thornclaw back from their own searches, he meowed, "Let's get back. We can't do any more."

Sandstorm stood still for a moment, gazing in the direction that the scent trail had seemed to lead. "It looks as if she was heading for Fourtrees."

That made sense, Firestar reflected. Fourtrees was the obvious place to go if Tawnypaw wanted to meet with a cat from another Clan, or to cross into another Clan's territory. Every hair on his pelt prickled with dread. He couldn't persuade himself any longer that Tawnypaw had just wandered off to hunt, and he could see from the troubled looks of his warriors that they shared his growing conviction: Tawnypaw had gone to ShadowClan.

When the patrol returned to the camp, Brackenfur and Bramblepaw were still anxiously waiting in the clearing. They had been joined by Tawnypaw's mother, Goldenflower, and Mousefur. All four cats looked bedraggled and despairing in the rain that was falling more heavily now.

"Well?" Goldenflower asked as Firestar came up to her. "What did you find?"

"Nothing," Firestar meowed quietly. "We don't know where she is."

"Then why aren't you still out there looking?" Goldenflower's voice was sharp.

Firestar shook his head. "There's nothing more we can do in the dark and the rain. She could be anywhere."

"You don't care, do you?" Goldenflower's meow rose, high-pitched with anger. "You think she left deliberately! You never trusted her!"

Firestar struggled to answer, knowing that her accusation was half-true. But Goldenflower did not wait. Instead, she spun around and disappeared beneath the branches of the warriors' den.

"Wait!" Firestar called, but she ignored him.

"She doesn't know what she's saying," Sandstorm meowed sympathetically. "I'll go and calm her down." She slipped into the den behind Goldenflower.

Tired and discouraged, Firestar turned to Bramblepaw, expecting a similar accusation from him. But his apprentice was standing quietly, and the look in his amber eyes was unreadable.

"It's okay, Firestar," he meowed. "I know you did all you could. Thank you." Head down and tail drooping, he made his way back to the apprentices' den.

Firestar watched him go. Exhaustion flooded over him; it seemed like several moons since Graystripe had first suggested going to RiverClan to see his kits. A chilly gray dawn was beginning to seep into the sky, and Firestar desperately needed to rest, but there was one more duty to perform first. He had to visit Cinderpelt, and make sure the RiverClan cats would recover from their ordeal.

As he padded across the clearing to the medicine cat's den,

Firestar felt all his doubts about his leadership welling up again. One warrior banished, and gone to join his enemy—and willing to kill to prove his new loyalties. One apprentice vanished. And the whole forest caught up in terror and hatred that Firestar saw no way to combat. The vision of himself wearing the mane of LionClan that he had seen in the stream seemed a long way away. If StarClan really had destined him for greatness, Firestar couldn't help wondering if they had chosen the wrong cat.

Standing on the Highrock, Firestar watched as his Clan emerged from their dens. It was the morning after his expedition to RiverClan territory, and he had called a meeting to tell his warriors exactly what had happened, and to explain the presence of the three RiverClan cats.

Mistyfoot and the two apprentices were sitting at the base of the Highrock with Graystripe and Cinderpelt. Firestar was pleased to see that they already looked stronger, as if their energy was coming back after a good meal and with Cinderpelt's care.

Ravenpaw had left at dawn, his injured ear swathed in cobweb and a gleam in his eyes as he recalled the battle on the stepping-stones.

"Amazing how my old training came back to me," he meowed to Firestar. "I hadn't forgotten the fighting moves."

"You did brilliantly," Firestar purred. "You're a real friend to ThunderClan."

"Now that Tigerstar is rising to power, I think Thunder-

Clan needs all the friends it can get," the loner mewed seriously.

Ravenpaw had spent a few moments by Bluestar's grave and then set out for the farm near Highstones. Firestar wondered if he would need to call on Ravenpaw for help again. Tigerstar's enemies would have to unite to drive him out of the forest—yet Firestar knew that the final confrontation must be his alone.

He waited until all the Clan cats had settled themselves around the Highrock, and then began to speak.

"You've all heard by now that Graystripe, Ravenpaw, and I went over to RiverClan territory last night." He described the Bonehill and the rotting prey strewn around the clearing, and how Tigerstar had whipped up the hatred of his warriors against half-Clans—cats whose parents came from two different Clans. Firestar's voice shook as he described the murder of Stonefur, and the cats below him shuddered and flattened themselves against the ground in sympathy and terror.

Dustpelt growled, "Why aren't we attacking ShadowClan right now, then, for revenge?"

"Because it's not as simple as that," Firestar replied. "ThunderClan alone can't take on ShadowClan and RiverClan combined, and expect to win."

"We can have a good try," retorted Cloudtail, springing to his paws.

"But where would we attack?" asked Firestar. "There'll be warriors from both Clans in the RiverClan camp, and I don't expect TigerStar has left the ShadowClan camp unguarded.

"I feel just the same as you," he went on. "I don't like what Tigerstar is doing, and I'm afraid of what he might do in the future. I'd like to know what StarClan want us to do, but so far I've had no word from them. Cinderpelt, have they spoken to you?"

The medicine cat glanced up at him. "No, not yet."

With an angry flick of his ears, Cloudtail sat down again, and Brightheart rubbed against his shoulder to calm him down.

In the brief pause, Firestar wondered if it was true to say that he had received no message from StarClan. There had been the vision of himself in the stream, wearing the glory of LionClan. He thought again of Bluestar's prophecy that *Four will become two; lion and tiger will join in battle.*

Suddenly understanding dawned on Firestar like a ray of sunlight striking through branches. Four *Clans* would become two; did that mean ThunderClan must join with WindClan?

"We're still here, Firestar!" Dustpelt's voice disturbed his thoughts.

Firestar started. "Sorry," he meowed. "I've called you here to welcome the three RiverClan cats we rescued. You all know Mistyfoot, and Featherpaw and Stormpaw, Graystripe's kits. I think we should offer them a place in ThunderClan until it's safe for them to go home."

Murmuring broke out around the clearing as he made the suggestion. Most cats agreed with him, Firestar could see, but a few others were looking uncertain.

Longtail was the first to voice his doubts. "That's all very well, Firestar, and I'm sorry for what they've been through, but if they stay here, what are they going to eat? It's the middle of leaf-bare. We've got our work cut out feeding ourselves."

"I'll hunt for them!" Graystripe sprang up to face the Clan. "I can feed all three of them, and more of the Clan as well."

"We're not helpless, you know," added Mistyfoot. "Give us a day or two to get stronger, and we'll hunt for ourselves and you as well."

Mousefur got up and spoke directly to Firestar. "It's not a question of who's going to hunt. This is a harder leaf-bare than usual, after the fire. We're all hungry, and we'll need all the strength we can get if we're going to have to fight this TigerClan. I say they should go home."

Sandstorm leaped to her paws before Firestar could speak."They *can't* go home," she pointed out. "Weren't you listening? They'll be murdered if they do, like Stonefur."

"Do you want it to be known that ThunderClan sent cats to their death?" Brackenfur added.

Mousefur looked down at her paws, anger making her fur bristle.

"It's worth mentioning," Whitestorm meowed calmly, "that all these cats are half ThunderClan. They have a right to ask us for shelter."

From his vantage point on top of the Highrock, Firestar saw a ripple of shock pass through his cats as they turned to look at Mistyfoot, standing like a living shadow of their former leader. Remembering the hostility some of them had shown when Mistyfoot and Stonefur had shared tongues with the dead Bluestar, Firestar realized that Whitestorm was taking quite a risk in reminding them.

But this time there was no hostility. Even Mousefur and Longtail stayed silent. The story of what had happened beside the Bonehill had swung the sympathy of the Clan over to the RiverClan cats. The warriors relaxed, their shock subsiding, and there were a few murmurs of agreement with what Whitestorm had said.

Firestar looked down at the RiverClan cats where they sat at the base of the rock with Graystripe and Cinderpelt.

"Welcome to ThunderClan," he meowed.

Mistyfoot bowed her head in gratitude. "Thank you, Firestar. We won't forget this."

"It was the right thing to do," Firestar meowed. "I just hope you'll feel completely better soon."

"They'll be fine, Firestar," meowed Cinderpelt. "All they need is good food and a warm place to sleep."

"Yes, there was no bedding in that horrible hole," Featherpaw fretted, her eyes wide and troubled.

"You don't need to think about that anymore," Mistyfoot promised with a comforting lick. "Just concentrate on getting strong again. As soon as you're fit, we'll have to get on with your training."

Firestar remembered that Mistyfoot was Featherpaw's mentor. He was wondering about the difficulties of training an apprentice in unfamiliar territory, when Graystripe broke in on his thoughts.

"Stonefur was Stormpaw's mentor, so he'll need another one now. Is it okay if I mentor him myself?"

"Good idea," Firestar meowed, and was rewarded by the glow of pride and pleasure in Graystripe's eyes as he looked at his son. "We'll hold the ceremony right away." He wasn't sure that it was necessary, given that Stormpaw wasn't truly a member of ThunderClan, but there was something inside him that longed to make contact with StarClan through the old, familiar rituals.

Leaping down from the Highrock he beckoned to Stormpaw with his tail. Stormpaw came to stand in front of him, still shaky on his paws but holding his head high.

"Stormpaw, you have already begun your apprenticeship," Firestar began. "Stonefur was a noble mentor, and ThunderClan grieves for him. Now you must continue to learn the skills of a warrior under a new mentor." Turning to Graystripe, he went on: "Graystripe, you will continue Stormpaw's training. You have borne suffering with a warrior's spirit, and I expect you to pass on what you have learned to this apprentice."

Graystripe nodded solemnly, then padded over to his son and touched noses with him. Firestar caught Brackenfur's eye; the young tom was obviously pleased that his old mentor had a new apprentice.

Firestar brought the meeting to an end and descended from the High Rock. Glancing around, he spotted Sandstorm not far away. "Sandstorm, I want to ask you a favor."

The ginger she-cat looked up at him. "What is it?"

"It's about Mistyfoot. She'll have trouble mentoring Featherpaw properly here. She doesn't know where the training places are, or the dangers, or the best places for prey."

Firestar hesitated, not sure if what he was about to suggest was a good idea. Not long ago he had chosen Brackenfur to mentor Tawnypaw, and Sandstorm had been deeply offended that he had passed her over. She might well take offense again at his new idea.

"Go on," mewed Sandstorm.

"I . . . I wanted to ask you if you'd help Mistyfoot with Featherpaw's training. I can't think of any cat who would be better."

Sandstorm gave him a long, measured look. "You think you can get around me with a bit of flattery, do you?"

"I don't—"

Sandstrom let out a purr of laughter. "Well, maybe you can. Of course I'll help her, you stupid furball. I'll have a word with her now."

Relief washed over Firestar. "Thank you, Sandstorm."

A loud wailing interrupted him. The cats still in the clearing were staring at the entrance from the gorse tunnel. Firestar could not see what had alarmed them, but he caught the tang of blood on the air, and unfamiliar cat scent.

Thrusting his way through his warriors, Firestar reached the entrance. Limping out of the tunnel was a cat that was almost wounded beyond recognition. Blood dripped from a long gash in his flank. His fur was matted with sand and dust, and one eye was closed.

Then Firestar made out the mottled dark pelt under the dirt and managed to distinguish the scent of WindClan. The newcomer was Mudclaw, barely able to stand from pain and exhaustion.

"Mudclaw!" Firestar exclaimed. "What happened?"

Mudclaw staggered toward him. "You've got to help us, Firestar!" he rasped. "TigerClan is attacking our camp!"

## CHAPTER 19

*Firestar leaped up the slope leading* into WindClan territory from Fourtrees. Behind him streamed a patrol of his warriors: Graystripe, Brackenfur, Sandstorm, Cloudtail, and Dustpelt with his apprentice, Ashpaw. Firestar had not dared bring more cats to WindClan's aid; he had left Whitestorm in charge of the ThunderClan camp with every other warrior on watch, in case Tigerstar planned to attack them as well.

His paws skimmed the springy moorland turf as his legs drove him toward the WindClan camp. A cold wind flattened his fur, carrying the distant scent of ShadowClan. Although Firestar knew he was still too far away, he imagined he could hear the screeches of battle as Tigerstar's warriors fell on the unsuspecting WindClan.

"We'll be too late," panted Graystripe at his shoulder. "How long did it take Mudclaw to reach us, wounded like that?"

Firestar did not waste breath in replying. He knew Graystripe was right. This was not the first time that ThunderClan had raced to help WindClan against an alliance of ShadowClan and RiverClan. But that time they had been given more warning and they had managed to drive the attacking warriors away. Now, by the time they reached the WindClan camp, the battle could be over, and yet Firestar knew that they had to try. The warrior code, his own friendships within WindClan, and the urgency of joining together to resist TigerClan, all forced him to lead his warriors to the rescue as quickly as he could.

As they drew nearer, the scent of ShadowClan was joined by a trace of RiverClan, mingling in a new scent that Firestar realized was the distinctive odor of TigerClan. They were near enough that he expected to hear the yowls of fighting cats, and the silence gripped his heart like cold claws. The battle must be over. Firestar slowed his pace as he and his patrol climbed the last slope toward the camp, his belly filling with dread at the thought of what they might find.

Firestar slipped quietly up to the ridge where he could look down over the camp. There was a strong scent of WindClan in the air, along with the tang of blood and fear. A single eerie wail broke the silence as Firestar breasted the rise and saw what Tigerstar had done.

The hollow where the WindClan cats had their camp was lined with gorse bushes. A few yellow flowers still showed on the spiny branches. Beyond, in the center of the camp, Firestar could see cats huddled together, scarcely moving. As he watched, a tortoiseshell queen raised her head and let out another chilling wail.

"Morningflower!" Firestar exclaimed.

Flicking his tail for his warriors to follow him, he raced down through the bushes and into the camp. Bursting out into the open, he was confronted by the WindClan leader, Tallstar. The black-and-white tom's fur was torn and covered in dust, and his long tail drooped with exhaustion.

"Firestar!" His voice was rough with pain. "I knew you would come."

"Not soon enough. I'm sorry."

The WindClan leader shook his head helplessly. "You did your best." He turned toward the cats who crouched on the floor of the clearing, too shocked or injured to move. "You can see what Tigerstar has done."

"Tell us what happened," urged Graystripe.

Tallstar twitched his ears. "You can see. Tigerstar and his warriors crept up on us . . . we had no warning, and in any case there were too many for us to fight."

Firestar padded forward, feeling his stomach turn over. None of the WindClan warriors had escaped without wounds. Deadfoot, the WindClan deputy, was lying very still with blood trickling from a gash on his flank; next to him lay Runningbrook, a she-cat whose pale gray fur was hanging off her shoulder in clumps. Their eyes stared at nothing, as if they couldn't believe what had happened.

Firestar could scarcely believe it either. This had been a completely unprovoked attack. There had been no warning at the last Gathering. Tigerstar had gained no extra territory for his Clan. The purpose of this attack had been nothing more than to bring *fear* to the WindClan cats.

"Hey, Firestar!" A weak voice made Firestar turn to see his old friend Onewhisker. The brown tabby warrior was lying on his side with deep wounds to his throat and shoulder. Barkface, the WindClan medicine cat, was pressing cobwebs to them, but the blood still oozed out sluggishly.

"Onewhisker . . ." Firestar trailed off, not knowing what to say.

Onewhisker's eyes were bright with pain. "It's not as bad as it looks." He grunted. "You should have seen the other cat."

"I wish we'd come in time," Firestar meowed.

"I wish you had, too. Look over there."

Onewhisker turned his head, and Barkface snapped, "Keep still!"

Firestar followed the injured warrior's gaze. Morningflower, the tortoiseshell queen who had been wailing aloud, was crouched over the motionless body of another cat. A small body, with torn ginger-and-white fur.

"No . . ." Firestar's throat closed so he had to choke out the words. "Not Gorsepaw."

"Tigerstar killed him." Onewhisker's voice was tight with rage. "He pinned him down in the center of the clearing, with his warriors around him so none of us could get close enough to stop him. He . . . he said he was going to kill him to show the rest of us what we could expect if we refused to join him."

Firestar closed his eyes, unable to bear the bloodstained scene in front of him, yet all he could see was an image of the massive leader of TigerClan, paws holding down the helpless apprentice while he challenged the WindClan warriors. A shiver ran through him. He thought back to the time that he and Graystripe had traveled to find WindClan and bring them home after ShadowClan had driven them into exile. Firestar had carried Gorsepaw, then a tiny kit, back across the Thunderpath.

All of that was wasted now, thanks to Tigerstar. Firestar could not help wondering if Tigerstar had deliberately chosen Gorsepaw because he knew of Firestar's bond with the young apprentice.

Opening his eyes, Firestar left Onewhisker and padded softly over to Morningflower, touching her shoulder with his nose to draw her attention.

She looked up, her beautiful eyes dulled with grief. "Firestar," she whispered. "I didn't ever think you'd saved my son for this. What have StarClan done to us?"

Firestar crouched down beside Morningflower, pressing himself against her side to comfort her, and touched his nose to Gorsepaw's fur. "He was growing into a fine warrior," he murmured.

The sound of another cat roused him; he looked up to see Graystripe. His friend bowed his head, too, and touched Gorsepaw's fur, mewing a few words of comfort to Morningflower.

"Firestar, what do you want us to do?" he asked, raising his head again. "We can't just leave them like this."

With a last gentle lick of Morningflower's ear, Firestar stood up and moved away with his friend. "Take two or three cats on a patrol," he ordered. "One or two of WindClan, too, if any of them are fit. They'll know their boundaries better than us. Check to make sure that there are no TigerClan warriors still lurking around. If you find any, you know what to do—chase them off, or kill them if you have to. And bring back as much fresh-kill as you can. WindClan need to eat, and they're not capable of hunting for themselves."

"Right," meowed Graystripe. He called Sandstorm, Cloudtail, and Dustpelt, and checked with Tallstar for permission to patrol in his territory. Tallstar agreed gratefully, and ordered Webfoot, who had escaped with torn fur and scratches, to go with them and show them the best places for prey.

"We need to talk," the WindClan leader mewed to Firestar as he watched the patrol leave. "Tigerstar left a message for you."

Firestar pricked his ears. "A message?"

"He wants both of us to meet him tomorrow at Fourtrees, at sunhigh," Tallstar replied. "He says he's tired of waiting. He wants our decision about whether we'll join TigerClan or not . . . and he's shown us what he'll do if we refuse."

He flicked his tail toward the wounded warriors and the limp body of the dead apprentice, all his grief contained in the simple gesture.

Firestar met his gaze, and the two leaders shared a long look of understanding.

"I'd rather die than join Tigerstar's Clan," Firestar declared at last.

"So would I," agreed Tallstar. "And I'm glad to hear you say that. Bluestar was right about you all along. Many cats thought you were too young and inexperienced when she made you her deputy, but you're showing your quality now. The forest needs cats like you."

Firestar bowed his head, humbled by the unexpected praise. "So—we'll meet tomorrow at Fourtrees," he meowed.

Tallstar nodded gravely. "Take my advice, Firestar, and bring some of your warriors with you. When we refuse to join Tigerstar, I don't imagine he'll let us walk away without a fight."

Firestar felt chilled to the tip of his tail. He could see that the older cat was right. "Then if we have to, we'll fight together?"

"Together," Tallstar promised. "Our Clans will join together like a lion to fight the tiger who prowls our forest."

Firestar stared at him in amazement. Tallstar could not know of Bluestar's prophecy, nor of Firestar's vision by the stream. And yet he had echoed the words of the prophecy. *Four will become two; lion and tiger will join in battle.* Had StarClan spoken to him as well? Firestar knew that the WindClan leader would not say—what passed between a Clan leader and the spirits of their warrior ancestors was for no other ears. But this echo reminded Firestar that they were leaders together, with the power of two mighty Clans behind them.

Gazing steadily at the noble black-and-white cat, Firestar meowed, "I swear by StarClan that my Clan will be the friend of yours, to fight this evil side by side."

"I swear it too," Tallstar replied solemnly.

Firestar raised his head, tasting the air, which still carried a faint trace of the raiding cats. He knew that this vow would run through their blood like cold fire until Tigerstar had been driven from the forest—or until they lost their ninth lives trying.

# CHAPTER 20

*The sun had begun to set* over the river, turning the water to a moving sheet of flame and sending a comforting warmth through Firestar's fur. He stood on the top of Sunningrocks, looking out over RiverClan territory.

"I wonder what tomorrow will bring," he murmured.

Beside him, Sandstorm shook her head, not replying in words but pressing her warm flank close to him. After their return from the devastated WindClan camp, Firestar had asked the pale ginger warrior to patrol with him. He had felt the need to get away from the rest of his Clan for a while to prepare himself for the meeting with Tigerstar. Yet he had not wanted to be completely alone, and Sandstorm's presence comforted him.

They had skirted Snakerocks and followed the Thunderpath up to the border with ShadowClan to renew the scent markings as far as Fourtrees; finally they returned along the RiverClan border.

There was no sign of TigerClan intruders. The borders were secure, and yet Firestar knew that if they had to fight TigerClan the battle would be about so much more than borders. It would be the climax of his conflict with Tigerstar, which had lasted almost since he had first set paw in the forest.

Firestar lingered on the rocks, savoring the comfort of being alone with Sandstorm. "Tigerstar is determined to make himself ruler of the whole forest," he meowed. "We must expect a battle."

"And ThunderClan will bear the worst of it," meowed Sandstorm. "How many warriors can WindClan offer us after today?"

Her voice was troubled, but Firestar knew that, with or without WindClan, every cat in ThunderClan would fight beside him bravely.

The fiery light was dying. Firestar turned to gaze across his beloved forest. A single star glittered in the violet sky.

*Is that you, Bluestar?* Firestar asked silently. *Are you still watching over us?*

Fervently he hoped that his former leader was still protecting the Clan she loved. If they survived the next day's meeting with Tigerstar, and managed to stay free from his quest for absolute power, it would be because StarClan knew that the forest needed four Clans.

Everything was still and silent. There was no breeze to ruffle the cats' fur, no sound of prey scuffling among the rocks. Firestar felt as if the whole forest were holding its breath, waiting for the coming dawn.

"I love you, Sandstorm," he murmured, pushing his muzzle against her side.

Sandstorm turned her head to meet his gaze, her green

eyes glowing. "I love you, too," she replied. "And I know that you'll bring us through tomorrow, whatever happens."

Firestar wished her could share her conviction. But he let himself be soothed by her trust in him. "We need to go and rest," he mewed.

The chill of night was gathering by the time they reached the ravine. Frost already sparkled on the grass and the surface of the rocks. As Firestar emerged from the gorse tunnel, a white shape loomed out of the darkness.

"I was starting to worry about you," Whitestorm meowed. "I thought you might have run into trouble."

"No, we're fine," Firestar replied. "There isn't even a mouse stirring out there."

"Pity. We could do with a few." Whitestorm gave Firestar a quick report on the patrols he had sent out and the watch he had set on the camp. "You get some sleep," he finished. "It's going to be a tough day tomorrow."

"I will," Firestar agreed. "Thanks, Whitestorm."

The white warrior faded back into the darkness again. "I'm going to check on the sentries," he meowed as he retreated.

"You couldn't have chosen a better deputy," Sandstorm commented when he was out of earshot.

"I know. I don't know what I'd do without him."

Sandstorm looked at Firestar, sadness and wisdom in her green eyes. "You might find out tomorrow," she meowed. "Or any of the others. If Tigerstar makes us fight, cats are going to die, Firestar."

"I know." But he had not truly thought about what that would mean until now. Some of the sleeping cats around him, the friends he loved, the warriors he trusted, would be lost to him. Win or lose, some of the cats Firestar led out to battle would not come back. And they would die because he had ordered them to fight. A pang of grief shook him, so deep and painful that he almost wailed aloud. "I know," he repeated. "But what can I do?"

"Go on." Sandstorm's voice was soft. "You're our leader, Firestar. You have to do your duty. And you do it brilliantly."

Humbled, Firestar found nothing to say, and after a moment Sandstorm pressed her muzzle against his. "I'd better get some sleep," she murmured.

"No, wait." Firestar found he could not face the prospect of that solitary den underneath the Highrock, full of shadows. "I don't want to be alone tonight. Come and share my den with me."

The ginger she-cat dipped her head. "All right, if you want me to."

Firestar gave her ear a quick lick and led the way across the clearing. Even though the curtain of lichen over the entrance to the den had still not grown back after the fire, the den lay in deep shadow.

More by scent than sight Firestar realized that one of the apprentices had left fresh-kill for him, and he remembered how hungry he was. The prey was a rabbit; he and Sandstorm crouched side by side to share it, swallowing with quick, famished gulps.

"I needed that," Sandstorm purred, extending her front paws and arching her back in a long, luxurious stretch. Then she yawned. "I could sleep for a moon."

Firestar arranged his mossy bedding to make a sleeping place for her, and she curled up and closed her eyes. "Good night, Firestar," she murmured.

Firestar touched his nose to her fur. "Good night."

Soon her soft, regular breathing told him she was asleep. For all his weariness, Firestar did not feel ready to curl up beside her. Instead he sat watching while the moon rose and spilled pale light through the entrance to the den, touching Sandstorm's fur to silver. She was so beautiful, Firestar thought, so precious to him. And yet she too might die tomorrow.

*This is what it means to be a leader*, he realized. He did not know if he could endure the pain of it, even though he knew that when dawn came, he would take up the burden StarClan had laid on him.

*Please, StarClan, help me to bear it well*, he thought as he settled himself into the moss beside Sandstorm. He took comfort from the warmth of her fur as he let sleep claim him at last.

# CHAPTER 21

*Firestar woke to see the den* floor washed by the pale light of sunrise. Beside him, Sandstorm still slept, the moss stirred by her breathing. Careful not to wake her, Firestar rose, stretched, and padded out into the chilly morning.

The clearing was deserted, but almost at once Whitestorm appeared from the warriors' den.

"I've sent out the dawn patrol," he reported. "Brackenfur, Mousefur, and Graystripe. I told them to do a quick sweep up the ShadowClan border and report back to us."

"Good," mewed Firestar. "It would be just like Tigerstar to arrange a meeting at Fourtrees and then mount a raid somewhere else. That's why I'm leaving you in charge of the camp, with as many warriors as I can spare."

"Take all the strength you need," Whitestorm meowed. "We'll be fine. Young Brightheart is shaping up to be a really useful fighter ever since she started training with Cloudtail. And the elders can still raise a few claws, if they're pushed."

"They'll *be* pushed, before all this is over," Firestar predicted. "Thanks, Whitestorm. I know I can rely on you."

The white warrior nodded and disappeared into the den

again. Firestar watched him go, then padded across the clearing to the fern tunnel that led to Cinderpelt's den.

When he reached the medicine cat's den, he could hear her voice coming from the cleft in the rock.

"Juniper berries, marigold leaves, poppy seeds . . ."

Looking inside, Firestar saw the small gray she-cat checking the heaps of healing herbs and berries ranged alongside the wall of the den.

"Hi, Cinderpelt," he mewed. "Everything in order?"

The medicine cat turned to him with a grave look in her blue eyes. "As much as it'll ever be."

"You think there will definitely be a battle?" Firestar asked her. "Have StarClan spoken to you?"

Cinderpelt came to join him at the mouth of the den. "No, not a word," she replied. "But common sense says there'll be a battle, Firestar. I don't need an omen from StarClan to tell me that."

She was right, Firestar knew, and yet her words chilled him. With such a momentous meeting ahead, *why* had there been no sign from StarClan? Had their warrior ancestors abandoned them in their time of greatest need? Too late, Firestar wondered if he should have traveled to Highstones to share tongues with StarClan.

"Do you know why StarClan are silent?" he asked Cinderpelt out loud.

The medicine cat shook her head. "But I do know something," she meowed, as if she had read his thoughts. "StarClan haven't forgotten us. They decreed long ago that there should be four Clans in the forest, and they won't stand by and let Tigerstar change that forever."

As Firestar thanked her and turned away to muster his warriors, he wished he shared her faith.

A stiff breeze was blowing as Firestar led his warriors up the slope to Fourtrees, rippling the grass and carrying the scent of many cats. Each gust brought a sting of rain from the gray clouds that pushed each other across the sky.

At the top of the slope, Firestar paused, crouching in the shelter of the bushes to look down into the clearing. Almost at once Cloudtail appeared at his side.

"Why are we standing about?" he demanded. "Let's get on with it."

"Not until I know what's going on," Firestar told him. "For all we know, we could be walking into an ambush." Facing his warriors, he raised his voice so that they could all hear him. "You all know why we're here," he began. "Tigerstar wants us to join his Clan, and he won't take no for an answer. I'd like to believe we can get out of this without a fight, but I can't be sure."

As he finished speaking, Cloudtail flicked Firestar on the shoulder with his tail and then pointed to the other side of the hollow. Turning, Firestar saw Tallstar approaching from WindClan territory, followed by his warriors.

"Good, WindClan are here," he mewed. "Let's go and meet them."

Firestar led the way along the lip of the hollow until he

came face-to-face with the long-tailed black-and-white tom.

The WindClan leader dipped his head in greeting. "Well met, Firestar. This is a black day for the forest."

"It is indeed," Firestar agreed. "But our Clans will stand for what is right by the warrior code, whatever happens."

Firestar was surprised at how many had come with Tallstar. Remembering the wounded and devastated cats in the WindClan camp the day before, he had expected only a small group to come to Fourtrees. Instead practically every warrior must have been there. They still showed the scars of the raid on their camp, but their eyes were bright and determined. Firestar recognized his friend Onewhisker, a long weal showing red along one flank, and Morningflower, her eyes cold with longing to avenge the death of her son.

Tigerstar might have a nasty shock, Firestar reflected, to see how many of WindClan's warriors were still ready to fight against him. Taking a deep breath, he meowed, "Let's go."

Tallstar dipped his head. "Lead on, Firestar."

Startled at being given such an honor by the older and more experienced leader, Firestar waved his tail to signal to the two united Clans—LionClan, he thought with a rush of pride. This was his destiny.

He stalked down the slope through the bushes, all his senses alert for attack. But he heard nothing except for the rustle of his own warriors following him. The scent of TigerClan was still some way off.

As Firestar led his cats into the clearing beneath the great oaks, the bushes on the opposite side parted and

Tigerstar stepped out to face him. Blackfoot, Darkstripe, and Leopardstar flanked him like vengeful shadows. The massive tabby's eyes gleamed as he spotted Firestar, and the young ThunderClan leader realized that this war was personal for him too. Tigerstar wanted nothing more than to sink his claws and teeth into Firestar's pelt and rip him to pieces.

Instead of making Firestar afraid, the knowledge exhilarated him. *Let him try!* he thought.

"Greetings, Tigerstar," he meowed coolly. "You came, then. Not still looking for those prisoners you lost from RiverClan territory?"

Tigerstar let out a snarl. "You'll regret that day's work, Firestar."

"Try and make me," Firestar retorted.

The TigerClan leader did not reply, but waited as more of his followers appeared through the bushes. They were a formidable group, Firestar realized, though some of them bore wounds and claw marks from the raid on WindClan the previous day. His heart began to thump painfully as he realized that the battle he had feared for so long might be unleashed any moment.

Tigerstar took a pace forward, his head raised challengingly. "Have you thought about my offer? I'm giving you the choice: Join with me now and accept my leadership, or be destroyed."

Firestar exchanged a single glance with Tallstar. There was no need for words. They had already decided what their response must be.

Firestar spoke for them both. "We reject your offer. The forest was never meant to be ruled by one Clan, especially not one led by a dishonorable murderer."

"But it will be." Tigerstar's voice was soft; he didn't even try to defend himself against Firestar's accusation. "With you or without you, Firestar, it will be. By sunset today, the time of four Clans will be over."

"The answer is still no," Firestar meowed. "ThunderClan will never submit."

"Nor will WindClan," added Tallstar.

"Then your courage is matched only by your stupidity," growled Tigerstar.

He paused, his gaze raking the warriors of WindClan and ThunderClan. Firestar heard snarls from the TigerClan warriors behind their leader and forced himself not to flinch away from their glittering eyes and bristling fur. For a few heartbeats not a cat moved, and Firestar braced himself for Tigerstar's order to attack.

Then he heard a choking sound behind him, and a single word gasped out: "Tawnypaw!"

Bramblepaw was standing rigid at Firestar's shoulder, staring into the ranks of their enemies. Following his gaze, Firestar spotted the young she-cat standing close beside Oakfur, a ShadowClan warrior.

"What is she doing there?" That was Brackenfur, thrusting himself forward to stand at Firestar's other side. "Tigerstar *did* steal her!"

"Steal her?" There was a purr in Tigerstar's voice. "Not at all. Tawnypaw came to us willingly."

Firestar didn't know whether to believe him or not. Tawnypaw was looking down at the ground as if she didn't want to meet the eyes of her brother and her former mentor. He had to admit that she didn't look like a prisoner; instead she just looked uncomfortable at being the center of attention.

"Tawnypaw!" Bramblepaw called. "What are you doing? You're a ThunderClan cat—come back to us!"

Firestar winced at the pain in the young cat's voice. He remembered the agony of losing Graystripe when his friend chose to leave and join RiverClan.

Tawnypaw said nothing.

"No, Bramblepaw," Tigerstar meowed. "*You* come to *us*. Your sister made the right choice. TigerClan will rule over the whole forest, and you can share our power."

Firestar saw Bramblepaw's muscles tense. At last, after all the doubts and suspicions Firestar had felt about him, the young cat was faced with a simple choice. Would he follow his father or stay loyal to his Clan?

"What do you say?" Tigerstar prompted. "ThunderClan is finished. There is nothing there for you."

"Join you?" Bramblepaw growled. He paused, swallowing as he fought to control his anger. When he spoke again his words rang out clearly so that every cat in the clearing could hear him.

"Join *you*?" he repeated. "After everything you've done? I'd rather die!"

A murmur of approval broke out among the ThunderClan cats.

Tigerstar's amber eyes smoldered with rage. "Are you sure?" he hissed. "I won't make the offer twice. Join me now, or you *will* die."

"Then at least I'll go to StarClan as a loyal ThunderClan cat," Bramblepaw retorted, his head high.

Firestar felt pride thrilling through him from nose to tail-tip. There could be no greater challenge to Tigerstar's power than for his own son to reject him in favor of the Clan his father despised.

"Fool!" Tigerstar spat. "Stay, then, and die with these other fools."

Firestar braced himself as he waited for his enemy to launch the attack, convinced that battle was upon them. Instead, to his surprise, Blackfoot raised his tail in a signal.

The bushes on the opposite slope rustled, and Firestar's eyes widened in shock as more cats emerged into the clearing. He had never seen any of them before. They were skinny, their fur ragged, but he sensed strength in their wiry limbs. The stench of crowfood and the Thunderpath rolled off them. These were no forest cats.

The warriors of ThunderClan and WindClan stared in disbelief as more and more of the strangers padded into the clearing. They fanned out into a semicircle around

TigerClan, row after row of them, more cats than Firestar could remember seeing all together in the forest, even at a Gathering.

"Well?" Tigerstar demanded silkily. "Are you still sure that you want to stand and fight?"

# CHAPTER 22

*Dismay kept Firestar's paws rooted to* the ground as he watched the newcomers approach. He noticed that some of them were wearing collars.

*"Collars?"* Ashpaw spat behind him, echoing his thoughts. The apprentice's voice was sharp with disgust. "Look at them—they're *kittypets*! We won't have any trouble beating them."

"Keep quiet," his mentor, Dustpelt, warned quietly, "until we have the full measure of our enemy. We don't know anything about these cats yet."

Firestar remained silent until all the strange cats had moved into the clearing and gathered around TigerClan. A huge black-and-white tom stepped out of their ranks and went to stand beside Tigerstar. Firestar presumed this was the leader of the newcomers. He was almost as big as Tigerstar himself, and he was muscular and battle-scarred. Even though they wore collars, Firestar knew these cats were far from being pampered kittypets.

Behind the black-and-white warrior appeared a much smaller black cat, who stalked light-footed through the grass to stand on Tigerstar's other side. Firestar could not imagine who he was; he looked more like a medicine cat than a warrior.

Firestar could feel every hair in his pelt tingling, and the air tasted thick, as if a storm were about to break. "So, Tigerstar," he meowed, forcing his voice to remain steady. "Do you want to tell us who your new friends are?"

"This is BloodClan," Tigerstar announced. "They come from Twolegplace. I have brought them to the forest to persuade you foolish cats to join with me. I knew you wouldn't have the sense to agree on your own."

A hiss of outrage rippled through ThunderClan and WindClan. Firestar heard Thornclaw whisper, "Remember those rogues we scented the day I was made a warrior? I bet they came from BloodClan."

He could well be right, Firestar thought. A patrol of these rogues from Twolegplace, checking out the forest to see what Tigerstar had to offer them. And what exactly had he offered? To share the forest in return for their help in battle?

"You see, Firestar?" Tigerstar's voice was exultant. "I am even more powerful than StarClan, for I have changed the Clans in the forest from four to two. TigerClan and BloodClan will rule together."

Firestar stared at his enemy in alarm. There was no possibility of reasoning with Tigerstar now. His hunger for power had twisted him so that in his mind his own huge figure dominated everything, blotting out even the light of StarClan.

"No, Tigerstar," he answered quietly. "If you want to fight, let us fight. StarClan will show who is more powerful."

"You mouse-brained fool!" Tigerstar spat. "I was prepared to come here and talk with you today. Just remember that it was you who drove us to this. And when your Clan mates are dying around you, they will blame you with their last breath." He swung around to face the mass of cats ranged behind him. "BloodClan, attack!"

Not a cat moved.

Tigerstar's amber eyes widened and he screeched, "Attack, I order you!"

Still none of the warriors moved, except for the small black cat who took a pace forward. He glanced toward Firestar. "I am Scourge, the leader of BloodClan," he meowed, his voice cold and quiet. "Tigerstar, my warriors are not yours to command. They will attack when *I* tell them, and not before."

The look Tigerstar gave him was incredulous and glittered with all the hatred he had ever shown to Firestar, as if he couldn't believe that this scrap of a cat was defying him. Firestar seized his opportunity. He paced forward until he stood right in front of the two leaders. Behind him, he heard Graystripe hiss, "Firestar, be careful!"

But this was no time for being careful. The very future of the forest was at stake, balanced on the breadth of a hair between Tigerstar's bloodthirsty quest for power, and the whims of the unknown BloodClan.

Now Firestar could see that the collar Scourge wore around his neck was studded with teeth—the teeth of dogs, and . . . *cats'* teeth, too. Great StarClan! Did they kill their own kind and wear the teeth as trophies?

Others of the cats were wearing the same grisly ornaments. Firestar's belly clenched and his mind reeled with a vision of blood flowing down the sides of the hollow, washing around the cats' paws in a sticky, reeking tide. His terror was not just for himself and his own Clan, but for every cat in the forest, friends and enemies alike.

Would blood truly rule the forest, as Bluestar had prophesied? Had she meant that Blood*Clan* would rule? Firestar shot a scorching glance at Tigerstar, wanting to express all the hatred he felt for the cat who had brought them to this.

But Firestar knew he had to hold on to his self-control if he were to make any impression on the BloodClan cats. Dipping his head toward their leader, he meowed clearly, so all the cats could hear him, "Greetings, Scourge. I am Firestar, leader of ThunderClan. I wish I could say you are welcome in the forest. But you would not believe me if I did, and I have no wish to lie to you. Unlike your supposed ally here, I am a cat of honor." He flicked his tail toward Tigerstar, trying to put all the contempt he felt into the single gesture. "If you've believed any promises he made to you, you're mistaken."

"Tigerstar told me he had enemies in the forest." There was all the cold of leaf-bare in the black cat's voice. When Firestar looked into his eyes it was like gazing into the deep places of the night, unrelieved by the smallest gleam of light from StarClan. "Why should I believe you instead of him?"

Firestar took a breath. This was the chance he had wanted all along, the chance he had missed at the last Gathering, when thunder and lightning had interrupted the meeting. At last he could stand in front of all the Clans of the forest and bring Tigerstar's dreadful history into the open. But now it was not just a matter of tarnishing Tigerstar's reputation, but of saving the whole forest from destruction.

"Cats of all Clans," Firestar began, "and especially cats of BloodClan, you have no need to believe or disbelieve me. Tigerstar's crimes speak for themselves. When he was still a warrior of ThunderClan, he murdered our deputy, Redtail, hoping to be made deputy himself. First Lionheart was chosen as deputy, but when that noble warrior died in a fight with ShadowClan, Tigerstar achieved his ambition at last."

He paused; a grim silence gripped the whole clearing, broken only by a contemptuous rumble from Tigerstar. "Mew away, little kittypet. It won't change anything."

Firestar ignored him. "Being deputy wasn't enough," he went on. "Tigerstar wanted to be leader of the Clan. He set a trap for Bluestar by the Thunderpath, but my own apprentice strayed into it instead. That's how Cinderpelt came by her crippled leg."

A shocked murmur swept through the clearing. Except for BloodClan, they all knew Cinderpelt, and she was popular even with cats of other Clans.

"Then Tigerstar conspired with Brokentail, the former leader of ShadowClan, who was ThunderClan's prisoner," Firestar told the listening cats. "He brought a pack of rogues into ThunderClan camp, and tried to murder Bluestar with his own claws. I stopped him, and when ThunderClan had beaten off the attack we drove him into exile. As a rogue, he slaughtered yet another of our warriors, Runningwind. Then before we knew what he was up to, he had made himself leader of ShadowClan."

Firestar paused and looked around him. He was not sure how BloodClan and their leader Scourge were taking all this, but he could see that he had the horrified attention of every other cat in the clearing. He steadied himself, wanting to be sure they heard the last, most dreadful part of his story.

"But Tigerstar still wanted revenge on ThunderClan. Three moons ago, a pack of dogs got loose in the forest. Tigerstar caught prey for them, then laid a trail of dead rabbits between the dogs' lair and the ThunderClan camp to lead them to us. He murdered one of our queens, Brindleface, and left her near the camp to give the dogs a taste for cat blood. If we hadn't found out in time to escape, the whole of ThunderClan would have been torn to pieces."

"Good riddance," Tigerstar growled.

"As it was," Firestar forced himself to go on, "our leader, Bluestar, died the bravest death of any cat, saving me and all her Clan from the pack."

He expected yowls of outrage, but only silence greeted him as his story came to an end. The eyes of every cat were fixed on him, stunned with shock.

Firestar glanced at Leopardstar, still standing with Blackfoot and Darkstripe a little way behind Tigerstar. The River-

Clan leader looked horrified. For a few heartbeats Firestar hoped that she might immediately break her agreement with Tigerstar and withdraw her Clan from his leadership, but she remained silent.

"This is Tigerstar's history," Firestar meowed urgently, turning back to Scourge. "It all shows one thing—that he'll do anything for power. If he promised you a share of the forest, don't believe him. He won't give up one pawprint, not to you or any cat."

Scourge's eyes narrowed; Firestar could see that he was thinking carefully about what he had heard, and hope flared inside him like a tiny flame. "Tigerstar told me what he was planning to do with the dogs when he visited me two moons ago." The black cat turned his head so that his gaze rested on the leader of ShadowClan. "He did not tell me that his plan failed."

"None of that matters now," Tigerstar broke in roughly. "We have an agreement with you, Scourge. Fight beside me now, and you'll have all I offered you."

"My Clan and I fight when I choose," Scourge meowed. To Firestar he added, "I will think about what you have said. There will be no battle today."

Tigerstar's fur bristled with rage and his tail lashed from side to side. His muscles bunched as he dropped into a crouch. "Traitor!" he screeched, and leaped at Scourge with claws extended.

Watching with horror, Firestar expected to see the smaller cat torn apart. He knew from bitter experience the strength in Tigerstar's muscles. But Scourge whipped to one side, avoiding Tigerstar as he landed. When the massive tabby turned to face him, Scourge lashed out with his front paws. The pale leaf-bare sun glinted unnaturally on the tips of each talon. Firestar felt his blood run cold. Scourge's claws were reinforced with long, sharpened dogs' teeth.

One blow to his shoulder unbalanced Tigerstar. He fell on his side, exposing his belly, and Scourge's vicious claws sank into his throat. Blood welled out as the smaller cat ripped him down to the tail with a single slash.

A desperate scream of fury erupted from Tigerstar, then broke off with a ghastly choking sound. His body convulsed, limbs jerking and tail flailing. For a heartbeat a stillness settled over him, and Firestar knew he was falling into the trance of a leader who loses a life, to wake after a little while restored to strength and with the rest of his lives intact.

But not even StarClan could heal this terrible wound. Scourge stood back and watched coldly as Tigerstar's body convulsed again. The dark red blood kept on flowing, spreading across the ground in a ceaseless tide. Tigerstar let out another shriek; Firestar wanted to cover his ears so he didn't have to listen anymore, but he was frozen to the spot.

Again the massive tabby's body grew still for a heartbeat, but again the wound was too terrible to yield to the healing trance. Another spasm seized Tigerstar's body. His claws tore up clumps of grass in his agony, while his screeches turned from fury to terror.

*He's dying nine times*, Firestar realized. *Oh, StarClan, no . . .*

It was a death he would not have wished on any cat, not even Tigerstar, and he thought it would never be over.

When they saw what was happening to the leader they had believed was invincible, horrified yowling came from the warriors of TigerClan. Firestar realized that they were all breaking rank; several cats pushed roughly past him in their mad haste to flee from the clearing. From somewhere behind him he heard Tallstar call out to his own warriors, "Wait! Hold the line!"

Firestar knew he did not have to give his own warriors the same order. They would stand with him to the end.

Tigerstar was panting now, his fight for life exhausting him. Firestar caught a glimpse of his amber eyes, glazed with pain and fear and hatred. Then his body gave one last jerk and lay still.

Tigerstar was dead.

Frozen in disbelief, Firestar stared down at the lifeless body. His oldest enemy, the most dangerous cat in the forest, the cat he had expected to fight to the death—gone, just like that.

Firestar was left facing Scourge. The small black cat looked unmoved. Now Firestar knew not to underestimate him due to his size. He knew he had never faced a cat more dangerous than this, who in a single blow could destroy a leader with nine lives.

Behind Scourge, the cats of BloodClan moved forward as if they were about to attack, and Firestar shot a glance at his own warriors to make sure they were ready. They stood in line with the warriors of WindClan, and Firestar braced himself to leap forward with them, but when he looked back at the enemy, Scourge raised one blood-soaked paw.

The cats behind him stopped.

"You see what happens to cats who defy BloodClan," the black cat warned calmly. "Your friend here"—he gave a contemptuous flick with his tail toward Tigerstar's motionless body—"thought he could control us. He was wrong."

"We don't want to control you," Firestar rasped. "All we want is to lead our lives in peace. We're sorry that Tigerstar brought you here with lies. Please feel free to hunt before you go home."

"Go home?" Scourge widened his eyes in scornful disbelief. "We're not going anywhere, forest fool. In the town where we come from, there are many, many cats, and live prey is scarce. Here in the forest we won't need to depend on Twoleg rubbish for our food."

His gaze slid past Firestar to where ThunderClan and WindClan stood ready for battle. "We are taking over this territory now," he went on. "I shall rule the forest as well as the town. But I understand that you may need some time to reflect on this. You have three days to leave—or meet my Clan in battle. I shall wait for your decision at dawn on the fourth day."

# CHAPTER 23

*Firestar stared, speechless with shock, as* Scourge turned away and disappeared through the lines of his own warriors. Silently the cats of BloodClan fell in behind him and vanished into the bushes with scarcely a rustle. Firestar tracked their departure through the movement of branches up the side of the hollow, and then they were gone.

Firestar looked down at the body of Tigerstar. The huge tabby's legs were splayed and his teeth bared in a last snarl of defiance at death. The amber eyes that had smoldered with savage ambition were blank and sightless.

Faced with the death of his enemy, Firestar knew he should feel triumphant. He had known for a long time now that the only hope for peace in the forest was the death of Tigerstar. But Firestar had always expected that he would be the cat that struck his enemy down, risking his own life in combat with the massive warrior. Instead, now that Tigerstar lay at his paws, staining them with his blood, he found himself struggling with the strangest feeling of all—grief. Tigerstar had received from StarClan all the strength, skill, and intelligence to make himself truly great, a legend among cats. But he had misused his gifts, murdered and lied and plotted revenge, until his ambition brought him to this terrible end. And nothing had been solved. The fate of every Clan still hung in the balance, and the tide of blood still flowed.

*We need your strength, Tigerstar,* Firestar whispered. *Just as we need every cat who can fight, to drive BloodClan out of the forest.*

He became aware that another cat was standing beside him, and he turned his head to see Graystripe. The rest of the ThunderClan cats were still drawn up in their battle lines at the far side of the clearing, with Tallstar and the WindClan warriors beside them.

"Firestar?" Graystripe's yellow eyes were huge with fear. "Are you okay?"

Firestar shook himself. "I will be. Don't worry, Graystripe. Come on—I need to talk to Tallstar."

As they turned away, Graystripe glanced down at the dead ShadowClan leader and a shudder passed through him. "I never want to see anything like that again," he meowed hoarsely.

"If we don't get rid of Scourge, you probably will," Firestar replied.

He paced slowly back toward the WindClan leader, using the time it took to cross the clearing to think. When he stood in front of Tallstar, he saw his own shock reflected in the eyes of the older cat.

"I can't believe what I've just seen," the WindClan leader. "Nine lives gone—just like that."

Firestar nodded. "No cat would blame you if you took your

Clan and left the forest to find another place to live." He did not doubt Tallstar's courage, but felt unable to assume that he would stay to fight such a terrible enemy.

Tallstar stiffened and his neck fur bristled. "WindClan was driven from the forest once," he hissed. "Never again. Our territory is *ours*, and we'll fight for it. Is ThunderClan with us?"

Even before Firestar replied he heard a murmuring from his own cats, defiance and determination mingled together. "We'll fight," he promised. "And we'll be proud to stand side by side with WindClan."

The two leaders looked into each other's eyes for a few heartbeats. Firestar could see that Tallstar shared the fear neither of them had spoken, that their resolve to fight the invading cats could mean the destruction of both their Clans.

"We'll go now to prepare ourselves," Tallstar meowed at last. "And we'll meet you here again in three days, at dawn."

"At dawn," Firestar echoed. "And may StarClan be with us all."

He watched the WindClan cats retreat up the slope toward their territory before he turned to his own warriors. They looked subdued, eyes wide with apprehension, yet Firestar knew that none of them would flinch from the coming battle. They had followed him to Fourtrees expecting to fight, and even though their enemies were more terrible than any cat could have imagined, they would still defy them to keep the forest that they loved.

"I'm proud of you all," Firestar mewed quietly. "If any

cats can drive out BloodClan, you can."

Sandstorm padded over to him and pressed her muzzle against his shoulder. "With you to lead us, we will do anything," she promised.

For a moment Firestar felt too overwhelmed to speak. Far from lifting his spirits, his warriors' expectations weighed on him heavily. "Let's get back to camp," he managed to meow at last. "We've a lot to do. Graystripe, Cloudtail, scout ahead. I wouldn't put it past Scourge to lay an ambush for us."

The two warriors bounded away in the direction of the ThunderClan camp. A few moments later Firestar led the rest of his cats after them, putting Dustpelt at the rear to keep watch. As they headed swiftly through the forest Firestar thought that he could feel Scourge's cold, malignant eyes following their pawsteps. Once before, when the dog pack was loose, Firestar had felt like prey in the forest, and now his enemy had a face all the more terrible for being one of his own kind.

But if the BloodClan leader was watching them he gave no sign of it, and the ThunderClan warriors reached the ravine unchallenged.

Firestar noticed that Bramblepaw had begun to lag behind, his tail trailing on the ground. "What's wrong?" he asked gently.

Bramblepaw raised his eyes to his mentor's, and Firestar was shocked by the depths of sick horror in his gaze.

"I thought I hated my father," he mewed quietly. "I didn't want to join his Clan. But I didn't want him to die like *that*."

"I know." Firestar pressed his muzzle against the young cat's side. "But it's over now, and you're free of him."

Bramblepaw turned his head away. "I don't think I'll ever be free of him," he murmured. "Even now that he's dead, no cat will forget that I'm his son. And what about Tawnypaw?" His voice choked. "How *could* she choose to follow him?"

"I don't know." Firestar understood how much pain Tawnypaw's betrayal must have caused her brother. "But if we come through this, I promise that we'll find a way of talking to her."

"Does that mean you will let her come back to Thunder-Clan?"

"I can't be sure of anything," Firestar admitted. "We don't even know if she *wants* to come back. But I'll give her a fair hearing, and do the best I can for her."

"Thank you, Firestar." Bramblepaw's voice was tired and defeated. "I suppose that's more than she deserves." He dipped his head to his mentor and padded on toward the gorse tunnel.

Firestar gazed down from the Highrock as the cats of ThunderClan emerged from their dens and gathered below him. He could see from their horror-struck expressions that the news of BloodClan's threat and Tigerstar's terrible death had already spread throughout the camp. He knew that it was his duty to give them hope and courage, but he did not know if he could, when he had so little for himself.

The sun was going down, and the rock cast a long shadow across the sandy floor of the clearing. The scarlet rays of the

dying sun made it too easy for Firestar to imagine that the camp was already washed in blood. He wondered if it wasn't a sign from StarClan, that all his friends, all his warriors, would be destroyed. After all, the warrior ancestors had shown no sign of anger when Scourge had ripped Tigerstar's nine lives out of him and let all his life's blood run into the sacred ground at Fourtrees.

*No*, Firestar told himself. To think like that was to despair and do nothing. He had to go on believing that BloodClan could be defeated.

Clearing his throat, he began to speak. "Cats of Thunder-Clan, you have heard of the threat that faces us. BloodClan has come from Twolegplace and laid claim to the forest. They want us to run away and let them take over without a fight. But three days from now, we will stand together with Wind-Clan and make BloodClan fight for every mouselength of the forest."

In the clearing below, Cloudtail leaped to his paws and yowled agreement. Several cats echoed him, but Firestar could see that some glanced doubtfully at one another, as if they were not sure they had a chance of surviving against BloodClan and their fearsome leader.

"What about RiverClan and ShadowClan?" asked White-storm. "Will they fight? And if they do, which side will they be on?"

"That's a good question," Firestar replied. "And I don't know the answer. The TigerClan warriors ran away when Tigerstar died."

"Then we need to know where they went," Whitestorm meowed.

"I could slip over into RiverClan territory to see," suggested Mistyfoot, getting up from where she sat at the base of the rock. "I know all the best places to hide."

"No," Firestar ordered. "You're in more danger over there than any cat. We don't know if TigerClan are still persecuting half-Clan cats, and I don't want to lose you. ThunderClan needs you."

For a moment Mistyfoot looked as if she would have liked to argue, but she dipped her head and sat down again as Whitestorm meowed, "We can find out most of what we need from border patrols."

Firestar nodded. "That's your job, Whitestorm. I want extra patrols along the ShadowClan and RiverClan borders. Their main task is to find out what the other Clans are doing, but they can keep their eyes open for BloodClan as well. If Scourge decides to attack before the three days are up, I don't want us to be caught napping."

Whitestorm flicked his tail in agreement. "Consider it done."

Firestar could see that his deputy's calm efficiency had encouraged the rest of the Clan, and he went on quickly before their fears could return. "Next, every cat in the Clan must be prepared to fight."

"Even the kits?" That was Sorrelkit, springing eagerly to her paws. "Can we be in the battle? Can we be apprentices?"

In spite of the danger they were in, Firestar suppressed a purr of amusement. "No, you're too young to be apprentices,"

he told Sorrelkit gently. "And I can't take you into battle. But if BloodClan win, they'll come here, and you'll need to be able to defend yourselves. Sandstorm, will you be responsible for training the kits?"

"I will, Firestar." Sandstorm's green eyes flashed with approval at Sorrelkit and her littermates, Sootkit and Rainkit, who had scrambled up to stand beside their sister. "They'll be able to give BloodClan a nasty surprise by the time I've finished with them."

"What about Brightheart?" Cloudtail called. "Her fighting moves are coming along well."

"I want to fight in the battle," Brightheart mewed determinedly. "Can I, Firestar?"

Firestar hesitated. Brightheart was stronger now, and she had been training hard with Cloudtail. "I'll think about it," he promised. "Are you ready for an assessment?"

Brightheart nodded. "Anytime, Firestar."

"We'll fight with you, too," Mistyfoot put in from where she sat near the base of the rock. Featherpaw and Stormpaw, sitting beside her, straightened up and looked determined. "We're all strong enough, thanks to you."

"Good. As for the rest of you"—Firestar's gaze swept the clearing—"warriors, apprentices, and elders, you have three days to prepare. Graystripe, will you supervise a training program?"

His friend's eyes lit up and his ears pricked. "No problem, Firestar."

"Get a couple of the others to help you . . . and rotate the training sessions so Whitestorm has enough cats for his patrols, and for hunting." Glancing around, he spotted the medicine cat sitting near the fern tunnel that led to her den. "Cinderpelt, are you ready to look after the wounded?"

Privately, Firestar knew there was no need to ask; he had never known Cinderpelt *not* to be ready, but he knew it would reassure the other cats to hear her say so out loud.

The look Cinderpelt gave him showed that she understood. "Everything's prepared," she replied. "But there'll be a lot to do once the fighting starts. If you could let me have an apprentice to help, that would be great."

"Of course." As Firestar wondered which apprentice to choose, his gaze rested on Fernpaw, and he remembered her gentleness and sensitivity to other cats' injuries. "You can have Fernpaw," he announced, and saw Dustpelt flash him a relieved look. "Fernpaw, if that's okay with you?"

The gray she-cat dipped her head in assent. For a moment Firestar wondered if he had forgotten anything, but he couldn't think what else they could do to prepare for what lay ahead.

Gazing down at his Clan, their shapes beginning to melt into the twilight, he took a deep breath. "Now eat well, and get a good sleep tonight," he ordered. "Tomorrow we'll begin—and in three days we'll be ready to show Scourge and his Clan that our forest will never be theirs for the taking."

# CHAPTER 24

*When Firestar emerged from his den* the following morning, the camp was already full of activity. Mousefur was leaving at the head of a patrol. Sandstorm was rounding up Willowpelt's three kits, who bounced around her in wild excitement as she herded them toward the gorse tunnel on their way to the training hollow. Mistyfoot and the two RiverClan apprentices followed them. Brackenfur passed them at the entrance to the camp, a piece of fresh-kill in his jaws.

Firestar spotted Whitestorm with Bramblepaw and Ashpaw beside the thorn wall that surrounded the camp, and padded across to join them. The white warrior came to meet him.

"I'm getting these two to inspect the defenses and patch any gaps," he meowed. "If BloodClan get this far . . ." He stopped, his blue eyes worried.

"Good idea." Firestar suppressed a shiver at the thought of BloodClan breaking into the camp. He turned sharply at the sight of movement in the gorse tunnel, and flashed a glance of astonishment at Whitestorm as Ravenpaw appeared, followed by Barley. The black-and-white loner had never been to the ThunderClan camp before.

Leaving his deputy to finish instructing the apprentices, Firestar padded toward them. Ravenpaw hurried forward confidently, but Barley lagged behind, glancing warily around, as if he wasn't sure of a welcome.

"We have to talk to you," Ravenpaw blurted out. "Last night we met Onewhisker on the border of his territory and he told us about Scourge and BloodClan." The raven-colored fur on his shoulders bristled. "We want to help, but more important, Barley has some information for you."

Firestar dipped his head in greeting. "It's good to see you both," he meowed. "And we're grateful for any help we can get. Perhaps you'd better come to my den."

Barley relaxed at Firestar's friendly greeting, and the two loners followed Firestar to the hollow beneath the Highrock. Early-morning sunshine slanted through the entrance and into the peaceful den. Firestar could almost forget the threat from Scourge and his bloodthirsty followers. But the serious expressions of his visitors reminded him all too clearly of the shadow over the future of the forest.

"What is it?" he prompted, once the two loners were settled.

Ravenpaw was gazing around him with an almost awe-struck look—Firestar guessed he was remembering Bluestar, and maybe wondering at how the apprentice who had trained with him had come to take the former leader's place. Barley, however, looked uneasy, crouching with his paws tucked under him as he began to speak.

"I was born in Twolegplace," he began quietly. "I know too much about Scourge and his warriors. I . . . I suppose you could say I was once a member of BloodClan."

Firestar's interest quickened. "Go on."

"The first thing I remember is playing with my littermates on a patch of waste ground," Barley explained. "Our mother taught us to hunt and find food among Twoleg rubbish. Later on she showed us how to defend ourselves."

"Your mother mentored you?" Firestar asked, surprised. "All of you?"

Barley nodded. "BloodClan doesn't have a proper system of mentors and apprentices. It's not a Clan at all in the way you forest cats understand it. Most cats listen to Scourge because he's the strongest and the most vicious, and Bone is a kind of deputy, insofar as he carries out Scourge's dirty work."

"Bone?" Fireheart asked. "Is that a big black-and-white cat? He was there at Fourtrees."

"That sounds like him, yes." The loner's voice was filled with disgust. "He's almost as bad as Scourge. Any cats who don't do as they're told are chased off, if they're lucky, or more likely killed."

Firestar stared at him. "But what about caring for kits and elders?"

Barley shrugged. "A she-cat's mate will probably hunt for her while she's nursing her kits," he mewed. "Even Scourge realizes that if there are no kits, sooner or later there's no Clan. But elders, or cats who are sick or injured—well, they're left to fend for themselves. It's kill or be killed, hunt or starve. There's no room for weakness."

Firestar felt every hair on his pelt bristle at the thought of a Clan that did not care for cats who were in need, where cats who had given good service were allowed to die if they could not care for themselves.

"Then why does any cat follow Scourge?" he burst out.

"Some of them enjoy killing." Barley's tone was cold and his eyes were bleak, staring at something Firestar could not see. "And others are too scared to do anything else. You can't lead your own life in Twolegplace if you're not a kittypet with a Twoleg nest to go to. Either you're with Scourge or against him, and cats who are against him don't last long."

Ravenpaw shifted closer to his friend and pressed his muzzle comfortingly against his flank. "That's why Barley left," he meowed. "Tell Firestar about it, Barley."

"There's nothing much to tell." Barley flinched, shrinking from some dark memory. "I couldn't bear what Scourge was doing, so one night I slipped away. I was terrified that Scourge or his warriors would catch me, but I reached the edge of Twolegplace and crossed the Thunderpath. I scented cats in the forest, but at the time I thought they would be just like Scourge and his lot, so I kept away from them. And finally I came to the farm, where it seemed I could live unchallenged. The Twolegs leave me in peace. They have no use for their mice."

He fell silent while Firestar thought rapidly. Barley's words confirmed what he had already known, that Scourge was a violent and dangerous enemy. "Scourge *must* have weaknesses," he meowed to Barley. "There must be some way of defeating him."

Barley met his eyes and leaned toward Firestar. "His one great strength is his one great weakness," he replied. "Scourge and his warriors don't believe in StarClan."

Firestar wondered what he meant. Cloudtail had no belief in StarClan, but he was still a loyal ThunderClan cat. What was Barley trying to tell him?

"BloodClan has no medicine cat," Barley went on. "I've already told you, they don't care for the sick, and if they don't believe in StarClan, there aren't any signs that could be interpreted."

"Then . . . they don't follow the warrior code?" That had been a stupid question, Firestar realized as soon as the words were out. Everything Barley had told him, everything he had seen for himself of the way Scourge and his cats behaved, confirmed that. "And you're telling me that's a weakness? All it means is they can do as they like, with no code of honor to stop them."

"That's true," Barley admitted. "But think, Firestar. Without the warrior code you might be just as bloodthirsty as Scourge. You might even be better at fighting him. But without the belief in StarClan—what are you then?"

He met Firestar's eyes steadily. Firestar's head reeled. After what Barley had told him he dreaded BloodClan even more, and yet somewhere in his mind there was a faint spark of hope, as if StarClan were trying to tell him something that he couldn't understand—or not yet.

"Thank you, Barley," he meowed. "I'll think about what you've told me. And I won't forget that you tried to help us."

"That's not all we'll do." Ravenpaw rose to his paws. "Onewhisker told us that you're meeting Scourge in battle in three days—two days, now. When you do, we'll both be with you."

Firestar stared at him, mouth open. "But you're loners," he began. "It's not your quarrel. . . ."

"Come on, Firestar," Barley mewed. "If Scourge and his gang take over the forest, how long do you think we would last? It wouldn't take them a quarter moon to find our barn and all the plump mice. We'd have the choice of getting out or being killed."

"We'd rather fight for our friends," Ravenpaw added quietly.

"Thank you." Firestar felt humbled by the depth of loyalty the two loners were showing to him. "All the Clans will honor you."

Barley snorted. "I don't know about that. All I want is a quiet life—but I won't get it until BloodClan is dealt with."

"None if us will." Firestar's ears twitched in agreement. "There's no hope for any of us while Scourge is in the forest."

Firestar had said good-bye to Ravenpaw and Barley and was heading for the sandy hollow to check up on the training program when he spotted Longtail and Frostfur leaping down the ravine. Firestar paused and waited for them.

"Any news?" he asked.

Longtail nodded. "We've been along the ShadowClan border as far as Fourtrees," he reported. "There's a reek of BloodClan coming from ShadowClan territory. You get the foul stink in your nose even from across the Thunderpath."

"They must be hiding out over there," Frostfur added.

"That makes sense," Firestar mewed thoughtfully. "But where has ShadowClan gone?"

"I was coming to that." Longtail's eyes were wide with excitement. "We picked up their scent at Fourtrees—the scent of many cats traveling in the same direction. I believe they crossed into RiverClan territory."

"So they went to their allies in RiverClan," Firestar mused. He wondered what sort of a welcome they would get. Would Leopardstar try to regain her old authority now that Tigerstar was dead?

Firestar shrugged. He had problems enough of his own without worrying about Leopardstar's. "Thanks, Longtail," he meowed. "We needed to know that. Go and get something to eat."

With a nod of acknowledgment, Longtail led the way into the gorse tunnel with Frostfur close behind him. Firestar stood watching them go, and when the tip of Frostfur's tail had vanished he went on to watch his cats training.

Graystripe was standing on a jutting slab of rock overlooking the apprentices. He pricked his ears in greeting as Firestar came to join him.

"How is it going?"

"Couldn't be better," Graystripe replied. "If Scourge could see us, he'd bolt straight back to Twolegplace with his tail between his legs."

The gray warrior was wearing a look of stubborn determination that Firestar remembered from the days of his forbidden relationship with Silverstream. Briefly he wished that he could tell Graystripe about seeing Silverstream in his dream at the Moonstone, but it wouldn't help his friend's grief. The beautiful she-cat was still dead, and Firestar hoped it would be a long time before Graystripe joined her in the ranks of StarClan.

"At any rate," Graystripe went on, "we're the best fighting force this forest has ever seen." His eyes widened as his gaze fell on a mock fight between Bramblepaw and Thornclaw. "Hang on a minute, I need to give Bramblepaw a tip about his clawing action."

He leaped down from the rock and bounded across the hollow, leaving Firestar to look around. Closest to him, Speckletail and Smallear were stalking around each other, waiting for a chance to spring. Sandstorm was instructing Willowpelt's three kits on the other side of the hollow. Firestar padded down to watch and he heard her meowing, "Okay, I'm a BloodClan warrior and I've just broken into your camp. What are you going to — "

The last word became a screech as Sorrelkit pounced and bit down hard on her tail. Sandstorm spun around, one forepaw raised with claws sheathed, but before she could bat Sorrelkit away, Sootkit and Rainkit jumped on her from behind. The ginger she-cat vanished under a writhing mass of kits.

By the time Firestar reached her, she was struggling free of them, her green eyes alight with laughter. "Well done!" she meowed. "If I really was from BloodClan, I'd be running scared by now." Turning to Firestar, she added, "Hi, there. Did you see these three? In a few moons they'll make great warriors!"

"I'm sure they will," Firestar mewed. "You're doing very well," he praised them. "And no cat could teach you better than Sandstorm."

"I want Sandstorm to be my mentor when I'm an apprentice," Sorrelkit meowed. "Can she, Firestar?"

"No, *I* want her!" Sootkit protested.

Rainkit added, "No, *I* do!"

Shaking her head, Sandstorm let out a *mrrow* of laughter. "Firestar will decide who your mentors will be," she told the kits. "Now let him see you practice those defensive moves."

Firestar watched while the kits scuffled together, pretending to attack and defend themselves. Even though they were excited, they managed to remember what Sandstorm had taught them, dodging expertly or dashing in to give their mock attacker a quick nip.

"They're good," Sandstorm commented quietly. "Especially that little Sorrelkit." With a sidelong glance at Firestar, she added, "If you asked me to mentor her, I wouldn't say no."

"Just between you and me, she's yours when the time comes," Firestar promised, blinking gently at her.

Even though he and Sandstorm, the kits, and all the Clan

were standing on the brink of disaster, Firestar still could not suppress a burst of pride and hope. Pressing his muzzle against Sandstorm's side, he murmured, "We'll win the battle. I have to believe that."

Sandstorm did not reply in words, but the look she gave him said everything.

Leaving her to go on with her lesson, Firestar crossed the hollow to the far side, where Cloudtail and Brightheart were training with Ashpaw and Dustpelt. Brightheart had just bowled Dustpelt over; he got up, spitting out sand, and meowed, "I never saw that move coming! Show me again."

Brightheart dropped into a crouch, but relaxed a moment later when she saw Firestar.

Cloudtail padded over to him, his tail held high. "Did you see that?" he asked proudly. "Brightheart fights really well now."

"Carry on," Firestar prompted her. "This looks interesting."

Brightheart flashed him a nervous look from her one good eye, and then turned back to concentrate. Dustpelt was trying to creep up on her blind side, but she weaved back and forth, keeping him in view the whole time. When he sprang, she slipped under his outstretched paws and hit his back legs to roll him onto the ground again.

"I see why you're called Dustpelt," Cloudtail joked as the brown warrior got up again, shaking his fur.

"Well done, Brightheart," Firestar called.

He twitched his ears to draw Cloudtail a little way away. "I hoped you'd be here," he meowed quietly. "I'm going to see Princess, and I thought you might want to come too."

Cloudtail's ears pricked. "Are you going to warn her?"

"Yes. With BloodClan on the prowl, she should know of the danger. I know she doesn't often go into the forest, but even so . . ."

"I'll be right with you," Cloudtail meowed, padding back for a word with Brightheart.

A moment later the two cats were heading for Tallpines, Firestar calling good-bye to Graystripe as they left the hollow. The pale sunlight of leaf-bare fell on the ash that still remained from the fire. The few plants that had returned were dry and shriveled, and there was neither sound nor scent of prey. This leaf-bare would have been hard enough, Firestar reflected, without the extra trouble from BloodClan.

When they reached the Twoleg nest where Princess lived, Firestar was relieved to see the pretty tabby she-cat sitting on the garden fence. She let out a trill of welcome as he raced across the open ground at the edge of the forest and leaped up onto the fence beside her. Cloudtail followed him in a couple of heartbeats.

"Fireheart!" Princess exclaimed, pressing her muzzle against his flank. "And Cloudtail! It's so good to see you both. Are you well?"

"Yes, we're fine," Firestar replied.

"He's Clan leader now," Cloudtail put in. "You have to call him Fire*star*."

"Clan leader? That's wonderful!" Princess let out a deep, delighted purr. Firestar knew she was proud of him even though she had no real understanding of what that meant—either the grief of Bluestar's death or the heavy weight of responsibility that went with leadership. "I'm so pleased for you," Princess went on. "But you're both very thin," she added doubtfully, drawing back to inspect her brother and her son. "Are you eating properly?"

It was hard to answer that question. Firestar and all the Clan cats were used to feeling hungry in this hard leaf-bare, but Princess had no way of knowing how scarce prey was, not when her Twolegs fed her the same kittypet food every day.

"We're doing well enough," Cloudtail repeated impatiently, before Firestar could reply. "But we came to tell you to stay out of the forest. There are evil cats around."

Firestar flashed an irritated look at his hotheaded kin; he would have tried to find a gentler way of warning Princess. "Cats from Twolegplace have come into the forest," he explained, pressing himself comfortingly against Princess's side. "They're fierce creatures, but they should leave you alone."

"I've seen them slinking through the trees," Princess admitted, her voice hushed. "And I've heard stories about them. Apparently they even kill dogs and other cats."

The tales were true, Firestar reflected, remembering the teeth studding Scourge's collar. And before very long, there would be more deaths to Scourge's name.

"All good storytellers exaggerate," he told Princess, hoping he sounded convincing. "You don't need to worry, but it would be best if you stayed in your own garden."

Princess held his gaze steadily, and Firestar realized that for once she wasn't deceived by his lighthearted tone. "I'll do that," she promised. "And I'll warn the other house cats."

"Good." Cloudtail meowed. "And don't worry about a thing. We'll soon get rid of BloodClan."

"BloodClan!" Princess echoed, and a shiver passed through her. "Firestar, you're in danger, aren't you?"

Firestar nodded, suddenly unwilling to treat her like a soft kittypet who couldn't cope with the truth. "Yes," he replied. "BloodClan have given us three days to get out of the forest. We don't intend to leave, so that means we have to fight them."

Princess went on giving him that long, thoughtful look. The tip of her tail swept around and touched a scar on his flank, an old wound from a battle so long ago that he had forgotten which one it was. Firestar had a sudden vision of how he must appear to her: gaunt and ragged in spite of his lean muscles, his battle-marked pelt a constant reminder of the harshness of his forest life.

"I know you'll do your best," she mewed quietly. "The Clan couldn't have a better leader."

"I hope you're right," Firestar meowed. "This is the worst threat to the Clan that we've ever had to face."

"And you'll come through it; I know you will." Princess rasped her tongue over his ear and pressed close against him. Firestar smelled her fear-scent, but she stayed calm, and her gentle features were unusually serious. "Come back safely, Firestar," she whispered. "Please."

# CHAPTER 25

*After they said good-bye to* Princess, Cloudtail went off to hunt, leaving Firestar to return to the camp alone. Twilight was gathering by the time he reached the ravine, and he scented Whitestorm before he spotted the pale warrior ahead of him. Firestar caught up to him just before he reached the gorse tunnel; he had a vole clamped in his jaws, and set it down when he saw Firestar.

"I was hoping for a word with you," he began, without even waiting for a greeting. "And it's best out here, where no cat will overhear us."

Firestar's heart lurched. "What's the matter? Has something gone wrong?"

"You mean apart from Scourge?" the older warrior meowed wryly. He settled himself on a flat rock and beckoned with his tail for Firestar to join him. "No, nothing's wrong. The patrols and the training are going well . . . but I keep asking myself, have we really thought about what we're doing?"

Firestar stared at him. "What do you mean?"

The ThunderClan deputy took a deep, painful breath.

"Scourge and his Clan outnumber us by many, even with WindClan fighting on our side. I know our warriors will fight to the last drop of blood to save the forest, but perhaps the price will be too high."

"Are you saying we should give in?" Firestar's voice sharpened; he had never expected to hear advice like this from his deputy. If Whitestorm's courage hadn't been beyond question, he would have said it was the speech of a coward. "Leave the forest?"

"I don't know." Whitestorm sounded tired, and Firestar was suddenly reminded of his age. "Things are changing, no cat can deny that, and perhaps it's time to move on. There must be territory beyond Highstones. We could find another place —"

"Never!" Firestar interrupted. "The forest is *ours*."

"You're young." Whitestorm looked solemnly at him. "You would see it that way. But cats are going to die, Firestar."

"I know." All day Firestar had kept busy, encouraging his warriors—and himself—with thoughts of a victory over Scourge. Now Whitestorm was forcing him to face the fact that even if they won, it would be at a terrible cost. ThunderClan might drive the invading cats from the forest and still be left with few survivors, as weakened as if they had been defeated.

"We *must* go on," he meowed. "We can't turn tail and run like mice. You're right, Whitestorm, I know you are, but what other choice have we? It *can't* be the will of StarClan for us to leave the forest."

Whitestorm nodded. "I thought you would say that. Well,

I've told you what I think. That's what a deputy's for."

"I'm grateful for it, Whitestorm."

The white warrior rose to his paws, turned toward his vole, and then glanced back at Firestar. "I've never had the kind of ambition that drove Tigerstar—or you," he meowed. "I've never wanted to be leader. But I'm particularly glad I'm not leader now. No sane cat would envy you the decisions you have to make."

Firestar blinked, not knowing what to say.

"All I hope for," Whitestorm went on, "is that I'll fight my hardest when the time comes."

A shadow of uncertainty crossed his face, and Firestar realized that many cats would have joined the elders by Whitestorm's age. It would be natural for him to fear that his fighting strength might fail.

"I know you will," he agreed. "There's no nobler warrior in the whole forest."

Whitestorm held his gaze for a long moment, saying nothing. Then he picked up his vole and padded into the camp.

Firestar stayed on the rock. Whitestorm's words had disturbed him, and he was suddenly reluctant to go back into camp and settle in his shadowy den under the Highrock. He knew he wouldn't be able to sleep.

After a few moments listening to the soft sounds of the gathering night, Firestar rose and headed back up the ravine. Faint red streaks showed where the sun had gone down, but overhead the sky was dark, and a few early warriors of StarClan looked down at him.

Firestar slipped silently through the undergrowth, and it was some time before he realized that his paws were taking him toward Sunningrocks. By the time he reached the edge of the trees it was completely dark. The rounded shapes of the rocks were outlined against the sky like the backs of crouching animals, with a shimmer of frost on the surface. Beyond them he could hear the soft bubble of the river over stones, and much closer a faint scuffling noise alerted him to the presence of prey.

Firestar's mouth watered as he identified the scent of a mouse. Barely letting his paws touch the ground, he crept up on it and sprang. He hadn't realized how hungry he was until his jaws closed on it, and he finished it in a few ravenous gulps.

Feeling better, Firestar sprang up to the top of the rock and found a place where he could sit and look down at the river. The dark water glittered with starlight. A breeze ruffled the surface, buffeting his fur and stirring the leafless forest around him.

Firestar turned his gaze upward to Silverpelt. The warriors of StarClan were watching—but they seemed cold and far away on this frosty night. Did they really care about what happened in the forest? Or had Bluestar been right all along, when she raged against them in her private war? For a moment Firestar caught a glimpse of his former leader's terrible sense of isolation. He could not truly share it, for unlike Bluestar he had never lost faith in the warriors of his own

Clan, but he was beginning to understand how she had come to doubt StarClan.

So many cats had already died in Tigerstar's fierce struggle for power, and StarClan had not saved them. Firestar wondered if he was being foolish to think that his warrior ancestors would help him now.

But without StarClan, how *could* his Clan survive? Lifting his head, he yowled to the glory of Silverpelt: "Show me what I should do! Show me that you're with us!"

No answer came from the white fire above him.

Painfully aware of how small and weak he was compared with the sky-spread StarClan, Firestar found a hollow in the rock that was sheltered from the chill breeze. He did not expect to sleep, but he was exhausted, and after a while his eyes closed.

He dreamed that he was seated in Fourtrees, his senses lulled by the warm air and sweet scents of greenleaf. The warriors of StarClan surrounded him on all four slopes, as they had done on his visit to the Moonstone when he received the nine lives of a Clan leader. He saw Spottedleaf and Yellowfang there, and all the warriors who were lost to ThunderClan, as well as others, newly added to the shining ranks: Stonefur and the young apprentice Gorsepaw.

In his dream Firestar sprang to his paws and confronted them. For the first time he did not feel in awe of his warrior ancestors. It seemed as if they had abandoned him, and the whole forest, to their terrifying fate. "You rule the forest!" hissed Firestar, letting all his anger at their betrayal spill out.

"You sent the storm on the night of the Gathering, so that I couldn't tell the Clans what Tigerstar had done. You allowed him to bring Scourge into the forest! Why are you doing this to us? Do you *want* us to be destroyed?"

A familiar figure stepped forward; Bluestar's gray-blue fur shimmered in the starshine, and her eyes were blue fire. "Firestar, you don't understand," she meowed. "StarClan do *not* rule the forest."

Firestar gaped at her, with nothing to say. Was everything wrong, then, that he had learned since he came into the forest as a kittypet, so long ago?

"StarClan cares for every cat in the forest," Bluestar continued, "from the blind, helpless kit to the oldest elder lying in the sun. We watch over them. We send omens and dreams to the medicine cats. But the storm was no doing of ours. Scourge and Tigerstar wade through blood to power because that is their nature. We watch," the former leader repeated, "but we do not interfere. If we did, would you truly be free? Firestar, you and every cat have the choice of whether or not to follow the warrior code. You are not the playthings of StarClan."

"But—" Firestar tried to interrupt.

Bluestar ignored him. "And now we're watching you. You are the cat we have chosen, Firestar. You are the fire who will save the Clan. No warrior of StarClan brought you here. You came of your own accord because you have a warrior's spirit and the heart of a true Clan cat. Your faith in StarClan will give you the strength you need."

As she spoke, a sense of peace crept over Firestar. He felt as though Bluestar's strength and the strength of all the warriors of StarClan were flowing into him. Whatever happened when his Clan met BloodClan in battle, Firestar knew StarClan had not abandoned him.

Bluestar rested her muzzle on his head just as she had done on the day he was made a warrior. At her touch, the pale fire of the assembled warriors began to fade, and Firestar sank into the warm darkness of deep sleep. When he opened his eyes, it was to see the first light of dawn staining the sky.

Firestar rose and stretched, the memory of his dream filling his paws with energy. It was his duty as leader to save his Clan. And with the strength of StarClan to help him, he would find a way to do it.

## CHAPTER 26

*Firestar wondered if the rest of* his Clan had noticed his absence, and if they were worrying about him. He knew that he should go back to the camp, but for a short time he stayed where he was on top of the rock, watching the dawn light spread above the forest.

The territory on the far side of the river was still and silent. Firestar tried to imagine how Leopardstar was coping. He guessed that the ShadowClan warriors who had fled into her territory would be unwelcome guests, with no prey to spare through the harsh moons of leaf-bare.

Then he sat bolt upright, fur bristling and ears pricked. Something had just occurred to him, and he couldn't think why he hadn't thought of it before. Maybe ThunderClan wasn't as outnumbered as he feared. Across the river were the warriors of two Clans, and with Tigerstar dead none of them had any reason to support BloodClan.

"Mouse-brain!" he murmured aloud. There was a chance that all four forest Clans could join together to drive out the lethal cats that threatened every pawstep of their lives. Four would not become two—four would become *one,* but not in

the way that Tigerstar had intended.

As the first glittering rays of the sun appeared above the horizon, Firestar leaped down from the rock and raced downstream toward the stepping-stones.

"Firestar! Firestar!" The yowl brought him up short just as he came in sight of the stones. He turned to see a ThunderClan patrol emerge from the trees behind him. Graystripe was in the lead, followed by Sandstorm, Cloudtail, and Bramblepaw.

"Where have you been?" Sandstorm mewed crossly as she picked her way toward him. "We've been worried sick."

"Sorry." Firestar gave her ear an apologetic lick. "I needed to think a few things out, that's all."

"Whitestorm said you would be okay," Graystripe meowed. "And Cinderpelt didn't seem worried. I got the feeling she knew more than she was telling."

"Well, I'm here now," Firestar mewed briskly. "And I'm glad I've met you. I'm going over into RiverClan territory, and it'll look better if I take some warriors with me."

"RiverClan?" Cloudtail looked amazed. "What do you want with them?"

"I'm going to ask them to fight with us against Scourge tomorrow."

The young warrior stared. "Are you out of your mind? Leopardstar will rip your fur off!"

"I don't think she will. Now that Tigerstar's dead, she won't want BloodClan in the forest any more than we do."

Cloudtail shrugged, and Graystripe was looking uncertain too, but Sandstorm's green eyes glowed with delight.

"I knew you would think of a way to defeat BloodClan," she purred. "Let's go."

Firestar turned to lead the way to the stepping-stones, but paused as Bramblepaw padded up to him.

"Firestar, can we talk to Tawnypaw if she's there?" his apprentice asked hopefully. His voice quavered. "There might not be another chance."

Firestar hesitated. "Yes, if you see her," he meowed. "Get her side of the story. Then we'll decide what to do."

"Thanks, Firestar!" Bramblepaw's eyes shone with relief.

Firestar slipped down the bank to the stepping-stones with his warriors behind him. As he led the way across he kept alert for movement on the opposite side of the river, but he saw nothing. There had not even been a RiverClan patrol, though by now the sun was well above the horizon.

Reaching the far bank, Firestar turned upriver toward the RiverClan camp. Before he reached it he came to the stream that led to the clearing of the Bonehill. A shudder ran through him as he remembered the last time he had been here. The reek of crowfood was fainter now, but the scent of many cats came to him on the breeze. Firestar recognized the mingled scent of TigerClan, once so ominous but now almost familiar compared with the stench of BloodClan.

"I think they must be in the clearing by the Bonehill," he mewed over his shoulder. "Some of them, at least. We'll go and see—Graystripe, keep a lookout."

Graystripe fell back as Firestar followed the stream, creeping quietly through the reeds until he came to the edge of the clearing. Peering out, he saw that the Bonehill was already beginning to crumble so that it looked like nothing more than a heap of rubbish. The stream was no longer choked with rotting prey, and there was a small heap of fresh-kill, as if cats had begun to establish a new camp.

Several warriors were huddled in the clearing, with ungroomed fur and dull, staring eyes. Firestar was surprised to see cats from both RiverClan and ShadowClan. He had expected to find only ShadowClan warriors setting up a camp here while RiverClan occupied their old camp on the island upriver.

Leopardstar was crouched at the foot of the Bonehill. She was gazing straight in front of her, and Firestar thought she must have seen him, but she gave no sign. The ShadowClan deputy, Blackfoot, lay close by. As his initial surprise ebbed, Firestar felt relieved that he would be able to deal straightaway with Leopardstar, who was obviously trying to rule both Clans.

He glanced back at Sandstorm. "What's wrong with them?" he murmured. He would almost have believed that the warriors were sick, but there was no taint of sickness in the air.

Sandstorm shook her head helplessly, and Firestar turned back to the clearing. He had come here looking for a fighting force, but these cats appeared to be half-dead. Still, there was no sense in going back. Signaling with his tail for his own cats to follow, he stepped into the clearing.

No cat challenged him, although one or two of the warriors raised their heads and gave him an incurious stare. With a glance at Firestar, Bramblepaw slipped away to look for Tawnypaw.

Leopardstar struggled to her paws. "Firestar." Her voice rasped, as if she had not used it in many days. "What do you want?"

"To talk to you," Firestar replied. "Leopardstar, what's going on here? What's the matter with you all? Why aren't you in your old camp?"

Leopardstar held his gaze for a long moment. "I am the sole leader of TigerClan now," she meowed at last, a spark of pride returning to her dull eyes.

"The old RiverClan camp is too small to hold both Clans. We let the queens and kits and the elders stay there, with some warriors to guard them." She let out a spurt of mocking laughter. "But what's the point? BloodClan will slaughter us all."

"You mustn't think like that," he urged the RiverClan leader. "If we all stand together, we can drive out BloodClan."

A wild light shone in Leopardstar's eyes. "You mouse-brained fool!" she spat. "Drive out BloodClan? How do you think you're going to do that? Tigerstar was the greatest warrior this forest has ever seen, and you saw what Scourge did to him."

"I know," Firestar replied steadily, hiding the shiver of sheer dread that ran through him. "But Tigerstar faced Scourge alone. We can join together as one to fight him so that afterward we can be four Clans again, according to the warrior code."

A sneering look crossed Leopardstar's face and she made no reply.

"What will you do, then?" Firestar asked. "Leave the forest?"

Leopardstar hesitated, tossing her head from side to side as if the effort of talking to Firestar irritated her. "I sent a scouting party to look for places to stay beyond Highstones," she admitted. "But we have young kits, and two of our elders are ill. Not every cat can go, and the ones that stay will die."

"They don't have to die," Firestar promised her desperately. "ThunderClan and WindClan are going to fight. Stand with us."

He expected further mockery, but Leopardstar was looking at him more intently now. Nearby, Blackfoot scrambled to his paws and padded over to stand beside her. As he faced the ThunderClan cats Firestar heard a low snarl from Graystripe did, and saw his friend begin to flex his claws. He gave the gray warrior a warning flick with his tail; he loathed Blackfoot just as much as Graystripe did, but for now they would have to be allies in order to face an even greater enemy.

"Are you mouse-brained?" the ShadowClan deputy growled. "You can't seriously be thinking of joining these fools? They're not strong enough to tackle BloodClan. They'll get us all torn apart."

Leopardstar gave him a cold look, and Firestar realized with a sudden burst of hope that she didn't like Blackfoot any more than he did. Stonefur, who had died under the black-and-white warrior's claws, had been her trusted deputy.

"I am leader here, Blackfoot," she pointed out. "I make the decisions. And I'm not ready to give up yet—not if there's a chance of driving out BloodClan. All right," she meowed, facing Firestar again. "What's your plan?"

Firestar wished he had some clever trick to offer, some way of driving out BloodClan that wouldn't risk the lives of every cat in the forest. But there was no trick; the path to victory, if there were one, would be hard and painful.

"At dawn tomorrow," he replied, "ThunderClan and WindClan will meet BloodClan at Fourtrees. If ShadowClan and RiverClan join us, we'll be twice as strong."

"And will you lead us?" asked Leopardstar. Reluctantly she added, "I haven't the strength now to take my cats into battle."

Firestar blinked in surprise. He had expected Leopardstar to demand authority over the other Clans. He wasn't at all sure that he himself was strong enough to take on the leadership in her place, but he could see that he had no choice.

"If that is your wish, then yes, I will," he replied.

"Lead us?" The voice, harsh with mockery, came from behind Firestar. "A kittypet? Are you out of your mind, Leopardstar?"

Firestar turned, knowing what he would see. Darkstripe was thrusting his way through the little group of his former Clan mates.

Firestar stared at him. In ThunderClan, Darkstripe had always been sleek; now his black-striped coat was dull, as if he had stopped caring for it. He looked gaunt, and the tip of his tail twitched nervously. Only the cold hostility in his eyes was familiar, and the insolence with which he looked Firestar up and down as he came to a stop in front of the leaders.

"Darkstripe." Firestar acknowledged him with a nod. Though he could never truly pity the dark warrior, he felt a pang to see how haunted he looked, his eyes empty, as if he were already being punished for betraying his birth Clan.

Leopardstar stepped forward. "Darkstripe, this isn't your decision," she meowed.

"We should kill you or drive you out," Darkstripe snarled at Firestar. "You turned Scourge against Tigerstar. It's your fault he died."

"My fault?" Firestar gasped in astonishment. The dark tabby's eyes burned with hatred, and Firestar knew that in his own way Darkstripe was grieving for the dead leader. Now that Tigerstar was dead, Darkstripe was utterly alone. "No, Darkstripe. It was Tigerstar's own fault. If he hadn't brought BloodClan into the forest, none of this would have happened."

"And how did it happen?" Graystripe broke in. "That's what I'd like to know. What was Tigerstar thinking of? Didn't he see what he was letting loose in the forest?"

"He thought it was for the best." Leopardstar tried to defend Tigerstar, though her words sounded hollow. "He believed the forest cats would be safer if they all joined together under his leadership, and he thought BloodClan would convince you he was right."

A snort of contempt came from Graystripe, but Leopardstar ignored it. Instead, she flicked her tail and another cat came up—a skinny gray tom with a ragged ear. Firestar recognized him as Boulder, one of the rogue cats Tigerstar had taken into ShadowClan.

"Boulder, tell Firestar what happened," Leopardstar ordered.

The ShadowClan warrior looked thin and tired as he met Firestar's gaze. "I belonged to BloodClan once," he confessed. "I left many moons ago, but Tigerstar knew about my past. He asked me to take him into Twolegplace because he needed more cats to make sure ShadowClan controlled the forest." He glanced down at his paws, his ears twitching uncomfortably. "I . . . I tried to tell Tigerstar that Scourge was dangerous, but neither of us imagined what he could do. Tigerstar offered Scourge a share of the forest if he would bring his cats to help him fight. He thought that once he'd made all the other Clans join TigerClan he could get rid of BloodClan."

"But he was wrong," Firestar murmured, feeling again that strange grief he had felt when he saw his oldest enemy lying dead at his paws.

"We couldn't believe it when he died." Boulder's eyes were stunned, as if he were sharing Firestar's memory. "We thought nothing could ever defeat Tigerstar. When BloodClan attacked our camp after Tigerstar died, we were too shocked to fight, though not all of us left. Some cats thought it would be safer to join Scourge. Jaggedtooth, for one." Boulder's voice grew bitter. "It would be worth fighting BloodClan to get my claws into that traitor's fur."

"Then will you do it?" Firestar glanced around and realized that all the cats in the clearing had drawn closer and were silently listening. Only Blackfoot and Darkstripe stood aloof, at the edge of the crowd. "Stand with us and WindClan tomorrow?"

The cats remained silent, waiting for Leopardstar to speak.

"I don't know," she mewed. "Maybe the battle is already lost. I need time to think."

"There's not much time left," Sandstorm pointed out.

Firestar gathered his own warriors together with a sweep of his tail and beckoned them over to the side of the clearing. "Think now, Leopardstar," he meowed. "We'll wait."

The RiverClan leader flashed him a defiant glance, as if she were going to insist that she would take as much time as she needed, but she said nothing, only drawing two or three of the RiverClan warriors closer to her and speaking to them in a low, urgent voice. Anger burning in his eyes, Blackfoot thrust his way forward to join them. The rest of the cats stayed in their frozen, wretched silence, and Firestar couldn't help wondering what kind of fighting force they would make.

"How mouse-brained can they be?" growled Cloudtail. "What's to discuss? Leopardstar says they can't leave safely—what else can they do but fight?"

"Be quiet, Cloudtail," Firestar ordered.

"Firestar." Bramblepaw's voice interrupted him. Firestar turned to see his apprentice standing a tail-length away with Tawnypaw close beside him. "Tawnypaw wants to talk to you."

The young she-cat returned Firestar's gaze steadily, reminding him irresistibly of her formidable mother, Goldenflower.

"Well, Tawnypaw?" he prompted.

"Bramblepaw says I should tell you why I left Thunder-Clan," Tawnypaw meowed without preamble. "But you already know, don't you? I wanted to be judged for what I was, not for what my father did. I needed to feel I belonged."

"No cat thought you didn't belong," Firestar protested.

Tawnypaw faced him with a glint in her eyes. "Firestar, I don't believe that," she meowed. "And neither do you."

Firestar felt his fur flush hot with guilt. "I made a mistake," he admitted. "I looked at both of you, and all I could see was your father. Other cats did, too. But I didn't want you to leave."

"Other cats did," Tawnypaw meowed quietly.

"She could still come back into the Clan, couldn't she?" Bramblepaw pleaded.

"Hang on a minute," Tawnypaw interrupted sharply. "I'm not asking you if I can come back. All I want is to be a loyal cat in my new Clan." Her eyes were shining. "I want to be the best warrior I can be," she went on. "And I can't be that in ThunderClan."

Firestar could hardly bear to see all the courage and loyalty that they were losing. "I'm sorry you left ThunderClan," he meowed, "and I wish you well. Tawnypaw, I really believe that if all four Clans fight tomorrow we can win back the forest. ShadowClan will survive, and be a Clan you can be proud of—a Clan that will be proud of you."

Tawnypaw gave him a short nod. "Thank you."

Bramblepaw looked distraught, but Firestar knew there was nothing more to say. The sound of his name distracted him, and he turned to see that Leopardstar was padding toward him across the clearing.

"I have made my decision," she told him.

Firestar felt his heart begin to pound. Everything rested on Leopardstar's choice. Without the support of RiverClan and ShadowClan—even with their warriors in such a pitiful state—there was no hope of driving BloodClan out of the forest. The few heartbeats before Leopardstar reached him seemed to stretch out to a moon.

"RiverClan will fight against BloodClan tomorrow," she announced.

"And so will ShadowClan," Blackfoot added, walking up behind her. His eyes flashed at Leopardstar as he silently asserted his authority.

Even though Firestar was relieved that the leaders had chosen to fight, he noticed some doubtful looks among the other cats. Darkstripe was the only one to speak out loud.

"You're all mad," he spat. "Joining a kittypet? Well, I'm not going to follow him, whatever any cat says."

"You'll obey orders," snapped Leopardstar.

"Make me," Darkstripe retorted. "You're not my leader."

For a few heartbeats Leopardstar looked at him with cold eyes. Then she shrugged. "Thank StarClan I'm not. You're about as much use as a dead fox. Very well, Darkstripe, do as you like."

The dark warrior hesitated, looking from Leopardstar to Blackfoot and back again, and then around at the rest of the clearing. The warriors were still murmuring among themselves, and none of them paid any attention to Darkstripe.

He glanced back at Leopardstar as if he were about to speak, but the RiverClan leader had already turned away. Darkstripe swung around with a vicious snarl at Firestar. "You fools—you'll all be ripped apart tomorrow."

He stalked away in dead silence. The cats parted to let him go and watched him until he disappeared into the reeds. Firestar wondered where the solitary warrior could possibly go now.

Leopardstar stepped forward. "I swear by StarClan that we will meet you at dawn tomorrow at Fourtrees. We will fight with you and WindClan against BloodClan." More briskly she added, "Shadepelt, will you send out hunting patrols? We'll need all our strength for tomorrow."

A dark gray RiverClan she-cat flicked her tail and began moving through the cats, choosing warriors for the patrols.

Leopardstar looked at the Bonehill with deep sadness in her eyes, and a shiver ran through her mottled pelt. "We must pull this down," she murmured. "It belongs to a darker time."

She dug her claws into the heap of prey bones. Slowly and hesitantly, as if they still thought that Tigerstar might appear and accuse them of treachery, her warriors joined her. Bone by bone, the pile was scattered across the clearing. Blackfoot and a few of the ShadowClan warriors stood watching a little way off. The deputy's face was shadowed, and it was impossible to guess what he was thinking.

Firestar drew his own followers away. He had succeeded in what he set out to do, and he could not help admiring Leopardstar's courage, but instead of satisfaction he felt a dark surge of foreboding as he cast one last glance at the two Clans in the clearing.

*What if I've condemned them all to death?*

## CHAPTER 27

*It was the time before dawn* when the moon had set, but the sun had yet to streak the horizon with milky fingers of light. The night was still and cold, black like frozen water.

Firestar padded out of his den. The clearing was empty, but he could hear the faint sounds of warriors waking up. Frost glittered on the ground, while above his head Silverpelt flowed like a river across the sky.

Pausing to drink in the night air filled with the scents of so many familiar cats, Firestar felt every hair on his pelt stand up. This could be the last morning he would ever spend in camp. It could be the last morning for any Clan. He felt as if everything were spinning out of his control, but when he looked for strength in the knowledge that StarClan controlled his fate, he found only uncertainty.

Firestar sighed and shook himself before walking over to the fern tunnel that led to Cinderpelt's den. The medicine cat was dragging herbs and berries into the clearing, where Fernpaw was making them into bundles ready to carry.

"Is everything ready?" Firestar asked.

"I think so." Pain filled Cinderpelt's blue eyes, as if she

were already seeing the wounded cats who would soon need her help. "I'll need more cats to carry all this up to Fourtrees. Fernpaw and I can't manage it on our own."

"You can have all the apprentices," Firestar meowed. "Fernpaw, will you go and tell them?"

The young she-cat dipped her head and hurried off.

"Once we get there, the other apprentices will be needed to fight," Firestar went on. "But Fernpaw can stay with you. Find somewhere well out of the way. I think there's a sheltered hollow on the other side of the stream—"

Cinderpelt bristled. "Firestar, you don't mean that? What use will I be if I'm not where the fighting is?"

"But the cats need you," Firestar insisted. "If you're injured, what happens to the rest of us?"

"Fernpaw and I can take care of ourselves. We're not helpless kits, you know." Cinderpelt's tart response reminded Firestar of her mentor, Yellowfang.

Sighing, he padded up to the medicine cat and touched noses with her. "Have it your own way," he meowed. "I know I can't say anything to change your mind. But please . . . be careful."

Cinderpelt let out a soft purr. "Don't worry, Firestar. We'll be fine."

"Have StarClan spoken to you about the battle?" Firestar forced himself to ask.

"No, I've seen no omens at all." The medicine cat raised her eyes to Silverpelt, where it was fading in the predawn sky. "It's not like StarClan to be silent when something so important is going to happen."

"I . . . I had a dream from them, Cinderpelt," Firestar told her hesitantly, "but I'm not sure I understand it, and there isn't time to tell you all of it now. I just hope it means something good for us."

There was curiosity in Cinderpelt's blue eyes as he spoke of his dream at Sunningrocks, but she did not question him.

Firestar returned through the fern tunnel and crossed the clearing to the elders' den. On the way he passed Brackenfur on watch, and waved a greeting with his tail.

When he reached the fallen tree, charred by the fire that had swept through the camp last greenleaf, Firestar found all the elders still sleeping except for Speckletail, who sat with her tail curled around her paws.

The she-cat rose to her paws as Firestar came toward her. "Is it time?"

"Yes," Firestar replied. "We'll be leaving soon . . . but you're not coming with us, Speckletail."

"What?" The fur on Speckletail's shoulders stiffened with annoyance. "Why not? We may be elders, but we're not useless. Do you really think we're going to sit back and—"

"Speckletail, listen. This is important. If you're honest, you know that Smallear and One-eye would barely make it to Fourtrees, never mind fight when they got there. And Dappletail's getting very frail. I can't lead them into battle against Scourge."

"And what about me?"

"I know you're a fighter, Speckletail." Firestar had thought carefully about what he was going to say, but with the elder glaring at him he felt like a raw apprentice again. "That's why I need you here. There'll be the other three elders here, and Willowpelt's kits. They've learned some defensive moves but they're not ready for battle. I'm putting you in charge of the camp while the rest of us are away."

"But I— Oh." Speckletail broke off as she understood what Firestar was asking her to do. Slowly the fur on her shoulders lay flat again. "I see. All right, Firestar. You can count on me."

"Thank you." Firestar blinked his gratitude at her. "If the battle goes badly, we'll try to fall back here and reinforce you, but we might not make it. If BloodClan comes here, you'll be all that's left of ThunderClan." His eyes met Speckletail's. "You'll need to get the kits and elders away. Try to cross the river, then head for Barley's farm."

"Right." Speckletail gave him a brisk nod. "I'll do the best I can." Turning, she looked over to where Brightheart slept in the shelter of the tree trunk. "What about her?"

"Brightheart is as strong as any warrior now," Fireheart meowed, his heart lifting. "She's coming with us." He padded over and nudged the young she-cat with one paw. "Wake up, Brightheart. It's time to go."

Brightheart blinked up at him with her good eye, then rose and stretched. "Okay, Firestar. I'm ready."

She was heading out into the clearing when Firestar called her back. "Brightheart, if we come through this, you'll be sleeping in the warriors' den from now on."

Brightheart's ears pricked and she seemed to stand taller. "Thank you, Firestar!" she meowed, and dashed off, all her drowsiness vanished.

Dipping his head in farewell to Speckletail, Firestar followed Brightheart into the clearing. By now the other cats had begun to emerge from their dens. The apprentices, Featherpaw and Stormpaw among them, were clustered around Cinderpelt, each carrying a bundle of herbs. Dustpelt was with them, speaking urgently in a low voice to Fernpaw.

Closer to the warriors' den, Brightheart had joined Cloudtail, while Mousefur and Longtail stalked around each other in a final practice of their fighting moves. As Firestar watched, Graystripe and Sandstorm slipped out from between the branches of the den with Thornclaw and Mistyfoot just behind. Whitestorm came up and urged the cats toward the nettle patch for a piece of fresh-kill.

Firestar felt a rush of pride. These were his cats, brave and loyal, every one of them.

Above him, the outlines of bare branches had begun to show black against the sky. Firestar felt a moment of sheer terror at the reminder of the approaching sunrise. He forced himself to stride confidently across the clearing until he joined Whitestorm beside the fresh-kill pile.

"This is it," the white warrior meowed.

Firestar took a vole from the pile of fresh-kill. His belly was churning with tension, but he forced himself to swallow a few mouthfuls.

"Firestar," Whitestorm continued after a moment, "I just

wanted to say that Bluestar could not have led us better in these terrible days. I've been proud to serve as your deputy."

Firestar stared at him. "Whitestorm, you're talking as if . . ." He couldn't put what he was afraid of into words. The older warrior's respect meant more to him than he could say, and he couldn't imagine how he would cope if Whitestorm did not come back from the battle.

Whitestorm concentrated on the blackbird he was eating, avoiding his eyes, and didn't say any more.

The camp was still dark when Speckletail emerged with the other elders to see the warriors off. Willowpelt's kits rushed out of the nursery to say good-bye to their mother and Sandstorm. They looked excited; they didn't fully understand what the Clan was going to face.

"Well, Firestar," Cloudtail meowed. "Is everything ready?" The tip of his tail twitched nervously as he admitted, "I'll be a lot happier when we're on the move."

Firestar swallowed the last of his vole. "So will I, Cloudtail," he replied. "Let's go."

Rising to his paws, he gathered his Clan with a flick of his tail. As his gaze met Sandstorm's, he felt strengthened to see her green eyes glow with trust and love.

"Cats of ThunderClan," Firestar called, "we go now to fight against BloodClan. But we're not alone. Remember there are four Clans in the forest, and always will be, and the other three will fight with us today. We *will* drive out these evil cats!"

His warriors sprang up, yowling their agreement. Firestar

turned, and began to lead them through the gorse tunnel and up the ravine toward Fourtrees.

When he paused at the top for a last glance back at the camp, he did not know if he would ever see his beloved home again.

# CHAPTER 28

❧

*The first faint streaks of dawn* were showing as Firestar approached Fourtrees. Pausing on the bank of the stream, he glanced back at the warriors who followed him. His heart swelled with pride as his gaze traveled over each one. Sandstorm, his beloved; Graystripe, the truest friend any cat ever had; Brackenfur, sensible and loyal; Whitestorm, his wise deputy; Thornclaw, the newest warrior of ThunderClan, looking tense and eager at the prospect of his first battle; Longtail, who had discovered at last where his heart lay; Frostfur and Mousefur, a formidable pair of she-cats; Dustpelt, reserved but true-hearted, and his apprentice, Ashpaw; Firestar's own apprentice, Bramblepaw, a glow in his amber eyes and his fur bristling; and Cloudtail, wayward but committed to his Clan, with Brightheart, the cat he had brought back from the brink of death. Pain like claws tore at Firestar's heart as he realized how much they meant to him, and what fearful danger they were facing now.

He raised his voice so that they could all hear him. "You know what lies ahead of us," he meowed. "I only want to say one thing. Ever since StarClan placed the four Clans in the forest, no leader ever had a band of warriors like you. Whatever happens, I want you to remember that."

"There was never a leader like you, Firestar," meowed Graystripe.

Firestar shook his head, his throat too choked for words. It was just like Graystripe to compare him to the truly great leaders like Bluestar, but he knew how far short of that he fell. He could only resolve to do his best to live up to his friends' trust in him.

Crossing the stream, he heard a whisper of movement from the direction of the river and glanced down the slope to see the cats of RiverClan and ShadowClan slipping quietly toward the meeting place. Firestar signaled a greeting with his tail as the warriors thronged around him, swelling the ranks of his own forces.

He was relieved to see that they had kept their promise, though the look of hostility from Blackfoot told him that even though ShadowClan might be fighting on their side this time, they would never be ThunderClan's friends.

Firestar spotted Boulder among the ShadowClan warriors. Tawnypaw was there too, looking nervous but determined. Mistyfoot went forward hesitantly to greet her friends among the RiverClan cats, touching noses with Shadepelt. Runningnose and Mudfur, the two medicine cats, arrived together, each with an apprentice carrying their supplies, and pushed their way through the throng until they found Cinderpelt. The three united Clans went on to Fourtrees together, with Firestar and Leopardstar in the lead.

When they came to the top of the hollow, everything was silent. The breeze was blowing away from them, toward ShadowClan territory, and Firestar felt his pelt prickle with dread. Their scent would be carried to the waiting BloodClan, while they themselves had no idea where their enemies might be.

"Graystripe, Mousefur," he whispered. "Scout around the hollow. Don't show yourselves. If you see any cats, come back and tell me."

The two cats slid off in opposite directions, barely visible shadows in the gray light. Firestar waited, trying to appear calm and confident, thankful for the presence of Whitestorm and Sandstorm close beside him. He had barely time to think about what might happen next when Graystripe returned with another cat close behind him. It was Tallstar.

"Greetings, Firestar," he murmured. "WindClan are here. All our warriors—and your friends, Barley and Ravenpaw."

The loners came up as the WindClan leader spoke their names. "We came to help as we promised," Ravenpaw meowed, twining his tail with Firestar's in greeting. "We'll fight alongside you, if you'll have us."

"If we'll have you?" Firestar echoed, a purr of gratitude swelling up inside him. "You're welcome; you know that."

"We're proud to fight with you," Barley mewed. Sandstorm came up to greet her former Clan mate, and the two loners took positions beside her.

"Do you know where BloodClan is?" Firestar asked Tallstar.

Tallstar's eyes were bleak as he gazed across the hollow to the ShadowClan territory. "Somewhere out there, watching us, I'd guess."

His voice was steady, and Firestar began to envy his calm, unshaking courage, until he caught the WindClan leader's fear-scent and heard him mutter under his breath, "StarClan help us! Show us an enemy we can fight!"

Somehow the knowledge that Tallstar was as afraid as he was himself only increased Firestar's respect for the older and more experienced leader. Tallstar would never show fear in front of his Clan. He would put aside his own feelings to do his duty as leader; Firestar only hoped that he could do the same.

He peered into the shadows, looking for a sign that Mousefur was on her way back. Almost at once he caught sight of her bounding toward him, and in the same heartbeat there was movement in the clearing below. Dark shapes appeared from the bushes at the foot of the opposite slope as BloodClan advanced in a single menacing line. Firestar's belly clenched in fear when the small figure of Scourge stepped out.

"I know you're there!" the BloodClan leader called. "Come and give me your answer."

Firestar paused for a heartbeat, and glanced at the cats behind him. Though he knew how terrified they must be, he could see nothing but fierce determination in their faces. LionClan was ready for battle.

"Go on, Firestar," Leopardstar mewed quietly. Her fur was

bristling and her ears lay flat against her head in a mixture of fear and defiance. "Lead us."

Firestar looked at Tallstar, who nodded. "You spoke for us before," he meowed. "You're the one who should lead us now. We all trust you."

Firestar led the united Clans down into the clearing. Scourge was waiting for him near the base of the Great Rock. His black pelt was neatly groomed and he sat with his paws tucked under him. His eyes were chips of ice, and the rising sun glinted on the teeth that studded his kittypet collar.

"Greetings," he meowed. He swiped his tongue around his jaws as if he were tasting a succulent piece of prey. "Have you decided to leave? Or do you presume you can fight against BloodClan?"

"We don't have to fight," Firestar replied steadily. To his surprise he felt icily calm. "We will let you go back to Twolegplace in peace."

Scourge let out a cold *mrrow* of laughter. "Go back? Do you really think we're such cowards? No, this is our home now."

Feeling the last spark of hope drain out of his paws, Firestar looked past Scourge at the ranks of his BloodClan warriors. These were lean, tough cats, most of them wearing collars studded with teeth like Scourge, the trophies of earlier battles. Some were flexing claws strengthened with dogs' teeth, and Firestar remembered the way Scourge's claws had ripped through Tigerstar's belly. Their eyes glittered as they waited for the order to attack.

"The forest is ours," Firestar told the black cat. "We rule here by the will of StarClan."

"StarClan!" Scourge sneered. "Tales for kits. Forest fool, StarClan won't help you now." He sprang to his paws, his fur suddenly bristling out so that he looked twice his size. "Attack!" he snarled.

The line of BloodClan warriors surged forward.

"LionClan, attack!" Firestar yowled.

He sprang toward Scourge, but the BloodClan leader dodged nimbly to one side. A huge tabby tom leaped into his place, hitting Firestar in the flank, knocking him off his paws. The clearing was silent no longer. As Firestar battered with his hind paws at the BloodClan warrior, he heard cats crashing through the undergrowth all around the hollow. Leopardstar bounded out of the bushes with Tallstar; Blackfoot raced forward at the head of a tight knot of ShadowClan warriors; and Whitestorm ran at the lead of the cats of ThunderClan, as all four forest Clans poured into the clearing and fell snarling on their enemies.

Firestar managed to throw off the BloodClan cat and scrambled to his paws. Scourge had vanished. Firestar was surrounded by a heaving mass of cats; he was amazed at how swiftly chaos had descended. He spotted Graystripe battling bravely with a huge black tom, and Willowpelt rolling on the ground, her teeth locked in the shoulder of a BloodClan tortoiseshell. Longtail was nearby, too, squirming helplessly under the weight of two BloodClan warriors. Firestar hurled himself into combat and dragged one of the cats away, feeling the strength of the muscular body as the enemy warrior turned on him. He felt claws slash into his shoulder, and raked his own claws across the warrior's face. Blood welled out of a gash on its forehead, dripping into its eyes; blinded, the cat lost its grip on Firestar, and he aimed a final blow before leaping back and whirling around in search of Longtail.

The pale tabby had driven off his other adversary, but he was bleeding deeply from his shoulder and flank. Firestar saw Cinderpelt limp rapidly out of the bushes; she nudged Longtail to his feet and helped him, staggering away from the thick of the fighting.

Firestar sprang back into the battle. Onewhisker flashed past him, pursuing a BloodClan warrior, and he caught a glimpse of Mistyfoot fighting shoulder-to-shoulder with Featherpaw and Stormpaw. Brightheart was weaving in front of a BloodClan tabby twice her size, her new fighting techniques already confusing the huge tomcat. Cloudtail fought beside her. Brightheart dodged beneath her enemy's outstretched paws, raking her claws down his nose. The tabby turned and fled. Cloudtail let out a yowl of triumph, and the two cats wheeled around as one and flung themselves back into the whirling mob of cats.

Not far away, Barley and Ravenpaw were battling side by side against a pair of identical gray tomcats, lean warriors whose collars bristled with teeth. "I know you!" one of them spat at Barley. "You didn't have the courage to stay with Scourge."

"At least I had the courage to leave," Barley hissed back at him, rearing up to swipe both forepaws at the gray warrior's ears. "It's your turn to run. You don't belong here."

Ravenpaw pressed forward beside him, and the two BloodClan warriors were gradually forced back into the bushes. A white BloodClan warrior burst into the open just beside them, with Morningflower slashing fiercely at his haunches as he fled from her. "Gorsepaw! Gorsepaw!" she yowled, giving voice to all her grief for her dead son. She leaped on the warrior and brought him down, clawing out pawfuls of white fur.

Firestar looked for Scourge. There could be no victory until the BloodClan leader was dead, and in a moment's breathing space Firestar reflected how strange it was that the final battle for the forest would not be with Tigerstar, but with Tigerstar's murderer.

But the BloodClan leader was nowhere to be seen. Fighting his way toward the base of the Great Rock, lashing out with teeth and claws, Firestar came face-to-face with a skinny gray she-cat. Her green eyes glinted with hatred as she launched herself at him, her teeth and claws digging deep into his shoulder. Firestar felt her tooth-studded collar crushing his face as she bit down. He twisted, tearing his neck fur free of the BloodClan warrior's teeth and launching himself at her unprotected belly, to score his claws down it. The she-cat sprang back and fled into the bushes.

Firestar stood panting, blood welling from his shoulder. How long could he keep this up, he wondered, before he grew too weak to carry on? There seemed as many BloodClan warriors as ever in the hollow, all strong and healthy and skilled in combat. Would the battle never end?

A BloodClan tortoiseshell loomed up in front of him, its face distorted with a screech of hatred. In the same heartbeat a dark shape shot out of the bushes, barreling into the tortoiseshell's side and shoving her away from Firestar. Astonished, Firestar recognized Darkstripe. Had the dark warrior decided at last that his loyalties belonged to ThunderClan?

A moment later he realized how wrong he was. Darkstripe whirled to face him, hissing, "You're mine, kittypet. It's time for you to die."

Firestar braced himself for the attack. "So now you're fighting on the side of Tigerstar's murderer?" he taunted Darkstripe. "Have you *no* loyalty in you?"

"Not anymore," Darkstripe snarled. "Every cat in the forest can turn to crowfood for all I care. All I want is to see you dead."

Firestar slipped to one side as Darkstripe leaped toward him, but one of the dark warrior's paws caught him on the side of the head and he lost his footing. Darkstripe landed on top of him and pinned him down. Firestar twisted, trying to free his hind paws. He scrabbled furiously at Darkstripe's belly but could not shake him off. The warrior bared his teeth, aiming for Firestar's neck. Firestar braced himself for a last desperate effort.

Suddenly Darkstripe's body rolled off him. Firestar got to

his paws to see Graystripe struggling with his old Clan mate in a screeching knot of fur and claws. Graystripe's pelt was torn and his shoulder glistened with blood from an earlier wound, but before Firestar could move to help him he flung Darkstripe to the ground and landed on top of him, panting.

"Traitor!" he hissed.

Darkstripe writhed violently, scoring deep gouges in the earth, but he couldn't throw off the gray warrior. "Fox dung!" he spat. He twisted his head, trying to sink his teeth into Graystripe's neck.

Graystripe lashed out with one forepaw. His claws pierced Darkstripe's throat and blood gushed out. The dark tabby gave one convulsive shudder. His jaws parted as he fought for breath. "There's nothing left . . ." he choked out. "It's all dark—everything's gone. . . ."

Firestar saw his eyes glazing, a terrible emptiness in them. His struggles faded and his body went limp.

Spitting contemptuously, Graystripe scrambled off him. "One less traitor in the forest," he snarled.

Firestar touched his nose to Graystripe's shoulder. Suddenly Graystripe went rigid, staring past his leader. "Firestar . . ." he rasped.

Firestar whirled around to see Sandstorm and Dustpelt fighting side by side at the edge of the battle. They didn't seem to need his help, and at first he couldn't understand what had distressed Graystripe. Then the mass of cats parted briefly to reveal Bone, the huge BloodClan deputy, crouched over another cat who moved feebly beneath him. So much blood clotted the victim's fur that Firestar could hardly make out its color, and it took him a couple of heartbeats to recognize Whitestorm.

"No!" he yowled, and he hurled himself at Bone with Graystripe hard on his paws.

Bone sprang backward, only to cannon into Bramblepaw and Ashpaw, who came charging across the clearing at the same moment. Firestar saw his apprentice leap onto the huge deputy's back, while Ashpaw bit down into his hind leg.

Confident that Bone would be distracted for a while, Firestar crouched beside Whitestorm, almost oblivious to the battle that surged around them. Recognition glimmered in the white warrior's eyes when he saw Firestar, and the tip of his tail twitched. "Good-bye, Firestar," he rasped.

"Whitestorm, no!" Firestar felt a wail of agony building up inside him. He should never have brought his deputy into this battle, when all along the white warrior had seemed to know that it would be his last. "Graystripe, find Cinderpelt."

"Too late," Whitestorm breathed. "I go to hunt with StarClan."

"You can't—the Clan needs you! I need you!"

"You will find others. . . ." The white warrior's gaze, growing rapidly dimmer, flickered to Graystripe and back again. "Trust your heart, Firestar. You have always known that Graystripe is the cat StarClan destined to be your deputy."

Letting out a long sigh, he closed his eyes.

"Whitestorm . . ." Firestar wanted to mewl his grief like a tiny kit. For a heartbeat he pushed his nose into his deputy's blood-soaked fur, the only mourning ritual that the battle allowed.

Then he turned to Graystripe, who was staring in shock at the old warrior's body. "You heard what he said," Firestar meowed. "*He* chose you." Rising to his paws, he lifted his voice above the tumult of battle. "I say these words before the body of Whitestorm, that his spirit may hear and approve my choice. Graystripe will be the new deputy of ThunderClan."

A yowl of agreement from behind startled him, and Firestar turned to see Sandstorm and Dustpelt pausing to nod briefly at Graystripe before dashing back into the battle again.

Graystripe had not moved, his yellow eyes fixed on Firestar. "Are you . . . are you sure?"

"Never surer," Firestar growled. "Now, Graystripe!"

Out of the corner of his eye, he saw the BloodClan deputy struggling free from Bramblepaw and Ashpaw. Before Firestar could spring at him, a screech of defiance sounded above the noise of battle and several more apprentices hurtled across the clearing. Bone was barely visible under the writhing heap of furious young cats. Bramblepaw and Ashpaw were there, with Featherpaw and Stormpaw and, yes, Tawnypaw, fighting beside her brother. Within a few heartbeats Bone had stopped trying to defend himself; his body went into a series of spasms, ending in his twitching tail, and as Firestar watched the twitching stopped. Ashpaw let out a hoarse cry of triumph.

At the same instant Jaggedtooth appeared out of nowhere.

Firestar felt his fur stand on end. Once a rogue, then a member of ShadowClan, and now part of the insult to the warrior code that was BloodClan. The massive warrior flung himself on the apprentices and fastened his teeth in the nearest—Bramblepaw—dragging him off Bone's body. At once Tawnypaw launched herself at the rogue cat. "Let go of my brother!" she spat. The rest of the apprentices sprang forward with her, and Jaggedtooth abruptly dropped Bramblepaw, turning tail and fleeing across the clearing with all the apprentices in pursuit.

Breathing hard, Firestar glanced around, and his stomach turned over as he tried to judge how the battle was going. Though Darkstripe and Bone were dead, and Jaggedtooth had been driven off, the clearing still seemed full of BloodClan warriors, and yet more were racing down the slope. ThunderClan had lost Whitestorm, and between the battling cats Firestar caught a glimpse of Tornear from WindClan lying motionless. Brackenfur and Mousefur fought on side by side, but Brackenfur was limping and Mousefur had deep claw marks stretching all along one side. At the edge of the clearing Frostfur was dragging herself into the bushes, with Fernpaw helping her, and not far away Runningnose, the ShadowClan medicine cat, was pressing cobwebs on a wound in Blackfoot's shoulder, until the ShadowClan deputy shook him off and threw himself back into the fray. Leopardstar appeared briefly, yowling hoarse encouragement to her warriors, before she vanished again in a surge of BloodClan cats.

*We're losing,* Firestar thought, fighting panic. *I must find Scourge!*

With the BloodClan leader's death, he knew the battle would be over. The cats from Twolegplace had no sense of tradition or loyalty to the warrior code. Scourge held them together, and without him they would be nothing.

Firestar felt his fur begin to bristle as his gaze found Scourge at last. The small black cat was crouched at the base of the Great Rock, his claws slicing at a warrior he had trapped there. Firestar's belly lurched as he recognized Onewhisker.

With a yowl of defiance he leaped across the clearing. Scourge whipped around, leaving Onewhisker to crawl away, bleeding.

The BloodClan leader bared his teeth in a snarl. "Firestar!"

Without warning, he leaped. Firestar rolled with the impact and landed on top of the smaller cat, planting one paw on his neck. But before he could bite down, Scourge wriggled away with the speed of a snake. The dogs' teeth on his claws flashed as he raked them across Firestar's shoulder.

Excruciating pain lanced through Firestar's body. He forced himself not to flinch but leaped forward again, sending Scourge flying back against the Great Rock. Briefly the black tom was stunned, and Firestar managed to bite down on his foreleg. Pain like fire seared through him again with another blow from the BloodClan leader's claws, and in the shock of it Firestar lost his grip on Scourge.

The BloodClan leader reared back, his paw raised for the death blow. Firestar scrabbled to get away, but he was not fast enough. Agony exploded in his head as the reinforced claws struck down. Flame washed over his eyes, fading to leave nothing but darkness. A soft, black tide was rising to engulf him; he made one final effort to get up, but his paws would not support him, and he fell back into nothingness.

# CHAPTER 29

*Firestar opened his eyes. He was* lying on the grass of Fourtrees with moonlight washing around him and the rustle of leaves above his head. For a few heartbeats he relaxed, reveling in the warm air of greenleaf.

Then he remembered Fourtrees as he had last seen it, the branches black and stark in the depths of leaf-bare and the clearing thronged with screeching, warring cats.

Abruptly he sat up. He was not alone. The warriors of StarClan lined the clearing, illuminating it with the shimmer of their pelts and the gleam in their eyes. In the front rank Firestar could see the cats who had given him his nine lives: Bluestar, Yellowfang, and Spottedleaf, Lionheart . . . and a newcomer, Whitestorm, restored to his youthful strength, with starlight glimmering in his thick fur.

"Welcome, Firestar," meowed the white warrior.

Firestar scrambled to his paws. "Why . . . why have you brought me here?" he demanded. "I should be back there, fighting to save my Clan."

It was Bluestar who replied. "Look, Firestar."

Firestar saw there was a space beside her. At first he thought it was empty, but suddenly he realized that it was filled by the faintest outline of a flame-colored cat. His green eyes glowed so pale they barely reflected the starlight that filled the hollow, but Firestar recognized him at once.

"You have lost your first life," Bluestar meowed gently.

A shiver ran through Firestar. So this was what it felt like to die. He stared in mingled curiosity and fear at the pale copy of himself in the middle of the clearing, and as his gaze locked with the ghost cat's he suddenly saw himself, hunched and bleeding, his fur ragged and the light of desperation burning in his eyes.

Firestar wrenched his head aside to break the contact. There was no time for this. Surely the whole point of having nine lives was so that he could keep going?

"Send me back," he begged. "If we're losing the battle, BloodClan will rule the forest!"

Bluestar stepped forward. "Patience, Firestar. Your body needs a moment to recover. You will go back soon enough."

"But it might not be in time! Bluestar, why are you letting this happen? Will StarClan not help us, even now?"

The former ThunderClan leader did not reply directly. Instead she sat down, her blue eyes glowing with wisdom. "No cat could have done more than you for ThunderClan," she meowed. "Even though you are not forest-born, you have the heart of a true Clan cat . . . more than ever Tigerstar or Darkstripe did, for though they taunted you with being a kittypet, they both ended up betraying the Clan of their birth for the sake of their own ambition."

Firestar's paws worked impatiently in the grass. What was the use of empty praise? He could not tear his mind away from what was happening in that other clearing, where loyal cats were fighting and dying. "Bluestar—"

The she-cat raised her tail to silence him. "Perhaps your quarrel with Tigerstar gave you the strength you need," she went on. "All along, you did what you thought was right, even when your Clan mates disagreed with you. You suffered loneliness and uncertainty, and that has made you what you are now . . . a gifted, intelligent leader with the courage to lead your Clan in its darkest hour."

"But I'm *not* leading them!" Firestar hissed. "And I can't save them—I'm not strong enough. We're going to lose the battle. Bluestar, this *can't* be the will of StarClan! We've always believed our warrior ancestors wanted there to be four Clans in the forest. Have we been so wrong?"

There was a ripple of movement from the front rank of the starry warriors. Bluestar rose to her paws as she was joined by the other eight cats who had given Firestar a life at the ceremony beside the Moonstone. All nine of them encircled the young cat who stood defiantly in the center of the clearing.

A voice spoke—not Bluestar this time, but an echo vibrating inside Firestar's head as if all nine cats were speaking to him at once. "Firestar, you are wrong. There were never four Clans in the forest."

As Firestar stared, rigid with shock, the voice went on: "There were always *five*."

Firestar felt nine pairs of eyes, alight with wisdom, rest on him. "Fight bravely, Firestar. You may return to the battle now, and the spirits of StarClan will go with you."

The shapes of the StarClan warriors seemed to dissolve into light. Firestar felt their strength flooding through him as water soaked into the thirsty ground, and he knew the courage that came with faith restored.

He opened his eyes. The sounds of battle rushed into his ears and he sprang to his paws. Straight in front of him he saw Cloudtail battling with Scourge. The young white warrior was on the ground, blood flowing freely from his wounds as Scourge shook him by the scruff and raked claws across his flank. But Cloudtail had his teeth fastened in Scourge's leg, and even though he was terribly injured he would not let go.

"Scourge!" Firestar yowled. "Turn and face me!"

The small black cat whipped around, letting go of Cloudtail in his shock. "How . . . I *killed* you."

"You did," Firestar spat back at him. "But I am a leader with nine lives who fights alongside StarClan. Can you say as much?"

For the first time he thought he saw a flicker of uncertainty in Scourge's cold eyes, and at last Firestar understood what Barley had told him. Scourge's lack of belief in StarClan was his greatest weakness. Without belief, without the laws and customs of the forest Clans, Scourge did not have the nine lives of a true leader. When he died, he would be dead forever.

The BloodClan leader's uncertainty lasted no more than a

heartbeat. He aimed a final blow at Cloudtail, dislodging the weakening warrior and tossing him up against the Great Rock.

Firestar launched himself at his enemy. And with every stride, he was aware of the StarClan warriors racing alongside him, matching his pace: Lionheart's golden strength; the lithe, muscular body of Runningwind; Redtail's dark fur, his bushy red tail streaming out behind him; Yellowfang with her claws outstretched; Spottedleaf, swift and determined; Bluestar with all her strength and skill in battle restored.

Firestar seemed to cover the ground on winged paws. His claws raked along Scourge's side and he dodged a blow to the head like the one that had claimed his first life.

But Scourge was fast. He flung himself between Firestar's outstretched paws and aimed for his belly, trying to rip him open with the same flick that had destroyed Tigerstar.

Firestar barely drew back in time. Now he was on the defensive, trying to avoid the gashing claws and still get close enough to Scourge to land a blow of his own. He managed to grip the BloodClan leader near the base of his tail, and the two cats rolled over and over on the grass, a shrieking whirl of teeth and claws. When they broke apart Firestar saw his own blood spattering the grass, and knew he had to finish this fight quickly before he weakened again.

When the old trick came back into his mind he scarcely believed it could work against a fighter like Scourge. But he could think of nothing else. He dug his front paws into the bloodstained turf, and crouched in front of his enemy as if he were giving in, every muscle tensed in readiness.

Scourge let out a yowl of triumph and leaped at him. In the same heartbeat, Firestar hurled himself upward, crashing into Scourge's belly and thrusting him backward onto the ground. His claws slashed through Scourge's pelt and his teeth met in the black cat's throat until he tasted the gush of warm blood. Firestar was dimly aware of Scourge's claws flailing viciously at his shoulders but he held on, raking his enemy's belly with his hind paws until the blows that were falling on him grew weaker.

Firestar shook his head, scattering thick drops of blood from his eyes. He released Scourge's throat and drew back to deal the death blow from an upraised paw. But there was no need. Scourge's eyes were fixed on him, dark pits of hatred, and his body jerked convulsively. He tried to snarl defiance, but the only sound was blood bubbling in his torn throat. His twitching limbs grew still and his eyes stared sightlessly at the sky.

Flanks heaving, his breath coming in agonizing gasps, Firestar gazed down at his dead enemy. Who knew where this cat's spirit was heading? Not to the ranks of StarClan, that was for sure.

A skinny black-and-white BloodClan cat was battling with Tallstar a couple of tail-lengths away. When he caught sight of Scourge's lifeless body, the BloodClan warrior froze, staring, and scarcely seemed to notice when Tallstar raked his claws down the side of his head. "Scourge!" he gasped. "No—no!"

He backed away, then turned and fled, blundering into another BloodClan warrior as he made for the bushes. The second warrior spat furiously and launched himself at Firestar, but before he could attack he too saw the body of his dead leader.

A terrible wailing broke from him. "Scourge! Scourge is dead!"

As the cry rose above the screeches of battling cats, Firestar saw the warriors of BloodClan falter and stop fighting. As they realized that they had lost their leader, they turned and fled. To Firestar's dazed eyes, the Twolegplace cats seemed to have shrunk. They were no longer fearsome warriors, but ordinary cats who had no place in the forest: slower than WindClan, duller than RiverClan, scrawnier than ShadowClan. All their menace was gone, and with a cry of triumph the forest cats surged after them and chased them out of the hollow.

Numb with exhaustion, Firestar hardly had the strength to understand that his cats—LionClan—had won. The forest belonged to StarClan once again.

# CHAPTER 30

*The clearing fell silent. Blood glistened* on the grass as cold sunlight sliced through the trees. Cloudtail struggled to his paws and staggered over to stand beside Firestar, looking down at Scourge's lifeless black body.

"You did it, Firestar," he panted. "You saved the forest."

Firestar gave the young warrior a lick. "We all did," he meowed. He thought back to the trouble his kin had caused when he first arrived in the forest. In those days, Firestar would never have imagined he could have felt so proud of his wayward nephew. "Go and find Cinderpelt, and get yourself something for those wounds."

Cloudtail nodded and limped off across the clearing.

Looking around, Firestar saw that warriors from each of the four Clans were gathering around their medicine cats at the edge of the clearing. One had become four again; LionClan was no more.

At first he couldn't see Sandstorm, and he felt panic welling up inside him. He was not sure he could bear it if he had lost her. Then he saw her stumbling wearily across the clearing. The fur along one flank was stiff with drying blood, but Firestar could see that her injuries were not serious.

"Thank StarClan!" he breathed.

He crossed the clearing in two bounds, and Sandstorm turned her head to look at him, her green gaze filled with relief. "We did it," she murmured. "We drove out BloodClan."

Firestar suddenly felt light-headed, as if the whole of Fourtrees were spinning around him.

"Steady," urged Sandstorm, supporting him with her shoulder. "You've lost a lot of blood. Come and see Cinderpelt."

Firestar staggered the rest of the way, drinking in Sandstorm's scent and feeling comforted by the softness of her fur. When they reached Cinderpelt he collapsed on the ground, wondering if he were about to lose another life. Then he realized he could still hear the sounds all around him in the clearing, and the pain of his scratches throbbed instead of fading as Fernpaw started pressing cobwebs to the worst of his wounds.

"Is he okay?" That was Graystripe's voice. "Hey, come on, Firestar—you can't give up now!"

"I'm not. I'm tired, that's all." Firestar blinked up at the gray warrior. "Don't worry; you won't have to be leader for a while yet."

"Firestar." Sandstorm gently prodded his shoulder. "There are more cats coming."

Firestar sat up to see a group of RiverClan cats padding toward him, headed by Leopardstar. The RiverClan leader dipped her head toward Firestar. Claw marks covered her pelt, but her eyes were clear and she carried her tail high.

"Well done, Firestar," she meowed. "They tell me you killed Scourge."

"Every cat fought well," Firestar replied. "We wouldn't have won unless all the Clans joined together."

"True enough," Leopardstar conceded. "But now we must separate again. I am going to take my Clan home. We must care for our wounded and grieve for our dead."

"And ShadowClan?" Firestar inquired.

"ShadowClan must go back to their own home," Leopardstar replied firmly. "I have a new deputy, and enough warriors to defend our territory if ShadowClan don't respect our borders."

"Who is the new deputy?" Firestar asked curiously.

"Mistyfoot," meowed the RiverClan leader, a glint in her eyes.

As Firestar stared in astonishment, Mistyfoot emerged from the ThunderClan cats, followed by Featherpaw and Stormpaw. "I'm going with Leopardstar," she explained, fixing Firestar with her mother's ice-blue gaze. "I'll always be grateful for what you did, but I'm a RiverClan cat at heart."

Firestar nodded. He had never expected Mistyfoot to change her allegiance completely from her birth Clan. "But . . . as deputy?" he meowed. "After what happened to Stonefur?"

There was deep grief in Mistyfoot's eyes, but her determination did not waver. "Leopardstar asked me just before the battle started," she explained. "I said I'd think about it, and now I know I have to do it for Stonefur's sake, and for the sake of the Clan."

Firestar dipped his head, respecting the hard decision she had made. "Then StarClan go with you," he meowed. "And may you always be a friend to ThunderClan."

The two young cats beside Mistyfoot glanced uncertainly from Firestar to Leopardstar. "We're going too," Stormpaw mewed. "RiverClan has lost many warriors. They need us."

Featherpaw padded up to Graystripe and touched noses with him. "You'll come and visit us, won't you?"

"Try to stop me." Graystripe's voice was muffled and his eyes were filled with the pain of his kits' divided heritage. "Be the best warriors you can, and make me proud of you."

"You've got something to live up to," Firestar added. "Your father is ThunderClan deputy now."

The two apprentices pressed close to their father and twined their tails with his. Leopardstar gave them a moment to be together before signaling to them, and the young cats fell in behind her. The RiverClan cats vanished into the bushes and up the slope toward their own territory.

Firestar's gaze fell on the group of ShadowClan cats not far away, and he noticed that Bramblepaw was with them, talking to his sister. Firestar rose to his paws and limped slowly toward them; Blackfoot got up to meet him as he approached.

"Firestar." The ShadowClan deputy narrowed his eyes. "So we won the battle after all."

"Yes, we did," Firestar agreed, adding, "What will you do now, Blackfoot?"

"Take my Clan home, and prepare for a journey to High-stones. I'm their leader now. We have much to do to recover, but life in the forest will go on as usual."

"Then I'll see you at the next Gathering. And Blackfoot, you would do well to learn from the mistakes of your predecessors. I saw what you did to Stonefur at the Bonehill."

A shadow flitted across Blackfoot's eyes, and he did not reply.

Firestar flicked his tail to beckon Bramblepaw, who pressed his muzzle briefly against Tawnypaw's flank and slipped through the ShadowClan cats to his mentor's side. Blackfoot rounded up his cats and led them out of the clearing. Runningnose, the medicine cat, brought up the rear with a glance at Firestar as he went. Firestar hoped he had better luck with this new leader, after the trouble he had endured with Nightstar and Tigerstar.

Firestar turned back to his own Clan and found himself face-to-face with Barley and Ravenpaw.

"I wouldn't trust Blackfoot," murmured Ravenpaw, watching the last of the ShadowClan warriors disappear into the bushes. "He's a troublemaker if I ever saw one."

"I know," Firestar replied. "Don't worry. ThunderClan will be ready if he starts anything."

"At least with Scourge dead, the cats from Twolegplace will have the chance to live in peace," Barley remarked with feeling. "They might have a better life now."

"You wouldn't go back to Twolegplace yourself?" Firestar inquired.

"Not on your life!" Barley's tail shot straight up. "We're heading straight for home."

"But it was good to fight with ThunderClan again," added Ravenpaw.

"ThunderClan will always be grateful to you," Firestar told them warmly. "You're free to come into our territory anytime."

"And you must visit us at the farm whenever you make the journey to Highstones," Barley mewed as they turned away. "I expect we'll be able to spare a mouse or two."

With RiverClan and ShadowClan accounted for, Firestar wanted to check in with WindClan before he gathered his own cats and headed back to camp. There was a small group of WindClan warriors clustered around Barkface, their medicine cat, but nowhere near as many as there should have been. Tallstar himself was missing. A prickle of fear ran through Firestar's flame-colored pelt.

Then he saw the WindClan leader emerging from the bushes on the far side of the clearing. Mudclaw and Morningflower and a couple of apprentices were with him. All five cats were panting hard, as if they had been running. Firestar bounded toward them, expecting to see enemy cats burst into the clearing in pursuit.

"What's going on?" he demanded. "Are BloodClan chasing you?"

Tallstar let out a satisfied purr. "No, Firestar. *We* chased *them*. We followed them as far as the Thunderpath. They won't be back here in a hurry."

"Good," Firestar meowed with deep appreciation.

He saw a similar glow in Morningflower's eyes, and realized that at last she felt avenged for the death of Gorsepaw.

Taking a deep breath, Firestar dipped his head toward Tallstar and meowed, "We have no further need for LionClan. There are four Clans in the forest again."

He could see that the older leader understood what he was saying. They were no longer allies, but rivals, who could meet in friendship only at Gatherings.

"We owe you our freedom," meowed the WindClan leader. He dipped his head and headed toward the rest of his warriors at the far side of the clearing.

Alone for the first time, Firestar scrambled up to the top of the Great Rock. The sickening stench of blood rose around him, but up here he could look out over the forest and dare to believe that soon the battle would be no more than a distant memory.

He imagined the spirits of StarClan all around him, sharing the leadership of his Clan. They would be beside him every pawstep until he gave up his last life and went to join them.

"Thank you, StarClan," he murmured. "Thank you for staying with us, fifth Clan of the forest. How could I ever have thought that I faced this battle alone?"

Suddenly he smelled a familiar scent and felt the soft touch of Spottedleaf's pelt brushing against his fur. Her breath was warm in his ear. "You are never alone, Firestar. Your Clan will live on, and I will watch over you forever."

For a moment Firestar felt all the pain of loss afresh, as if his beloved medicine cat had not died many moons ago, but in this very battle. Then his ears pricked at the sound of claws on rock, and as Spottedleaf's scent faded, Firestar saw Graystripe and Sandstorm climbing toward him, with Bramblepaw scrambling up behind.

Sandstorm pressed her flank to Firestar's. "Bluestar was right. Fire did save the Clan."

"And now there are four Clans again," Graystripe added. "Just as there should be."

*No, there are five*, Firestar thought. He looked down over the clearing and the trees that stretched as far as he could see, and his senses filled with the sounds and the scents of his forest home. A thousand secret whispers told him that newleaf was stirring in the cold earth, shooting up new green fronds and rousing the prey from its long leaf-bare sleep.

The rising sun broke over the trees and flooded the clearing with light and warmth, and it seemed to Firestar that no dawn had ever been brighter.